Praise for A Lady in Havana

"…a young wife… is caught in a web of forbidden romance and political intrigue. Morgan's debut is an engaging, compulsively readable work of historical fiction bolstered by compelling characters and a fast-paced narrative… vivid descriptions… A thoughtful, thrilling portrait of one woman's personal and political self-discovery."
—*Kirkus Reviews*

"…entertaining novel of passion and persuasion…A colorful blend of glamour, betrayal and old fashioned… dreaming… a pure delight… a fascinating depiction of lasting memories."
—*Foreward Reviews*

"*A Lady in Havana* offers a quick pace, engaging characters… the glamour and danger of Cuba on the eve of the revolution… an action-packed story that will appeal to fans of historical fiction…"
—*Blueink Review*

"…delightfully well written… riveting descriptions captivate the reader's attention from beginning to end."
—Jose Manuel Garcia
Author of *Voices from Mariel: Oral Histories Of the 1980 Cuban Boatlift*

"A fun and frothy read, delightful as a daiquiri on a sultry summer night."
—Rosa Lowinger
Bestselling author of *Tropicana Nights*

To - Jim -

A Lady in Havana

A Novel

Frank Foster
writing as

Ashley Morgan

Ashley Morgan

gatekeeper press

Columbus, Ohio

A Lady in Havana

Published by Gatekeeper Press
2167 Stringtown Rd, Suite 109
Columbus, OH 43123-2989
www.GatekeeperPress.com

ISBN: 9781642371420
eISBN: 9781642371437

Printed in the United States of America

About The Author

A Lady in Havana is the first work of historical women's fiction from Ashley Morgan, a pseudonym for an author whose bestselling novels have been previously published under another name.

A native Floridian, Morgan splits time between homes in central Florida and the mountains of western North Carolina and enjoys traveling, opera and fine wines.

For my mother. I loved her more than either of us knew.

"Others go to bed with their mistresses; I with my ideas"
-José Martí

"All things truly wicked start from innocence"
-Ernest Hemingway

"A revolution is not a bed of roses"
-Fidel Castro

Chapter One

Dimple

I've always liked my name. At least after I finally overcame my childish embarrassment of being called Dimple. I mean, really. Dimple?

It might have helped if I'd seen the name in print instead of my first exposure to it being called Dimple. But that was before I became aware that cute, pinchy dimples in your cheeks, especially if you're a girl, were not viewed as a deformity but as a charming physical attribute. Some have called me "Dimp" but I've never liked that as much. Maybe that was because Southerners typically don't abbreviate given names. Barbara is usually Barbara, not Barb. I don't have a middle name but I confess to becoming envious of girls with classic southern couplet given names like Mary Catherine or Mary Claire. I've always loved the way people pronounce them as though they were one word, not two.

Growing up, my real name of Dorothy Card made it easy for my girlfriends to call me by my family name saying they thought I was one. A card, that is. They may have been right.

Unfortunately, having a middle name wasn't all I was envious of; I have a long list. I could start with my envy of girls who grew up with a father, or a mother they could be proud of. Of girls who had the gumption to stand up to their parents. Of girls who didn't have to deal with some of the *horrors* I had to. And of girls who had a pretty chiffon dress to wear to the tea dances we had then and some pretty pearls to go with it. I suppose it's not a very attractive quality to have—envy—but I have a long list of those, too. Unattractive qualities, I mean.

Being envious was bad enough, but couple it with shame and it's a *horrid* combination for a young girl. I was ashamed that other girls had fathers and I didn't. I was ashamed of my mother and . . . well, I could continue but I'm thankfully over most of that. I mean, what does it matter now anyway after the stroke?

The stroke. That damn stroke. I can't walk; my mouth is contorted on the same side as my dead leg. My angel of a daughter, Hallie, feels obligated to come here to The Meadows almost every day and sit with me. I'm a useless burden to everybody and, intellectually, I just wish I could go ahead and die. But I'd miss Hallie and I'd miss doing something for her she's been begging me to do for years. And since my mind and my speech have inexplicably bounced back a little, my mission for what remains of my life is to accommodate Hallie's request.

I'm watching my lovely daughter standing beside my nursing home bed. I see her notice me resting at an odd angle and use the remote control to crank the metal-frame contraption a little more upright and fluff the pillows around my elderly, snow-white head which she tenderly strokes a couple times. It makes me more comfortable and I thank her with a smile that I know is crooked but it's the best I can do. I see Hallie lean toward the now-running recorder on the bedside table to make sure it will capture what I realize are my greatly anticipated first words on the topic she is so anxious to hear about. I watch my good hand on the swing-away table across my bed. It's manicured with red nail polish and I drum my nails on the table, a life-long nervous habit of mine.

It's time. Time to do what I've promised my Angel (which is what I've called Hallie most of her life). I must gather myself and use this brain that, for the moment at least, still somehow works. I look out the window for a long time trying to bring it all back. I sense Hallie getting restless. I must start. I promised her.

So, I begin to talk.

Oh heck, Angel, why don't I just start with the juicy stuff?

I'd never met anybody like Roberto. I'd never even met anybody with a name ending in a vowel, much less a man like that. I'll tell you, he was *gorgeous*.

I'd never thought Latin men were particularly attractive, but Roberto was different. He was the most mysterious and intriguing man I'd ever met. He had jet black hair; a thin mustache; dark, brooding eyes which could be mischievous, and—this is *so* ironic— dimples you could get lost in. Especially when he smiled. Lord, could he smile. That smile of his could melt a fifty-pound block of ice in seconds.

Roberto had this kind of percolating confidence that was almost . . . insolent. He just sort of took charge of you. It was disarming; it was . . . it was more than disarming, it was devastating. I had never had a man affect me that way except Dallis, but even he was nothing like Roberto. I don't know what would have happened if I'd met him before I married Dallis.

What do I mean by that, you ask? Just hang on, Angel; you'll find out. Then you'll have to ask yourself if you really wanted to.

Of course, I never would have met Roberto if it hadn't been for Dallis. I mean that's how I met Roberto—through your daddy. That was when Dallis was representing that company up in Illinois that made the school buses and ambulances. He covered the state of Florida for them. Ye gads, it was *so* embarrassing when he would drive a hearse home he'd been showing to a funeral home. After he'd been doing it a while, the neighbors finally stopped rushing over to see which one of us had died.

I wish now I hadn't burned all Roberto's letters, but I had no choice. We were living in Miami at the time and I can still remember the day I walked into the post office there and rented that box. I shouldn't say walked in, *slunk* in was more like it. I was *so* embarrassed and felt *so* guilty. I just knew that stern-looking postal worker behind the counter knew exactly why I was there. I kept waiting for him to say, "Well. Renting a box to get letters from your lover so your husband won't find out, eh?"

I know, I know, you're shocked. And you should be—I'd be disappointed if you weren't. But I may as well get it out right away, Angel. You've been after me to talk and tell you everything so, as they say, be careful what you ask for. Yes, I was unfaithful to your father. But with everything that goes on in this day and time, that may be the dullest thing I'm going to tell you.

Before you go to pieces or anything like that, let me assure you that Roberto is *not* your father. Let me also assure you that I loved Dallis. But I loved Roberto, too. Just in a different way. I'll never forget the day your daddy came home and told me something that changed our lives.

"We're going *where?*" I said.

"Cuba," Dallis said.

"You're drunk," I said.

His face spread into his wide grin that always made his eyes look like they were squinting. "Haven't had a drop."

"Cuba?" I said. "We can't afford to go to Cuba. We can't even afford to go to Miami Beach and it's just across the bridge."

"With all the money I can make down there, we can't afford not to go."

"Dallis Duncan, how in the world are you going to make any money in Cuba?" I asked. "On my two trips to Cuba with Judy and Muffy, the only people I saw making money were the prostitutes and the bartenders and I don't see you as either one of those. The people with money are the ones with . . . land and . . . sugar . . . and tobacco."

"So, you don't want to go to Cuba," Dallis said, deadpanning.

I playfully hit him on the chest with my fist. "Of *course* I want to go to Cuba. I will *always* want to go to Cuba. You know how I love it. But what in heaven's name are you talking about? *Moving* there? *Living* there?"

One reason it occurred to me that we might move there is that we were living in a little two-bedroom stucco house near Coral Gables. Notice I said *near* Coral Gables, not in it. That house would never have been in the Gables; it wasn't nice enough. Bungalows, they were called. It was the fifties. We were renting the place for sixty dollars a month and straining to do that. Of course, you hadn't come yet.

"We might live there eventually," Dallis said, answering my question. "But I'm just talking about making some trips there to start." He took me by the shoulders and looked at me hard with those dreamy blue eyes of his I loved to look at. "I really need for you to come with me. They tell me that getting in with the powers that be down there involves socializing and nobody's better at that than you are." He finished with one of his looks that were always so special to me. It wasn't one of his crinkly-faced grins but one of his thin smiles with those blues eyes looking so earnest that the devil would have converted to Christianity if Dallis had asked him to.

I can't even smile any more but you remember what it looked like when I could. When I was really happy I knew my upper gums showed and I hated knowing it. I knew it happened when something really tickled me or really made me happy but there was no stopping it. Well, this was one of those times because we were going to Cuba. I gave your daddy what I'm sure was one of my gummiest grins ever.

Actually, that's not all I gave him that night, if you know what I mean. But it was hard to remember because it was after we came home from a little German place in Miami I can't even remember the name of—the something, something House. The House part was spelled H-A-U-S, German style. Anyway, for some strange reason, this German restaurant always served all the Florida lobster you could eat for something like three dollars. It was ridiculous. I've always liked Florida lobster better than Maine, primarily because of the firmer texture. Maine lobster was always kind of *slimy* to me.

Anyway, we drank way too much bourbon, smoked a million Lucky Strikes, and stuffed ourselves with lobster. I was celebrating going back to Cuba with Dallis—we had never been there together—and Dallis was celebrating in advance all the money he was going to make and how it was going to change our lives.

At the lobster place that night, when I got back from a trip to the ladies room, your daddy was almost in an *embrace* with our cute blonde waitress.

"I could just get my own table across the room," I said icily as I stood waiting for the encounter to end and for Dallis to stand and pull my chair out. The cute waitress just smiled at me and promised to check on our food. I didn't even look at her as I waited with as much dignity as I could muster for Dallis to hustle around behind my chair and seat me.

"Don't tell me," I deadpanned. "Her husband wants to buy a hearse."

Dallis didn't say anything—he couldn't—he just sat down and gave me the look I'd seen too many times: the look of a little boy who had just stuffed his pockets with extra cookies when his mother had given permission for only one. It was a look meshing guilt with contrived innocence that resulted in a countenance so preposterous and indefensible that it almost made me want to burst out laughing. In these situations, I usually maintained my deep freeze for a while, sometimes up to several days, not that it ever did any good. But that night, I thawed pretty quickly because it was a special night and I didn't want to ruin it.

Ten days later, we left for Havana.

Chapter Two

Hallie

That first day of capturing her mother's recollections on a recorder still burned in Hallie's memory. When she'd learned it was actually going to happen, she'd rushed to the nursing home while glancing nervously at the rear-view mirror of her maroon Honda Accord. She knew that collecting yet another speeding ticket would make her insurance premiums, which already amounted to what she imagined to be the country's average personal income, soar once again. What was almost more upsetting to her was the possibility of having to attend another court-mandated session of driving school.

Even in her learner's-permit days, Hallie had a heavy foot and she applied it now, gunning the Japanese sedan to fifty-five in a thirty-five zone. She felt speeding was her only option because her mind was still replaying Mrs. Price's phone call.

"She's a talkin' again. You might want to get over here, honey," Mrs. Price had said. Hallie had measured the palpable excitement in the woman's voice and felt her own skin tingle as she anticipated what might be in store.

"Oh, damn," she said out loud in response to a horrifying thought, then exhaled a long breath of relief as her eye caught her slim briefcase on the floor by the passenger seat. It contained the digital recorder—not spying it would have meant a quick, possibly illegal U-turn.

The drive would last another eight to ten minutes and she used it to recall the very first time her mother began to talk intelligibly after the stroke, a session Hallie, unfortunately, did not record. Hallie's mouth, covered by Revlon's Cherries in the Snow pink lipstick, curled in pleasure as her mind replayed those first precious words. She remembered walking into her mother's room at The Meadows, worried that the "roll" the elderly lady had been on would have subsided and resulted in her mother fading back to her normal morose, incommunicative state.

"Mother, do you still feel like talking a little bit?" Hallie had asked. Mrs. Price, in her crisp nursing uniform, was on the other side of the bed and her large eyes—almost as black as her skin—were wide with anticipation.

Hallie did not get an answer; instead, she heard a stream of consciousness that kept her spellbound. The voice she heard amazed her. It was far stronger than it had been over the last year but it retained its refined dignity and soft, musical lilt. And, of course, it lingered on its vowels, as did the voice of any lady of that age who had been reared in the Deep South.

At one point, her mother dwelt on her Southern cooking prowess. Hallie wondered why her mother was telling her about homemade mayonnaise, greens, cornbread, and put-up sweet pickles. She already knew all that and was expert herself at preparing all those things, thanks solely to her mother's careful instruction during Hallie's adult years. But then she remembered what the doctors had told her about strokes and the peculiar and unpredictable behavior they could cause.

Her mother had exhibited the gamut. While at times she had shown some signs of aphasia, she had at other times been effusive—and lucid—in her conversations. Now, amazingly, she was unleashing a stream of intelligible recollections about her previously mysterious life. Hallie was thankful that, at the moment anyway, her mother's interest seemed to be in talking, and doing lots of it. Some of her mother's other activities at The Meadows recently had gotten her into hot water: sneaking cigarettes and climbing into bed with other male residents of the nursing home. The latter is something she knew her mother would never be morally capable of doing had her synapses and neurons not been altered by the oxygen-sapping stroke.

Hallie's mother's life was indeed mysterious to Hallie, at least the part of it which occurred before Hallie grew up. Before boarding school and college, Hallie had spent a good deal of time with her paternal grandmother as a child. Rumors, snippets, hints of things were all she had to go on, but something told Hallie that hearing the details for the first time could be the answer to her dream.

One of Hallie's two dreams had spent last night with her at her small house. That was the norm when she and Rich Rodino slept together. Even after his expensive divorce, Rodino still had his mansion, but Hallie was uncomfortable staying over there with all his staff around.

Rodino was quite the cook; when Hallie arrived from the nursing home, he was already busy in her kitchen. He'd let himself in with his key and was working on one of his specialties: lobster mac 'n cheese made with Vermont smoked white cheddar and topped with a drizzle of white truffle oil. Rodino came by his innate culinary skills honestly; his ethnicity was pure Italian and so were most of his dishes. He had a glass of chardonnay going. Hallie took one look at him and knew it wasn't his first.

"Hello, Angel," he boomed, using Hallie's mother's affectionate term for her. He wore a bright smile when she came in and folded herself into his arms.

She glanced at his wine glass. "Any more of that?"

"Gallons," he said, reaching for the bottle and opening a kitchen cabinet for a stem. In short order, she was holding a glass of Rombauer chardonnay and studying her boyfriend of some five months now. He was three years younger than she but he insisted that age made no difference to him.

"But," she had said, "what if we . . . you know, really get . . . you know, *involved* and something permanent happens. You'll just get better looking; I'll start looking like Grandma Moses and you'll dump me."

He'd just smiled broadly and taken her in her arms. "You're beautiful now and you always will be," he'd said and she had melted.

"So how's your mom today?" he asked.

Hallie climbed on a bar stool next to her kitchen island and took a long pull on the wine. "She's turned into Chatty Cathy. Can't shut her up."

Rodino stopped chopping shallots and looked up at her. "Well, that's great. I mean, it's what you want, right? You know, for your idea?"

"That's right," she answered. "And I especially need my idea to work now."

"Oh?"

She reached toward a little filing tray on the end of the kitchen island, drew out two envelopes, and tossed them his way like a couple of playing cards. "These came yesterday. Two more rejections of my short stories." Her tone was despondent.

Rodino put down his chopping knife and quickly wiped his hands on a dish towel. In a flash, he was around the kitchen island at Hallie's side with her hands in his. He looked at her with eyes which were the darkest Hallie had ever seen in a man, perhaps somewhere between brown and black, if that was possible.

"Those magazine editors are nuts," he said. "Your stories are the best I've ever read. You're a fabulous writer and you know it."

She smiled up at him and squeezed his hands gratefully. "You are very prejudiced, my dear."

"No I'm not. And your novel is going to get published *immediately*."

She knew one of her dreams—Rich Rodino—had put his finger precisely on her other dream. She pulled her hands away from his and took another wine drink. "Ha. I have to write it first."

"Well, if your mother comes through with your story idea like you're hoping, you'll be on your way. Can you start now?"

"Not really," she said. "She's only just begun. This afternoon, she and my father were on their way to Cuba where it all happened. Whatever it is that *did* happen. Maybe tomorrow she'll really get into it."

Chapter Three

Dimple

I'm staring at a still life giclee on the wall opposite my bed at The Meadows. The subject is a lovely, flowered blue bowl containing fruit. I sense Hallie has walked in my room. When I continue staring at the giclee, I realize she is panicked wondering if my previous day's loquaciousness was a fleeting thing. I turn to her and erupt in what I know is one of my twisted, stroke-mangled smiles. Then I begin speaking in my customary South Georgia drawl.

"Hey, Angel. I'll bet you want to find out more about Cuba."

I see her smile then I turn back to the picture on the wall to gather my thoughts. She waits in patient silence for what I know is long enough for an oral thermometer to register one's body temperature. Finally, I start:

Well, on that first trip, your daddy and I flew to Havana from Miami on a Pan Am DC-3. My goodness, I think the fare was only fifty dollars or so round trip. Of course, I'll never fly again but I still miss the DC-3. It had two motors and the plane sat on its tail wheel, so when you got on you walked uphill to get to where the pilots were. All the airlines used them back in the fifties; I don't think jets came along until the sixties. It had a single row of seats on each side and one stewardess. Everybody calls them flight attendants these days. She wore one of those smart powder blue Pan Am uniforms with a little side cap perched at an angle on her head as she handed out Chiclets. Gracious, I'll bet you don't even know what Chiclets are. They were those little things that were hard like a piece of candy until you started chewing them; then they ended up like gum. They were sweet and just *divine.* They kept my ears from popping even though the flight from Miami to Havana was under an hour; no sooner had we climbed than it was time to come back down to land.

We were so broke then, but somehow your daddy convinced Challenger Manufacturing Corporation, the company that made the buses and hearses—they were in Illinois south of Chicago—to pay for a lot of our travel expenses. Your daddy was a *wonderful* salesman and talked them into it. What they didn't know was how much Dallis and I loved mojitos, Cuba Libres, and daiquiris. In Florida, we would put a huge dent in a bottle of Early Times bourbon, but in Cuba how could you drink anything but rum? And dancing? Lord, we'd go at it to that Cuban music until the wee hours. In fact, somewhere I'll bet I still have an album I bought down there. I still remember the title: *Havana at 2 a.m.* Sometimes, when we were back in Miami and had had enough bourbon, we'd play it and do the rhumba. Which we got pretty good at, by the way. Lord, what a dancer your daddy was. And all the women knew it. I wish they hadn't; we had our worst fights when he'd get in a clinch on the dance floor with some *hussy* he didn't even know. In some cases, hadn't even *met.*

Anyway, we flew from Miami to Havana and rode from the airport southwest of the city in a taxi. It was a Chevrolet, I think. All the cars were American and, if I'm not mistaken, the very same ones I rode in are still being used today. Except I think a lot of them now have Russian engines, or at least Russian parts.

I was simply a wife accompanying her husband on a business trip and Dallis had made all the arrangements. I hadn't asked much of anything about what we'd be doing; I was just so glad to be going back to Cuba. I'd been twice with Judy and Muffy and loved it to death. We'd had *the* best time. Everybody was so nice, especially since they served us girls just out of college all the daiquiris we wanted. We learned the rhumba from strange Cuban men with mustaches. But all we did with them is dance, nothing more. We mostly drank too much, smoked too much, and giggled. And on each trip I won a little over ten dollars playing blackjack, which was a fortune back then. In fact, I could never have afforded the trip if Muffy's daddy hadn't been an executive with Pan Am. The flights were free and he got us a deal at some little hotel I can't even remember the name of. It was clean and nice but nothing special.

That hotel we girls stayed at was the sort of place I expected Dallis and I would drive up to as we made our way into Havana—Dallis had handed the driver a piece of paper with the address—but instead, the driver pulled right up to the world-famous Hotel Nacional de Cuba. I just stared at Dallis.

"Dallis?" I said, barely able to talk.

He gave me one of his grins that made him look like he was squinting. "What?"

"Dallis, this is the Hotel Nacional. Why did he stop here?"

"Why shouldn't he?"

"Dallis, we can't be staying here."

The squinting grin persisted. "And why not?"

"Because . . . because . . . we can't afford it, that's why not. This is the fanciest, most expensive hotel in Cuba, maybe in the whole Caribbean. What'd you do, rob a bank?"

Dallis leaned over toward me, took my hand, and gave me one of his earnest looks. "Let's just hope we do as well selling school buses as I did selling Challenger on putting us up at the Nacional."

I couldn't help myself. I kissed him hard right on the lips and said, "Don't worry, honey; we will."

After I said that, I realized I'd surprised myself. What in heaven's name did I know about school buses, much less how to sell them? So why did I say it? I suppose it was because of Dallis's comments about "needing my help" and that "socializing is very important when doing business in Cuba." I momentarily wondered what I might be getting myself into. I would soon find out.

This Challenger Manufacturing Corporation put us up in a pretty-much standard room, but it *was* at the Hotel Nacional de Cuba and it overlooked Havana Harbor. Not only that, it was a corner room and had a little balcony. The very first thing I did was throw open all the draperies and step out onto that balcony. It was early April and a cool breeze blew right in my face from the north. Right from Key West, I remember thinking, as I squinted to focus on the horizon, wondering if the naked eye could see ninety miles from the sixth floor. But, of course, it couldn't. Mainly because the bay started at the Malecon and went to El Morro, the entrance to the harbor. The breeze felt good, although it annoyed me that it was not being kind to my hair I'd worked on so hard before we left Miami. I wore mine in typical wavy mid-fifties style—not long but not a bob either. I usually put a small pompadour in front and patterned my "do" a little after Ava Gardner. But who wouldn't try to do that? Especially after my girlfriends and I had caught a glimpse of her on the street on our last trip to Havana.

Did I just say Habana? With a "b"? I think so. On my trips there I picked up only a little Spanish; it was later that I became fluent but I'll get to that.

What? Oh, that's right; I suppose you didn't know that. Well, hang on, Angel, it's coming.

You really didn't need to learn much Spanish to function in Cuba either as a tourist or a businessman because English was so prevalent. In fact, almost everything was American, not just the cars. Americans owned much of the country, including the sugar industry, the mines, many of the farms. Even the casinos. And even the Cuban president, Batista, spoke English well. And he made sure other Cubans did too because he was all about bringing the *Yanqui* dollar to Cuba. He knew tourism made Cuba prosper, and in those days it did, but Fulgencio Batista—yes, that was his name, Fulgencio—always got his cut of everything. And it was a *big* cut. Word is he left with $300 million when he went into exile.

So we got settled in our room in the Nacional and I wanted to go to the bar for some daiquiris. So did Dallis but, as always, he wanted to do something else first. You and I have never talked about sex that much but, if you have your daddy's DNA, lordie you must be a nymphomaniac. It's funny how when we women want sex all the time we're nymphomaniacs but when men want it all the time they're . . . well, just men, I guess. Or sex fiends, or mashers or whatever. Masher. You've probably never even heard that one. I know I'm dating myself, but that's not hard to do at this stage of the game. Don't get me wrong; I liked sex too. It's just that I could be equally as happy with a blender of daiquiris, a pack of Luckies, a great Cuban orchestra, and a crowd of cute people.

Anyway, as almost always, I saw to Dallis's wishes. I mean, after all, he'd brought me to Cuba and we were at the Nacional. Afterwards, he said we could go to the Casino Internacional which was run by Meyer Lansky, the American gangster who was Batista's "gambling consultant." Actually, Lansky was the casino operator and Batista was his partner.

Dallis looked at his watch. "We'll have almost an hour to have a drink or two and play a little blackjack."

I was puzzled. "Then what?" I asked.

"Then Roberto will meet us."

"Roberto? Who's Roberto?"

Dallis took me by the arms and gave me one of his looks. This one was animated; his blue eyes seemed to flicker and dance all at the same time. "Roberto is our man in Cuba. He's going to help us sell buses for all Batista's schools."

"Really?" I said, properly awed.

He still held my arms. "Well, I hope so. It depends on how this meeting goes."

I'm not sure why but that remark made me a little nervous. We proceeded to each have probably two mojitos while we played a little blackjack. But very little because we were mostly into the mojitos and our Lucky Strikes. You probably never even heard of Luckies; they were these short little cigarettes. They didn't have filters like the current ones have. Lord, they were *loaded* with nicotine and just *divine.* I'd do anything for one right now.

Anyway, it was probably good that we had a couple of drinks before Roberto showed up. Because if he'd come before I'd had a drink, I probably wouldn't have been able to talk. Dallis spotted him first across the casino floor. Dallis and I were standing at the blackjack table when Roberto strode up to us from a distance. He looked almost incandescent from the combined impact of his white teeth, his white dinner jacket, and the casino lights reflecting off his rather slick, jet black hair.

I remember it just like it was this morning. That walk toward us was like a slow-motion scene from a movie where everything else faded into background. A scene about a . . . king or a . . . president walking; the only thing missing was his throng of attendants and handlers. As he approached us, I realized that he wasn't even looking at Dallis. Instead, his eyes and that smile were directed at me like some kind of laser beam. Actually, the mojitos didn't help me talk; they just kept me from *fainting* because this was the best-looking man I'd ever laid eyes on and he had the most commanding presence I'd ever experienced.

I know I should have looked away but our eyes were locked. I'm sure my face was beet red as I stood right by my dear husband staring at this strange man approaching us. He never did look at Dallis; he just walked right up to me and held out his hand. I gave him mine and he bent and kissed it. *That's* when I would have fainted without the mojitos. I almost did anyway.

"And you must be Mrs. Duncan," he said, in the most charming Cuban accent I'd ever heard.

"Why . . . yes," I was stammering. "How do you do?"

He didn't answer; he just released my hand, turned to Dallis, and extended his hand again with a smile. "Dallis, right?"

Dallis took his hand. "I assume you're Roberto."

The smile was continuous. "I am Luis Roberto Alvarez Montero. The casino manager kindly directed me to you." His Cuban accent was profound but not thick, melodic but not comedic, completely enchanting.

Of course, Dallis pronounced the second syllable of Roberto like "Bert" or "Gert," but I soon began pronouncing it the proper way—*Roe-bair-toe*—and loved hearing myself do it. It was much later that I learned to roll the second R slightly.

Roberto looked at our almost-empty glasses, then, with a grandiose wave of his hand, he said, "May I suggest that we leave here and go to a little classier place where the mojitos are better?"

Dallis and I exchanged glances. I knew mine was one of incredulity because, I mean . . . leave the Casino Internacional for someplace *classier*? Are you serious? But Dallis quickly said, "Whatever you say, Roberto," using his best *gringo* pronunciation.

"Excellent," said the dreamy man who had walked up a few seconds before. He bowed slightly and extended his hand toward the casino entrance.

Chapter Four

I had no earthly idea where this Roberto character was taking us, but I had a feeling it would be a place far more important than the places I'd been with Judy and Muffy on our quest for Havana's best daiquiris. As we strode out of the Casino Internacional, the staff actually bowed as they smiled at us. I say "us" but their eyes were clearly on Roberto. I don't remember anybody even *noticing* us when we walked in.

Once outside, Roberto stopped and looked at us. "Perhaps you would not mind walking," he said. "It is a very short distance and the evening is beautiful."

He was right about that. The earlier breeze had diminished just enough to make the warm evening a delight, but the residual of the previous wind had Havana Harbor's waves still flinging sea spray high in the air as they struck the seawall called the Malecon—a sight even more spectacular in Havana's city lights. Prior to reaching the city streets, we walked through the open space adjacent to the Nacional among coconut palms, gumbo limbo trees and hibiscus. There are some lyrics in some song I can't remember about "tropical splendor;" well, Angel, this was it and I *adored* it.

Almost by the time Dallis got around to asking Roberto where we were going, we were there. We'd arrived at a building with an understated exterior, actually one of many buildings on a city street just two blocks from the Nacional. It had a neon sign hanging out front which read "Cabaret Montemartre."

Roberto pushed open the door and the tuxedo-clad staff fell all over themselves almost immediately, fawning over Roberto and jabbering in Spanish which I understood little of at that time. I said a silent prayer of thanks that Dallis had listened to me and worn a sport coat and a tie instead of the guayabera he'd wanted to, because *everybody* in this place was dressed to the nines. As well they should have been because this place was just *divine*. One entire wall was filled with an enormous curved bar which had huge fountains on either side that went all the way to the tall, tall ceiling. The fountains had *gorgeous* sculptures of nudes, both men and women, and the chandeliers were spectacular. The place certainly turned my young head at the time; I know I was smiling from ear to ear and showing my upper gums but I couldn't help myself.

The tuxedoed manager, maître d', or whoever he was, called Roberto by name and said some things to him in Spanish which obviously had to do with showing us to our table. Roberto made a sweeping gesture for us to follow the man and we did until we reached a round table right on the dance floor, clearly *the* table to have in the entire place. Behind the dance floor was an enormous stage which looked almost like it was made of black patent leather but accented with all manner of shiny stuff. On the stage was an orchestra playing Cuban music which sounded far better than I'd heard on either of my two trips with Judy and Muffy.

Roberto beat Dallis to the punch and, with a sweeping dramatic flair, pulled my chair out for me, after which I said, "Gracias."

"De nada, Señora," he said with a broad smile. "I did not know you spoke Spanish."

He was still standing sort of behind me and I was trying to figure out if he was being attentive or just trying to look down my dress. Not that it was that low, just a little. "Unfortunately, *gracias* and *de nada* are about the extent of my vocabulary," I said, cutting my eyes back up at him in a way I used to have back then.

"Well, Señora," he said, still smiling. "That is about all you need to know." Then those dark eyes seem to focus in on me more. "At least when you are with me."

I don't know why but I blushed profusely. I mean, I wasn't looking at myself but I could feel the heat in my cheeks. I looked at Dallis and his expression was one of irritation but I think I could read his thoughts: business is business.

In one motion, Roberto seated himself, snapped his fingers, and made some sort of clicking noise with his mouth. In less than five seconds, two tuxedoed waiters swarmed upon us. In just minutes after that, we all had freshly made mojitos in spectacular glasses like I'd never seen before, with the Montmartre's signature swizzle sticks shaped like a nude woman. With a large smile, Roberto raised his glass. We followed suit and all clinked. "To my new American friends," he toasted.

"Amigos," I said and immediately felt like an idiot. Which I was for blurting out the third and final word of my Spanish vocabulary when Roberto was speaking impeccable English to us and probably hadn't even finished his toast. He just looked at me, bemused but in a tolerant, almost intrigued way.

"Yes," he said. "Amigos. I welcome you to my beloved Cuba and wish you happiness and prosperity."

We all drank up. Dallis put his glass down and gave us one of his squinty-eyed grins. "That prosperity part sounds good to me."

I cut a glance at Roberto and saw that I wasn't the only one to say the wrong thing. You could see it in Roberto's face but then he underscored it by holding up his hand in a pausing motion. His grin was forced as he said, "Relax, my friend, we can talk business later. It is a beautiful night and you and I have the company of a beautiful woman. Let us enjoy it."

I blushed again at the beautiful woman part. Mainly because he was wrong. Oh, I wasn't bad back then; it was way before I started battling my weight. But I always thought my lips were too big. Some of these girls these days who have their lips shot up with God-knows-what to make them bigger would have killed for my lips back then. Then there was the matter of my gums always showing when I smiled. That's not to mention that I was still, as an adult, a little self-conscious about my nickname Dimple and how I got it. I just prayed Dimple would not slip out around Roberto; I needed to be Dorothy with him. I mean, this was business.

Anyway, the mojitos flowed and the orchestra played and Roberto ordered arroz con pollo for us.

Arroz con pollo is chicken and yellow rice, kind of a signature Cuban dish. It came along with more mojitos—which really were the best I'd ever had—and then the floor show.

Angel, you wouldn't have believed this floor show. They always called Havana "Las Vegas South" and the costumes were just spectacular. The five-foot-long bongo drums, the songs—all of the lyrics in Spanish, but I didn't care—were spellbinding. And their dancing. Ye gods, those people knew how to wiggle everything but their wigglers and I soon learned how to as well.

Actually, Roberto taught me. He started with a sort of bow to Dallis and said, smiling, "Dallis, I wonder if you would permit me to ask your beautiful wife to dance."

Dallis seemed to momentarily rotate his neck around his shoulders in a tick I'd never seen before—he obviously didn't like the way things were going—before saying, "Of course, Roberto, you two show me how the natives do it." He tried to add a grin but it didn't quite come off. I hoped Roberto didn't see me roll my eyes at the "natives" crack which mortified me.

Dallis was always the best dancer in any room; all the women swooned. But Roberto . . . lord, lord, lord. He did things with his hips that didn't seem physiologically possible. I did my best to keep up with him and tried my best to imitate him. The rhumba is really very simple. He kept repeating the count: *One,* two, three. *One,* two, three. It's much less about the feet than it is the hips and Roberto kept stressing that. "It's all in the *heeps,*" he would say in his delightful Cuban accent. My problem was deciding where to look—at his "heeps" or into those dark, inscrutable eyes of his.

When the orchestra slowed and began playing "Besame Mucho," that sort of narrowed it down to his eyes. Roberto danced with me right in front of my wonderful husband in a way no other man had unless he was drunk. He held me just a little closer than he should have and those eyes seemed to bore right through me like some kind of laser drill. I tried to avert his gaze but couldn't seem to. I was at the same time thrilled, embarrassed, weak-kneed, and terrified that Dallis would bust a gusset. I was relieved when the music stopped between songs because, between the mojitos and Roberto, I again began to fear I might faint.

Gallant as he was, Roberto later also taught Dallis how to wiggle his hips to Cuban music while all three of us were on the dance floor together, laughing hysterically, our mood and camaraderie no doubt helped along by our increasing count of mojitos. Our condition made me glad that dessert was on the table—*flan*, the delicious Cuban egg custard.

We were halfway through our dessert when one of the staff came to the table and whispered in Roberto's ear. He listened intently for a moment and then nodded, seeming to agree to something. As they brought us cups of that incredible Cuban coffee, Roberto looked at Dallis instead of me one of the few times during the evening.

"There is someone I would like for you to meet," Roberto said. "A fellow American of yours. I doubt that you know him but he is on his way over to our table."

Dallis and I looked in the direction of Roberto's glance and saw a strange-looking, small man in a dinner jacket heading our way. He was barely taller than I was, and had dark, slicked back hair. My mother would have said he looked very Jewish. Which I later found out he indeed was. A Russian one. Well, Belarus, actually.

Roberto stood and so did Dallis. I, of course, didn't. "Mr. and Mrs. Duncan, please meet my friend, Mr. Meyer Lansky." The man shook hands with Dallis. I did not offer my hand—ladies never did back then—and, to his credit, he did not reach for it but simply bowed slightly. Roberto invited him to join us, the staff scurried, and a chair appeared.

I had never heard of Meyer Lansky but Dallis obviously had. "*The* Meyer Lansky?" he asked, with a not-too-cordial and amazed expression.

Lansky paused several moments and studied Dallis before answering. "If you mean, am I the 'gangster' Meyer Lansky, the answer is yes. The only problem is that press reports about me are patently false. I am a legitimate businessman whose success has annoyed certain members of the press who are having trouble making ends meet themselves on their salaries. Simply put, they are jealous of my business success and try to build themselves up by tearing me down. It's a rather unattractive trait of human nature that has been around since the beginning of time."

Roberto spoke up. "Meyer is quite correct. He has been unfairly treated by the American press based on nothing but rumors and lies."

Dallis spoke. "So, Mr. Lansky, what exactly *is* your business?" There was still no cordiality in Dallis's tone.

Lansky broke out in a thin smile, looked around the room and then back at Dallis. "You're looking at it, Mr. Duncan. Part of it, at least."

That stopped Dallis. "You . . . you mean you own this place?"

Lansky's thin smile widened. "You people are my customers tonight and I thank you for your business. Now, Mr. Duncan, I ask you: was your food and drink and service satisfactory tonight?"

"Yeah, you bet," Dallis said, loosening up considerably now.

"And have you seen anything dishonest or criminal going on in this establishment?

Dallis grinned now. "No, of course not. It's a terrific place. Best I've ever been in. Your people do a fine job."

Meyer Lansky bowed almost imperceptibly. "Thank you, Mr. Duncan. Perhaps I can now increase your enjoyment of our little club."

At that moment I neither saw nor heard anything—no hand motions, no raising of an eyebrow, nothing like that. So I don't know how he did it, but somehow at that very moment, a tuxedoed man appeared with one of the most beautiful finished wooden boxes I'd ever seen —probably of Cuban mahogany—and held it in front of Meyer Lansky. It was large enough to require the man to hold it with both hands. I was about to ask what the box was when Meyer opened it and I saw what was inside.

Meyer looked at Dallis and said, "Mr. Duncan, with your permission, I will make a selection for us." Then he looked at me and said, "Assuming Mrs. Duncan does not object."

I smiled obediently and said, "Certainly not. I just *love* the smell of a good cigar. Especially a Cuban one."

I was lying through my teeth. As much as I loved as many Lucky Strikes as I could get my hands on, I'd always *loathed* the smell of cigars. Maybe it was because a boy I dated from Georgia Tech once told me they sometimes put cow manure in them, even those fancy Cuban ones. I never did find out if that was true.

Meyer, Dallis and Roberto all engaged in the obligatory affected ritual which seems to accompany lighting up an important cigar. It was nauseating to watch, particularly when my dear, usually unaffected, husband engaged in it.

Lansky leaned back, drew on his cigar and blew a big ring of smoke toward the ceiling. Then he leaned in toward the table and his tone changed. "We were just speaking of business. Roberto tells me you'd like to do some. School buses and ambulances, I believe?"

Chapter Five

For the first time that evening, Dallis perked up. I thought I understood. All he'd done all night is try to stay sober while throwing down endless mojitos and watching his wife wiggle her hips on the dance floor while flirting with some apparent Latin lothario. Now he had a chance to be in his element: talking business. His mission was on. It was why he was here. I thought I saw him shake his head slightly to sort of revive himself. He took his glasses off and pulled out his handkerchief for his ritual cleaning, which I had learned was as much to gather his thoughts as anything else.

"Yes, Mr. Lansky," Dallis said in his best business speak. "My company is most interested in the Cuban market. Our biggest competitor has been getting all the country's business and I'm sure we can make President Batista a much better deal."

I was so proud of Dallis and the important way he spoke about this until Meyer Lansky's reply. "So, you've come down here to cut the price of your products? What about the quality of your vehicles? Are they better than what Cuba is using now? Perhaps they are not as good and that's why you will sell them so cheap?"

Dallis was a bit flustered. "No, no, that's not the case. On the contrary, Mr. Lansky, Cuba is paying more than they should for a product that our customers in the United States will tell you is far inferior to ours."

Lansky wore a thin, derisive smile as he said, "So, let me get this straight: You somehow know how much the Cuban government is paying for school buses and you've apparently come to Cuba to disparage your competitor."

Off came Dallis's glasses again and out came the handkerchief. "I'm sorry, Mr. Lansky, I know I'm not making myself clear. No, I don't know exactly how much you're paying—"

Lansky held up his hand. "Not me, sir, I am an American, just like you. We are talking about the Cuban government."

"Right. I meant to say I'm not exactly sure how much the Cuban government is paying for buses, but my company is extremely interested in the Caribbean market and will be very aggressive on price. As far as my competitor is concerned, I believe they make a decent product; it's just that ours is much better. Is that a better way to put things?"

I had been dying a thousand deaths for Dallis but after that last rejoinder I felt better.

"Well, I really don't think I can help you, Mr. Duncan. I barely know President Batista. Your best bet is Roberto here. He's the one with the connections in the president's office. In fact, he's the one with connections in *everybody's* office. He's a good man to know, and to do business in Cuba, you have to know the right people." He leaned back again for a pull on the cigar.

I was studying Roberto for some reaction. I would have been blushing again if someone talked like that about me in my presence, but Roberto was just absently tapping a Montmartre swizzle on the table with one hand and holding his cigar in the other. He seemed to be studying the nude woman swizzle stick.

"By the way, how do you know Roberto?" Lansky asked.

Dallis began to reply. "Well, he—"

"I have a relative in Miami who knows Mr. Duncan's cousin," Roberto said, interrupting. I looked at Dallis and his expression confirmed what I was thinking: that Roberto had just fabricated what he said, on the spot. I couldn't wait until later to ask Dallis the *real* way he knew Roberto, something which had never occurred to me until now.

Lansky looked to Dallis for confirmation. "Yes, that's right," Dallis said, staring at Roberto with a hint of a scowl. "My cousin."

Roberto spoke now. "I am afraid Mr. Lansky is a bit modest. President Batista is well aware of Mr. Lansky and holds him in high regard. Perhaps if I keep him updated on our progress and our business discussions, he will consider at least putting in a good word for you with the president. That, of course, assumes that I decide to represent you in these matters."

Dallis was always a great salesman and somewhere along the line was taught to always ask for the order. "So what has to happen for you to decide to represent me?" he asked.

That beautiful mouth of Roberto's spread into a wide grin. "We have to spend more time together. I need to get to know you better, get comfortable with you. And we have to talk about our arrangement. How long can you stay here in Havana?"

Dallis removed his glasses but didn't go for the handkerchief this time. "Well, I don't know, maybe a week. Maybe longer if I could convince the company."

Roberto was still smiling. "Excellent."

Meyer Lansky stood. "Well, I must excuse myself. Duty calls. It was a pleasure to meet you, Mr. and Mrs. Duncan, and I wish you success in your venture. Tell me, do you enjoy gambling?"

"You mean blackjack?" I asked.

"Blackjack, craps, just about anything you like. I own the casino at the Hotel Nacional—"

"That's where we're staying," I said.

"But I also have an intimate casino here in another room. I'll tell the cashier that your credit is good."

"Oh, that's wonderful," I said as I cut a glance at Dallis, who obviously thought it was anything but.

Lansky bowed slightly as he made his exit from our table.

"What an interesting man," I said. "He seemed nice to me; why do people think he's a gangster?"

"Probably because he's in the gambling business," Roberto said. "Some people in it are engaged in other things which are illegal. Meyer obviously is not or he would be in prison. His casinos and hotels—and he owns more of them than just this one and the

Nacional—are very well run and fair. Would you like to take him up on his offer and give some blackjack a try?"

Like my mother, I loved to gamble and loved blackjack. But out of the corner of my eye, I could see Dallis dying a thousand deaths. We were on thin financial ice anyway and all we needed was to make a mistake in the casino. Even a little one.

"Oh, let's do!" I said as I watched the color drain from Dallis's face.

Roberto started to stand, but Dallis, who had quickly recovered from my blurting our acceptance of the blackjack invitation, stopped him. "Just a minute, Roberto. Before we do that, what's this business about your friend in Miami and my cousin?"

Roberto actually became a bit sheepish as he raised both hands. "Forgive me, Dallis. That was purely for Meyer Lansky's benefit. He is a good man and I trust him. I just do not want him to necessarily know all the details of my business with you. I hope you do not mind."

Dallis seemed to be mulling that one over. Finally, he simply said, "Okay. No problem."

Once again, I thought to myself: business is business.

We rose and went into another room. This was a small, but completely elegant chandelier-adorned casino filled with elegantly dressed people, which is the way things were in Cuba in the fifties. Roberto took us to the cashier where Dallis signed a marker for $100. I thought he was going to have a heart attack right there. Maybe me, too. But I felt better when he only took twenty-five chips worth a dollar each and we went to the dollar table. We watched Dallis play for a short while and he was only down three or four dollars so I didn't feel terrible. The problem was, I wanted to play too and said so.

Roberto spoke up. "It is bad luck for a husband and wife to play at the same table. Dallis, with your permission, I will take your lovely wife to another table to play and keep an eye on her so she will not lose too much money." He was beaming one of his smiles. The color seemed to drain from Dallis's face but, once again, business was business, so he nodded quickly and then looked back at the hand he was being dealt.

Roberto took me gently by the elbow and steered me all the way across the room, out of sight of Dallis's table, to another table that had a small sign on it in Spanish and English. It said: five hundred dollar limit.

"Roberto! My stars, look at that sign; we can't play here," I said, close to hyperventilation. "Dallis and I don't have that kind of money."

He just smiled down at me—maybe I didn't tell you, but he was about six-two—and said, "Let us form a little partnership. I will put up the money and you play. If you win, you keep the money you win and if you lose, I will take the loss."

He just smiled and waited for my reply, gazing with those dark eyes of his. His gaze cut right through my very being and made my knees feel as if they would buckle any second. Looking back, this was a seminal moment that profoundly affected many events to follow. It was, of course, highly improper of him, and his bearing suggested many possibilities about what might be in his . . . what? His mind? His heart? His . . . well, I won't go into that because I don't want to embarrass Ladasha. As he continued to direct his absolute attention to me during the moments I considered his gambling proposition, I asked myself: what's really happening here?

I tried to instantly measure him. The look he was invading me with was certainly not a leer. I would have found anything like that unbecoming and revolting; after all, I loved my husband to death. Whatever was going on was something I was susceptible to because of a certain sense I had of his probity. He genuinely seemed interested in *me*. But, all things considered, tempting as it was, there was no way I could accept his proposal. I made up my mind to decline immediately and made myself look back into his eyes.

" . . . Well . . .," I said, "maybe just a few hands?"

My word, what had I said? What would I tell Dallis?

Roberto beamed. "Excellent. He reached in his pocket and pulled out an enormous stack of Cuban pesos and exchanged them with the dealer for an equally enormous stack of chips. "By the way," he said, "I have been meaning to ask you all evening. May I call you by your given name?"

The eyes were boring in again. I felt my own divert; I mean, how much could I take? I looked back at him. "Please . . . call me Dorothy," I said quietly.

"Dorothy." He softly repeated my name, smiling and seeming to study me all over again. "It is beautiful. Like you." As he said it, he put his hand gently on my arm for a moment. When he removed his hand, my arm felt like a hot coal had just been on it.

"Shall we play?" he said, gesturing toward the blackjack table.

"I'm ready," I said with what I know was girlish gaiety, and sat on the only empty stool on the table. Of course, cocktails were offered and I took a crème de menthe while he ordered cognac. He stood right behind me and very close. I could feel his breath on my neck which made concentrating on the game almost impossible. Despite that, somehow before Dallis found us, I was up $230 and trying to keep from squealing with every hand I won. One look at Dallis gave me a sinking feeling. How was I going to explain it to him?

Chapter Six

Hallie

"Have you considered winging it?"

Hallie was so taken aback by the question that she had to think a moment to be sure she understood it.

"Surely you don't mean . . ." Her response trailed off.

Ian Lightbourne, her companion at the bar at Tampa's Palma Ceia Golf and Country Club, nodded. "That's exactly what I mean," he said.

Hallie emitted a nervous laugh and rolled her eyes. It only took her a moment to become exercised. "Of *course* I haven't considered winging it. You see, I have this MFA professor named Ian Lightbourne who threatens expulsion from the university if I even *think* about writing a novel from anything other than a damn detailed outline." She folded her arms over her chest and exhaled sharply. "Wing it," she repeated with derision that was part contrived, part not. She reached for her glass of Acacia chardonnay and took an aggressive, and hopefully calming, pull.

Her professor smiled ruefully. "So you think I'm that inflexible."

"Inflexible?" she answered. "For God's sake, how do I reconcile flexibility with the writing dogma you've pounded into me for every college course I've taken from you? That's like the pope all of a sudden saying he thinks divorce and abortion are just *wonderful* ideas."

Lightbourne was silent for a few moments as he gazed at her with a bemused expression down his rather aquiline, but nonetheless attractive, British nose. "Point well taken," he said, "but it sounds to me as if your circumstances are unique and may require a drastic approach."

Hallie just shrugged and sat with her arms folded. She felt too confused and discombobulated to respond.

"Just listen to me," Ian Lightbourne said. "You must realize two important things. One is that this is not your story and the other is that you don't know how it ends." He reached over and put his hand gently on her arm. "And forgive me, but there is a chance you may never know how the actual story ends."

She looked up at him and nodded, appreciative of his empathy for her mother's tenuous remaining existence on Earth.

He continued. "When one writes a novel, there is always a plot idea but the story is inside the writer." He clutched his chest for emphasis. "This story is not inside you because it's not yours. Now I think what you're doing is fantastic and can be a great success, but your tape recordings are not going to totally carry the day. I think you need to get started writing this book as your mother is telling the story to you. That's the only way it will become a part of you and the only way you can get your muse involved. And, yes, that means starting now, winging it, with no outline."

She felt a mix of gratitude, excitement, and relief. "I don't know why I got angry there for a moment. I'm sorry."

"No worries," he said.

"It's actually a big relief," she said, "because it means I can get started. And the sooner I get started, the sooner I have a chance to finish the work, sell it, and start the royalties—"

His hand was up. "Uh-uh. Remember I told you that any first-timer is a fool to assume their novel will even be published, much less ever generate any meaningful money. You know how much fiction is being published every year, and self-publishing alone is bringing another million books a year on the market."

She smiled at him. "I know. But there are two reasons I'll be different. My work will be better and I have no choice but to succeed because my financial situation is, well . . ."

He touched her arm again. "You are very talented, my dear. And I hope you are a smashing success straightaway."

This made Hallie look at her professor and measure him. As she did so, she tried to measure herself and her relationship with him. This was the third time they had gone for drinks. The first two times they had reviewed class work, but this time he'd just smiled after class and said, "Glass of wine? No work, just to unwind?" She'd hesitated, but only for a moment, and now she wondered why. Wondered what she was doing here. It wasn't to butter him up to get a good grade. She got those anyway, was definitely going to get her MFA, and mainly just wanted to learn.

She figured Ian Lightbourne for maybe fifty-five or so, barely older than she. He looked as British as he sounded, often wearing tweedy jackets and corduroys and wearing his salt-and-pepper hair rather long, especially in the back, but no facial hair. Unlike her lover, Lightbourne's eyes were the color of the Gulfstream, and they alternated between being brooding and alive with mischief—an engaging and captivating combination. His appearance, humor, creativity, and knowledge Hallie found to be a very attractive package. But . . . she had Rich—and Ian knew it—plus Ian was married to one of the most successful lawyers in Tampa.

But still, this was the third time for drinks. She'd met his wife once when she'd come to class to get a house key she'd misplaced. Mrs. Ian Lightbourne had zoomed in and out, almost making the papers fly off the desks as a short little flounce on the jacket of her navy blue suit seemed to create turbulence in her wake. Off to another court date, Hallie assumed.

As she considered these things, Hallie noticed Ian looking at her in a way he never had. He erupted in a smile as he said, "Are you as hungry as I am? We had an impromptu conference call with the provost today and lunch was a handful of almonds." He looked at his watch. "I'll bet we could get a table at Mise en Place." Then he nodded in the direction of the Club's dining room. "This place can be kind of a zoo this time of year."

Hallie wondered if his last comment translated to: "Besides, my wife might come in here with a group of clients and see us."

"Ian, you need to go home and have dinner with your wife tonight," Hallie said.

He threw back his head and laughed out loud. "Silly girl," he said. "My wife almost *never* has dinner with me. And when she's not preparing for a trial, she's going to some charity event trying to get on another civic board—why, I don't know. We really don't see terribly much of each other."

That comment spawned new emotions in Hallie. One was empathy for his obvious loneliness, something with which she had become quite familiar since becoming single. But another was a somewhat empty feeling of disappointment that his invitation was less about her than it was about his own loneliness.

She leaned in toward him and flashed her best smile, now putting her hand on *his* arm. "Ian, thank you so much for the kind invitation, but I've just been given my marching orders by this dashing British professor to get off dead center and write my novel without an outline. You're very sweet. Say hi to your wife for me." She stood and did something she'd never done—leaned over and kissed him on the forehead—and left.

Chapter Seven

Dimple

I'm in my wheelchair in a somewhat private alcove in a room The Meadows calls their solarium. I see Hallie switch on the digital recorder as she sits beside me in a chair. Ladasha has already "groomed" me—fixing my snow-white hair and putting some lipstick on. The morning sun streams in from a lovely garden outside the solarium. It's a more pleasant spot than my room, to be sure. Maybe it will get me to talking more. Hallie is ready; she asks me what happened after her daddy and I joined Roberto at the casino that first night in Havana.

I hear her but my gaze is locked in, trance-like, to the blossoms on a magnificent magnolia tree in the garden. I know Hallie is panicked again but I still proceed at my own pace. I slowly turn to her, put on the best smile the effects of my stroke will allow, and begin.

Your daddy was *so* mad at me for winning all that money at blackjack. It wasn't that I won that upset him because even that amount of money was important to us then. No, it was the fact that Roberto had staked me that just *infuriated* him. We went back to our wonderful room at The Nacional and he didn't even want to . . . well, you know.

But he got over his anger quickly. I think it was because he clearly saw Roberto as a way to change our financial lives and he was willing to overlook certain things. Up to a point, at least.

However, Roberto's attention to me wasn't the only thing frustrating Dallis. It seemed that, no matter what Dallis said or did to move things along, Roberto never wanted to actually get down to talking business, to discussing exactly how Dallis was going to sell all those school buses to the Cuban government. Roberto kept insisting that before they could have meaningful and effective discussions, they must get to know one another well. Get comfortable with each other. He told Dallis his family came from Spain and that was the European approach to doing business.

Well honey, I can tell you this: it was just fine with me because it was one continuous party, and I was in on everything. It started the next night when we joined Meyer Lansky for dinner at the Riviera Hotel he owned. We had *the* absolute best table in the place. And talk about people falling all over themselves to serve us. I'll tell you, Angel, my head was turned. My biggest worry became clothes because it was beginning to be obvious that we were in for this kind of life every night we were there. I told Dallis that he and Roberto were going to be seeing the same outfits on me multiple nights and asked if I should buy just a few more things while we were there. Of course you know what he said: "Hell, no; we can't afford it." And you know what I said: "What about all this money we're going to make?" Ha, he didn't even answer me.

After dinner at the Riviera's elegant restaurant, Dallis and Roberto and I went into their nightclub for the floor show. I'm not sure why, but I chose when your daddy was in the men's room to finally ask Roberto, "Other than being from Spain, you haven't said much about your family. And are you married? Do you have children?" I sort of gulped after I croaked the words out.

Roberto didn't have to turn to look at me; he already was. It was the look that seemed to redefine the concept of attentiveness. A look that seemed to say that his thoughts of me consumed his entire being. Once again, I couldn't meet his eyes; I had to look away.

"Dorothy, you may be the most beautiful woman I have ever known," he said.

That stunned me for a moment until—and I've no idea where it came from—I surprised myself by blurting, "Roberto, in the first place, you shouldn't be saying something like that to me unless it's in the presence of my husband. And in the second place, what in heaven's name does that have to do with telling me about your family?"

As soon as I said it, I had a sinking feeling in the pit of my stomach which told me that my impulsiveness had just queered Dallis's bus deal and ruined our chance for a better financial life. What in the world gets into me? I thought.

Roberto surprised me by breaking out in wide grin and raising his index finger in the air. "That is a point well taken, Señora." Then he leaned toward me and lowered his voice. "But it is unfair to blame me for the beauty and grace God has given you. I admire not only your beauty but also your courage and loyalty and it is difficult for me to refrain from sharing those feelings with you. All I know to do is to ask for your forgiveness each time I do so."

Despite my efforts not to, I felt myself smiling. "Okay, so what about your family? In fact, what about *you*, while we're at it?"

He leaned back now and seemed to measure either me or the words he was about to speak. His expression and tone became reflective in a sort of respectful way as he began. "My grandfather was an importer of sugar in Spain but having trouble with supply. So he and his partner decided one of them would move to Cuba. They actually drew lots to decide which of them would go and it was my grandfather who moved his family to Cuba and began acquiring sugar lands. By the time my father was a man and ready to join my grandfather in the business, slavery had been abolished in Cuba; the business had become more mechanized and technical, and the large U. S. companies had begun consolidating the industry. But it did not matter, because my father preferred to become a physician; a surgeon, in fact, which he still is today right here in Havana." He looked at me and smiled. "Is there anything you need removed from your body? He is your man." He seemed to revel in his little quip, but only momentarily as he allowed his eyes to roam all over me while he added,

"However, I would not recommend you do anything of that sort." Then he laughed out loud at his own joke.

It was infectious and I giggled before asking, "Okay, but what about you?"

He looked back with an impish smile. "What *about* me?"

"Well . . . are you a doctor, too? Like your father?"

He threw his head back and laughed again. "No, no, I failed my science classes and I cannot stand the sight of blood. I am a big— how would you say?—a baby. I decided to study the law."

"So you're a lawyer? Then what are you doing selling school buses?"

The throaty, head-back laugh again. "You are a charming girl. I am considering representing your husband and his company to provide certain client services which may assist him in dealing with the Cuban government."

Well, Angel, as you know, I was a housewife who was also an accomplished party girl who knew which fork to use, kept the conversations going, and used proper grammar. And I tried to be as lady-like as I could while still living it up pretty good. But there's one thing I wasn't and that was stupid. I had heard about all the graft and corruption in Cuba. How nothing got done unless somebody got paid off. In fact, I had avoided the subject with Dallis because he was so excited about the Cuban business opportunity and I was equally excited about being along for the ride. So, without really thinking it over, here I went again.

"Roberto, those . . . certain client services. Would that have something to do with paying money to certain people to make sure the buses get sold?"

I couldn't believe I'd said it and immediately wished I could take it back. Roberto just studied me for some long moments with a very serious expression on his face. Heavens, I thought, what if Dallis chooses this moment to come back from the men's room? I cut my eyes to expand my peripheral vision and didn't see him. Then I had a disgusting thought: Dallis was probably trying to get a phone number from a cocktail waitress. Roberto finally spoke.

"Of *course* it has something to do with that. That is the way business is done in Cuba. At least right now."

"What do you mean 'right now'?" I asked.

"Nothing. Just that it is the way business is done. Tell me, does that bother you?"

I had to think that one over. I considered myself a very honest person and always found the "everybody does it" excuse for doing something you shouldn't to be pretty lame. Even worse was the "he'll never know" gambit. My answer to that was always, "yes, but *I'll* know." At that moment, I already knew I was getting in too deep with Roberto but the irony of the moral dilemma I was heading toward with him had not yet struck me. But on the bribery question, it became clear at that moment that it was the only way Dallis was going to pull this bus deal off and change our lives. And it was obvious to me that Dallis knew how the game was played before he decided to pursue the opportunity; he just hadn't told me.

"Yes, it bothers me a great deal," I said. "But it doesn't look like I'll be giving anybody a brown paper bag and it doesn't look like I could do anything to stop it."

"Just look at it as a local custom," Roberto said.

"A local custom," I repeated. I smiled and said, "It's the only local custom so far I don't like."

He leaned toward me with one of his "looks." "There are some other local customs with which you have not yet become familiar."

"Like . . . ?"

"Like when a man and a woman are attracted to each other, even though they may have another in their life, they can enjoy each other's company in a very special way."

As he said it, he gently allowed his hand to rest on my knee under the table and at that very moment Dallis walked up. We both looked up at him simultaneously.

Chapter Eight

Hallie

The parking lot of the Rodino & Ross building was almost full; Hallie had to park at the far end and walk with her wind-buffeted umbrella through a Tampa thunderstorm to the main entrance of the building. Her route took her past a covered parking area connected to the building by a breezeway. The parking space closest to the door had a sign that read Richard Rodino and she saw Rich's red Bentley GT convertible parked there, staying dry despite its top being down. She caught a whiff of leather scent from the camel-colored seats as she walked by.

The receptionist greeted Hallie, called her by name and waved her to the elevator of the four-story building. On her way to the elevator, Hallie experienced the pleasure of walking by an enormous work in multi-colored glass by Dale Chihuly. Rich had never told her what he paid for it but she suspected it might have cost more than many people in Tampa earned in a year. Rich had his own reception area on the eighth (and top) floor where his office was and it sported its own Chihuly, albeit a smaller one. His assistant greeted her warmly as had the first floor receptionist. "Hi. He's on the phone. Can I get you something?"

"No thanks, Karen," Hallie said. "I'll just try to dry off for a minute."

A minute is about all it took for Rodino to emerge from his office, take Hallie by the shoulders, give her a brief hug, then lead her into his office. "Honey, you're wet. We should have just met somewhere for lunch."

She smiled up at him. "It's okay. I don't come to your office that much and I always like seeing how important you are."

Rodino pursed his lips in an expression of modesty as he motioned her to one of the chairs across from his desk and walked around to his high-backed executive chair. Although the matching coat was in a closet, Rodino was wearing the pants of a custom tailored suit with a custom white dress shirt to go with it and a Burberry four-in-hand necktie. "The most important person in this room right now is you," he said, and she felt a glow of pleasure. She recognized that it was a pattern, a trait of his: Rich Rodino always knew just the right thing to say at just the right moment.

She looked past him and out his broad window down on I-275 but could see little besides her own reflection because the rain was still pouring. He followed her glance then turned back toward her and grinned. "Not a very good day to go to lunch in a convertible, is it?"

She shook her head.

He nodded in the direction of his desk telephone. "If you're not rushed, it may work out anyway because I have no choice but to wait for a call I'm expecting. A big new investor in our latest settlement fund is supposed to tell me if he's going to pull the trigger on five million."

"Do you think he will?"

Rodino grinned. "I made the presentation myself yesterday."

Although the display of hubris gave her a slight sinking feeling in her stomach, she nevertheless smiled. "See, I told you you're important."

Just then his phone rang. "Hello," he said. "Yeah, put him on."

Hallie sat and listened to one side of a phone conversation and saw quickly that it was not going well.

"You can't be serious," Rodino said and then paused for a long time as he listened. The he said, "Look, uh . . . can you hang on just a second?" He covered the mouthpiece with his hand and looked up at Hallie.

"Why don't you wait outside for me," he said. "I'm going to have to turn up the heat on this guy." He smiled at her. "Don't want to bruise your pretty ears."

Hallie shrugged and obediently withdrew. She sat in his waiting room next to Karen's desk and chatted with her, mainly about the weather. Through Rodino's door she could hear his voice, the volume and passion high, but she could understand nothing. After perhaps five minutes, there was silence and Karen's phone rang. She listened a moment and said simply, "Okay." Then she nodded for Hallie to go back in.

Back in his office, Hallie first saw Rodino's back. He was standing, staring out his window at the rain. The rain had made his window a mirror and Hallie could see Rodino's facial expression even though his back was to her. It was an expression she'd never seen him wear—a sort of dark fury. She wished she hadn't seen it but it lasted only a few seconds before he whirled to face her. He was now wearing a broad grin.

"So, what sounds good for lunch?" he asked, brightly. "Palma Ceia, the Yacht Club, a Cuban place?

"I'm always partial to Palma Ceia," she said

By the time they got downstairs it had stopped raining, but Rodino put the top up on the Bentley anyway. In less than fifteen minutes, they were sitting at their lunch table.

"Glass of wine?" Rodino asked her.

She was taken aback. "I've never seen you drink wine at lunch."

He grinned, sheepishly she thought. "I kind of need one after that phone call." And he ordered a glass of pinot noir for both of them.

"I take it your new investor is not going to become your new investor?" she said.

He smiled at her warmly and touched his temple with his fore-finger. "Very perceptive, as usual. Win some, lose some; it's just that I hate losing. But we win our share and the good news is we don't need that guy that badly. Plenty more smart money still rolling in."

"Well, I'm glad to hear that," she said brightly.

"Yeah, not to worry," he said. His smile then turned to a frown. "But, damn, I hate to lose."

Hallie had seen this competitive incinerator burning before and knew it never subsided below a smolder. It was part of what made Rodino attractive to her; her former husband, whom she had divorced, had been a counter opposite, almost to the point of rank indolence. In fact, the only resourcefulness her ex-husband had ever exhibited was when he essentially stole all her money, which was one of the reasons Hallie took back her maiden name of Duncan.

"Hey," Rodino said. "Changing the subject: what's up with the book? Is your mom still jabbering away every time you go see her?"

Hallie rolled her eyes. "Is she ever. She's in Cuba now trying to help my father sell school buses but about to start having an affair with the Cuban lawyer my dad is working with to help him make the right contacts with the government."

"Hmmm. Sounds juicy. Have you finally started to write it?"

She thought several long moments contemplating her reply and said nothing.

He gestured with both hands. "I said have you started to write it yet?"

She gave him a pursed-lips smile. "Actually, I'm planning to start tonight after I see my mother this afternoon."

She wasn't exactly sure why she said what came next. "Last night I had drinks–here at the Club actually–with my professor and we discussed that very thing. In all the classes I've taken from him, he's stressed the importance of a complete outline before beginning a novel. But last night, he changed his tune after I told him how things are unfolding with Mother."

She waited for his response with anticipation.

"Makes sense to me. Why fool around with a bunch of extra work if you know what the plot is?"

"Well, that's not the exact reason he gave for changing his recommendation but it's in the ballpark."

They finally ordered lunch; Rodino uncharacteristically had a second glass of wine, and Hallie left for The Meadows feeling unsettled and not knowing why.

Chapter Nine

Dimple

I'm in a bit of pickle today. It's because Hallie is champing at the bit to find out what happened when Dallis came back from the men's room at the Montmartre Club just when Roberto's hand was on my knee under the table. She arrives with her recorder as I'm in the middle of looking at some old snapshots from my childhood in Smithtown, Georgia. Ladasha found them in my things and, now that my noggin is working a little better, I'm keenly interested. Hallie sits down but does not turn on the recorder. I start to talk but I'm not sure it's what she wants me to talk about. Actually, I'm sure it's not.

You know, Angel, these pictures just bring it all back. My first memory is of Thanksgiving at Granny's house. I must have been five or six, I'm not sure. That house is gone now—torn down for a shopping center, I think—but I can still remember every room and could describe the furniture in it if you asked me.

You do want me to? Well, I'm not going to describe everything, Angel, but I can tell you that every room in the house except the bathrooms had a fireplace. That was the heating system. Thank goodness I was a girl and didn't have to go out to the coal bin on winter mornings with that big old pail and load it with coal then tote it in to build a fire. One of my uncles was usually staying at Granny's house when I was there and they would gently knock on my bedroom door about dawn. Actually, it wasn't *my* bedroom; it was Momma's, but it was where I slept. My uncle would gently tap on the door, wait a second or two, then come in and start that fire with the coal he'd brought in and some newspapers. Momma and I would just turn over in our beds and burrow deeper into the comforter, but not before Momma would, in a kind of languid, half-groan say to her brother, "Thank you, Harrison."

That was my favorite uncle's name: Harrison. I guess he was my favorite because I was a favorite of his. And also because I somehow knew he was so *worldly* compared with the rest of my family. He'd been in the Navy and traveled all over the place and continued to while my other uncle never left Smithtown and had no desire to. Auntie ended up marrying a wealthy wholesale grocer named Reavis Yancey and rarely left Smithtown either. But they sure rode around in a brand-new Buick he bought every year.

Granny's house was a big, sprawling frame place with a tin roof and a front porch which ran the entire width of the house. It didn't have all that much property and it was a block from the town square and right next door to Smithtown's little bus station. It had lots of bedrooms, a huge living room, a dining room almost as big as the living room, and an *enormous* kitchen.

Just about everything happened in that kitchen except eating. That we did in the dining room except for Sunday night when we cooked scrambled eggs, country ham and biscuits, and ate in the kitchen. Don't ask me why we ate breakfast food on Sunday nights and why that meal was taken in the kitchen because I have no earthly idea. But I do know that Granny's biscuits were *divine* and that I couldn't add to them enough of the fresh Georgia cane syrup we always had. I'd cut the biscuit in half and lay the two halves out on a separate plate, paste them up good with the fresh butter we churned, then pour *gallons* of that cane syrup on top. We always had cane syrup by the case because my grandfather was a country doctor and took the syrup instead of a fee from one of his patients. *Lord,* was it good.

I guess the reason I remember that first Thanksgiving was because of the turkey. I can still remember the hatred I had as a child for my other uncle who always seemed to torment me: Uncle Buck. It all came to a head that day.

"Uncle Buck, why did you do it?" I screamed as I kicked his shins repeatedly. My ferociousness made him pick me up in his arms to protect himself and to try to console me.

"Dimple, don't you want some nice hot turkey for Thanksgiving?" he said. "It's gone taste mighty good."

"No!" I said, still yelling at the top of my lungs. "You're a meanie! I want you put that turkey's head back on right now!"

Of course he couldn't replace the turkey's head but I didn't know that. All I knew is that he'd let me watch him cut the turkey's head off and in my mind's eye–at least what's left of my mind–I can still see that huge turkey running around Granny's back yard in circles. It was long time before I warmed back up to Uncle Buck.

That was the last Thanksgiving Daddy came and it was the last time I ever saw him. He and Momma were barely speaking by then. In fact, I don't think he spoke to her at all that day. His name was Jordan Card and most Georgia folks pronounced it "Jerden". Another one of those Southern things, I guess. My mother, Maudie, was eighteen when they married and he was in his mid-thirties. She called him "Mr. Card" then and that never changed.

It's hard for me to remember what I felt for my father then. I suppose it was love, but mainly I was terrified of him; he was so formal and stern. Maybe he knew he would never see me again after that day. I say that because something very unusual happened. He walked over to me after my little *tête à tête* with Uncle Buck and uncharacteristically picked me up and held me in his arms. I remember seeing something unfamiliar for my father: the hint of a smile. Believe it or not, to this day I can still remember the smell of his hands after he put one of them on my cheek. It was a smell I really can't describe except to say it was masculine, kind of leathery but still fresh and clean, if you know what I mean.

The smell of his breath was something else again. It was a putrid combination of hangover breath and fresh whiskey breath, neither of which was unfamiliar to me because it was a regular occurrence with both Momma and Daddy.

After Daddy left us, Momma and I lived in a little two-room apartment on the second floor above Flossie's Fine Dresses on the square and I would walk to Smithtown Elementary. Lots of nights we'd stay at my grandmother's house and sometimes I would stay at Granny's by myself. These arrangements didn't seem peculiar to me at the time, but as I got older and learned more about my parents, and particularly my mother, I realized why we didn't just move in with Granny. The reason was simple; Momma didn't want to give up her social life. That term "social life" meant one thing in proper Southern circles in Smithtown, Georgia but, as I grew older, I learned it meant something totally different to Momma. It meant whiskey, men, and gambling. She had a healthy appetite for all three.

"Where have you been, Momma?" I asked the question when she came in one night, more than a little unsteady.

It was the middle of the night but I was awake because a *horrible* storm had come through. To this day, I can still remember how loud the thunder was. It must be what war sounds like, I thought. When I discovered my mother wasn't there with me, I got more scared. I suppose if that happened today some government agency would charge her with child neglect.

"Just out doin' a little drinkin' and smokin', Angel," she said. She called me "Angel" just as I do you.

"Why can't you stand up right, Momma? And why are you talking so funny?"

I got only a genteel grunt as she tumbled into her bed which was next to mine. She didn't bother taking off her clothes; she just kicked off her shoes. It was the first time I'd ever seen stockings down around a lady's ankles. I got back in my bed but I couldn't go back to sleep. One reason was the way my mother smelled. When I was older and frequenting bars myself, I recognized that distinctive aroma, the mixture of spilled whiskey residue and stale cigarette smoke which combined to make a smell similar to clothes which had been worn way too long without washing. I hated that smell as a child. As an adult, I smelled it when I walked in a cocktail lounge early in the day when the previous night's *fragrance,* if you know what I mean, was still in the air. It would put a damper on things for me. At least until my first bourbon and soda went to work.

"Drinkin' and smokin'," she'd said. Well, amen to that. Especially on the smoking part. Heavens to Betsy, I started when I was fifteen and have *never* been able to quit. Thank God for Ladasha slipping me one every now and then.

Somehow, Momma managed to hold a job. She was the secretary to the director of the Smithtown Chamber of Commerce. The director was a man named Joe Saluda. He was Italian, I guess, and not very attractive. On top of that he was *married.* But that didn't stop Momma. On more than one occasion, I saw him slip out of our apartment early in the morning. When I got older, I wondered how he did that. I mean, where did he tell his wife he'd spent the night? Then, when I got even older and had been exposed to the art of deception, I knew he'd probably told her he had to go to a big place like Columbus, Atlanta or Macon to see someone who was considering moving their business to Smithtown.

Momma was a living paradox. When she was sober, she was sweet to me. She actually doted on me. And on her good behavior, she was a modicum of probity—dignified and proper, and always striving to get the details of Southern refinement and propriety correct, almost fanatically. She taught me everything I know about china, flatware, furniture, linens, housekeeping, and cooking.

Oh, could she cook. Most people call it country cooking now, but to us it was just the way you did things. We wouldn't *dream* of buying mayonnaise; we made our own. I can still remember the expression on Momma's face when she'd look at a jar of Hellman's mayonnaise. "That's old *bought*," she'd say. We churned our own ice cream and made our own sweet pickles. And our fresh cornbread and collards–both with *lots* of sugar–were simply *divine.* But the thing I wish I had right now was what we made more often than anything else: fudge. It was *heavenly.*

As I continue to look at one old photo after another, I'm so engrossed in nostalgia that I barely hear Hallie trying to get me back to talking about Cuba and Roberto's hand on my knee. Then I feel myself getting a little tired.

Chapter Ten

Hallie

Despite her mother's many faults, more than she even *knew* about, Hallie loved her dearly. She regretted not having spent more time with her and not getting to know her better when she was young. But they'd been apart during the time Hallie lived with her paternal grandmother in Florida who had a little bit of money. Enough to pay for boarding school, then college at the University of South Florida. It was her senior year that she'd met her husband, Morris, who was already the general sales manager at a huge Chevrolet dealership in Tampa. Not long after they were married, he was in line to get his own dealership in another city with his boss putting up most of the money. It would have meant moving from Tampa which Hallie had not been excited about. But becoming an automobile dealer, even buying out Morris's boss over time, would have changed their financial lives dramatically.

Such a change had been needed because Hallie and Morris were about as good at spending money as making it. And financial planning was perpetually something they "needed to sit down and look at." She had let Morris keep track of their money which made it easy for him to conceal his gambling losses he'd incurred on his regular trips to Las Vegas, the expenses of which he claimed were "comped" by the casino. When she accidentally came across two used plane tickets to Vegas for her husband and somebody named Suzanne something or other, her world crumbled, the acrimonious split ensued, and, under Florida's quirky divorce laws, Hallie didn't even get alimony.

After the divorce, Hallie kept her part-time job writing copy at Tampa's largest advertising firm. She took the small settlement from her divorce and invested it in one of Rich Rodino's structured settlement funds that were an offshoot of his thriving law firm. The twelve-percent return she was getting via monthly checks, together with her earnings from her part-time job, were making ends meet but nothing more. The cash to pay for three or perhaps four months living expenses was her only cushion. Thank God for Rich's law firm and her investment with him, she often thought.

Those same circumstances over her financial circumstances were at the root of the moral dilemma she faced. She thought she was in love with Rich, but there were times when she wondered how much those emotions were being influenced by her tenuous financial situation. If Rich asked her to marry him, her life would change far more drastically than if Morris had become a Chevrolet dealer somewhere.

After all, she was sure Rodino & Ross was easily one of the most successful law firms in Tampa. Rich's firm had over forty lawyers in his Tampa office alone and had other offices in Orlando, Sarasota, and Tallahassee. Rich ran things from his fabulous office and lived in a virtual mansion. His Bentley was just part of his fleet; he had his own jet, a 120-foot yacht, and he was always at the top of the list of contributors to local charitable causes. His divorce, which was purported to have been very expensive, had not seemed to slow him down a bit. He was a superstar in Tampa and one of its most highly regarded citizens. Hallie knew her participation in all of that, were she to become his wife, would be, well, just indescribable, and she wouldn't have to leave Tampa. She found herself forcing out of her head daydreams of the kind of life she would have as Mrs. Richard Rodino because she wanted to be sure she was in love with *him* and not his lifestyle and his bank account. Adding to the churning nature of her feelings was whatever might be going on—or not—with her natty, and married, British professor.

But she knew there was a surefire antidote to whatever poison might afflict her, and that was her writing. Hallie could still remember the day, soon after her divorce, that her best friend—also her boss—took her to lunch.

"I want you know I hope you stay with us forever," Grace Lamont had said. "You're the best copywriter in the Western Hemisphere."

She remembered flushing with pleasure and some embarrassment.

"But," she continued, "You're wasting your talent. If I were you, I'd get in the master of fine arts program at the university, take all the creative writing classes you can, join some focus groups, and get busy writing something you can publish. Probably a novel if there's a story in you somewhere. You could do all of that and keep your job here. In fact, if you need some help paying for it, I'll give it to you. You can pay me back out of all the royalties you'll get someday." Grace had added a warm smile to that last statement.

It had been one of those moments. Mainly because she'd been thinking along the exact same lines. But she had little money and needed more confidence than she had. The push and the help her great friend gave her was a godsend and she welled up with tears at the lunch table that day. She told Grace she was the best friend and the best *boss* in the Western Hemisphere.

Chapter Eleven

Dimple

Hallie is coming to have supper with me tonight. It's at 5:30. Ye gads, I can remember when that was bourbon and soda time. I rest all afternoon because I know she's *suffering* to hear what happened with Roberto's hand on my knee. After supper, Hallie wheels me into the alcove in the solarium and I put her out of her misery.

All right, Angel, I know what you want to hear. What happened after Roberto put his hand on my knee, right?

Well, you're going to be disappointed because not much of anything happened. I mean, what *could* have happened? Oh, I watched Dallis's face and he had the same look he got every time he sensed that Roberto was up to no good with me, which seemed to be more and more often. But he didn't know Roberto's hand was on my knee.

So, did Roberto take his hand away when your daddy walked up? Heck, no! He left it there. But I took his hand very softly for second, making him think for an instant that I was going to hold it or caress it, but then all in one motion, I moved it off my knee and bent his pinkie back in the process as hard as I could. He grunted in pain so loudly that Dallis asked him what was the matter.

"Oh, nothing," he said.

Well, that evening came to a close with Dallis still champing at the bit wanting to know when he and Roberto were going to get down to business and start selling some school buses. And Roberto finally acted like he might be ready to talk business, suggesting we meet for lunch the next day at the Nacional.

When Roberto showed up at that lunch the next day, it was the first time I had seen him wearing anything other than a white dinner jacket or a suit. Today he was wearing a guayabera. That's the casual Cuban, typically white sport shirt with the two rows of vertical pleats on the front and back, always worn out and never tucked in the trousers. Lord, he looked just as dashing in that silly sport shirt as he had in a dinner jacket. He had a briefcase with him and we sat outside on the hotel's terrace dining area. It was two o'clock in the afternoon, but that's Cuba for you.

Roberto seemed serious. He didn't even order a drink of any kind, just café con leche . . . uh, that's Cuban coffee with lots of milk. Then he started talking. "Dallis, I assume you do not mind if Dorothy sits in on our business discussions. It may actually be helpful because there will be some degree of social activities required with some of the government officials making decisions on purchases of school buses."

Dallis gave the thumbs-up sign but never even looked at me. "No problem."

"Excellent. Well, Dallis, I have given this a great deal of thought and analyzed this situation very carefully." He fell silent.

"And?" Dallis said.

Roberto smiled now. "I have decided to represent you."

Dallis smiled too. "Well, that's great." He gestured to Roberto's briefcase. "Do you have some kind of proposed agreement to show me?"

"No. All I have in my attaché are some lists and locations and names of people you will need to see to assess the size and nature of the school bus fleet so you will have the information you will need to prepare a proposal. Our agreement will be one among gentlemen based on our trust and a handshake. That is why I wanted to spend time with you. To get comfortable." He was still smiling.

Dallis studied Roberto for a few long moments. "Well, Roberto, I normally favor that type of agreement too, and I certainly feel comfortable with you also."

I knew Dallis was lying through his teeth when he said that. Only a fool would have not noticed the attention Roberto had been paying to his wife, and Dallis was no fool.

Dallis continued. "But I see some possible problems with your approach. One is that I'm doing business in a foreign country, another is what happens if you or I forget something, and maybe the biggest problem is that I'm not sure the company I represent, Challenger, will go for a verbal agreement."

I was proud of the way Dallis presented his summary and I turned to Roberto with interest to see what he would say.

"Those are excellent points, Dallis. Please allow me to answer them carefully. Challenger should have no problem because, if we are successful, they will be issued formal purchase orders by the Cuban government and be paid for the buses under the normal irrevocable letter of credit from a U.S. bank, probably based in Miami. As for this being a foreign country, that should not make a difference—business is business. And, Dallis, I am not planning on forgetting anything, are you?" He grinned when he said it.

"No, but—"

"The verbal part will govern the agreement between you and me for payment for my services of introducing you to the right people and arranging for certain marketing activities, all of which will be paid for in cash. Now some of these amounts may be large and that is something you may have to use some persuasion with Challenger for but, believe me Dallis, it is the way business is done in Cuba. The only way."

"Marketing activities paid for in cash," Dallis repeated slowly. "Roberto, can we just call a spade a spade? We're talking about bribing government officials to get the bus business, aren't we?"

Roberto eyes met Dallis's stare unwaveringly for several long moments before he answered in a flat tone. "You can call it what you want, Dallis. You have to recognize that business practices and customs in this world vary from country to country and that you must be tolerant of the customs of others. But please understand that the only way you may experience the privilege of conducting late-stage marketing activities involving cash is if certain other events take place successfully. The first of those events is getting introduced to the right people in first place. The next is convincing those people that your product is a superior one. Only then will you be allowed to conduct special, final marketing activities that involve cash. Have I been clear?"

Out came Dallis's handkerchief and off came his glasses again. At that moment, it struck me that moral conundrums seemed to abound. On the one hand, Dallis had to wrestle with deciding whether to get involved in bribery, and on the other I had to deal with going to bed nights finding myself dreaming of doing certain things with Roberto I shouldn't be doing with anyone but my dear husband. It made me wonder if we were sitting at the lunch table across from the devil himself. Well, if we were, the devil was far more handsome and charming than I ever thought possible. The whole thing made me feel strangely excited, yet creepy.

Dallis finished cleaning his glasses and put them back on. I knew him to be unfailingly honest, priding himself on it. So he was clearly struggling. He then did something that almost made me well up with tears. He looked right at me and said, "What do you think we ought to do?"

Our eyes met in an effort to search each other's souls. In those moments I prayed for an answer to come from somewhere within me. When it came, I wasn't sure if my prayer was answered by God or the devil.

I choked back my feelings of . . . what? . . . revulsion, I suppose, and said, "Honey, it's no secret how things are done in all of Latin America. I think deep down, in our heart of hearts, we probably knew before we came down here we were going to be faced with this. And you need the business."

Dallis just nodded. Then he turned to Roberto and said, "How much cash for you and how much for the . . . marketing? And can you assure me that the pricing can be robust enough to support all the . . . fees?"

Roberto smiled and extended his hand across the table to Dallis who took it and shook. "Excellent decision, my friend. Let me assure you this will be a good deal for your company and that the pricing can be structured to cover all costs and provide an attractive profit margin. However, I cannot get specific on the cash portion until"—he tapped his attaché case—"you meet with some of these people to assess the fleet and develop at least a rough idea of what vehicles you will propose. Then, we'll have to meet with Meyer."

"Meyer," Dallis repeated. "Meyer Lansky?"

Roberto nodded.

"My God, what does he have to do with this?"

Roberto smiled, almost sheepishly. "Despite his modest statements to the contrary, Meyer and Fulgencio Batista are like this." He held up his first two fingers very close together. "Perhaps you did not know that they are partners in all Meyer's casinos. That is how the casinos operate with no problems. I know the president, of course, but on things like this, Meyer is sort of his gatekeeper."

"So when do we meet with him?" Dallis asked.

"Very soon. But first I have something else in mind." He was smiling. "I would like to invite you both to accompany me to my parents' beach house at Varadero. It is quite spectacular, right on the sea, and very relaxing. The drive is just under two hours from Havana. We can spend the night there, or two if you like; then, Dallis, I can take you to the places you will need to go to meet with the managers of the school bus fleets to discuss their needs while Dorothy stays at the beach house and relaxes. How does that sound?"

Dallis and I looked at each other for a moment before giving each other a simultaneous "why not?" shrug. "When do we leave?" Dallis said.

"We could leave this afternoon but I do not want to."

"Oh?"

Roberto was smiling. "We must wait until tomorrow. Otherwise we would miss the dinner dance at the Biltmore tonight. Do you have a dinner jacket?"

Dallis cut a glance at me then looked back at Roberto. "That's a no on the dinner jacket, and–"

"No problem," said Roberto. "I'll have my tailor call on you this afternoon. He'll take care of everything."

"Listen, Roberto, I—"

Roberto held his hand up. "Do not worry, my friend; I will take care of everything."

Dallis emitted a long sigh. "Okay, so what's this Biltmore?"

Roberto was still smiling. "The Havana Biltmore Yacht and Country Club. It is a wonderful, historic old private club and you will love it. My father is a member; I am a member . . ." He leaned in and lowered his voice. "Unfortunately for him, President Batista has never been admitted to membership and he is not happy about it. I am frankly surprised that he has not had the place blown up."

While all this talk of fancy private clubs and dinner jackets was going on, I was in a panic. Was Roberto going to send a dressmaker along with a tailor? I'm telling you, Angel, I didn't have a *stitch* to wear to that club. I'd almost worn everything I'd brought. And on top of that I hadn't brought a solitary *thread* of anything that would pass for beach clothes at Roberto's parents' place. Two things were obvious. One was I had to go shopping that afternoon and the other was that Dallis and I were going to have a knock-down, drag-out over it.

"So, it is all set," Roberto was saying jauntily as he rose from the table. "I will send a car for you at eight." And he left abruptly.

Dallis and I sat for several minutes saying nothing, just reflecting on what, for us, was a rather extraordinary meeting because neither of us had ever operated at this level before. But—and I didn't know about Dallis—deep within me I felt that somehow it was our destiny.

Finally, Dallis spoke. "Well, things are more clear now, aren't they?"

I nodded my agreement, but it was only to be accommodating because there were many things still unclear to me, not the least of which was what was going on—or not—between me and this Roberto character I had really only just met, but who seemed to be occupying way too many of my thoughts.

"Honey, let me ask you something," I said. "You never did say how you found Roberto."

He had been fumbling for a Lucky for both of us and, before answering, he struck a match from a small book with the Hotel Nacional logo and lit us both up.

"I didn't," he said. "He contacted me."

Chapter Twelve

Even though it was one of the smallest ones, Roberto's parents' beach house at Varadero was just *divine*. Roberto's father was a successful surgeon but still had trouble keeping up with his Varadero neighbors like Al Capone and Irénée du Pont. In fact, Batista himself had a place there. My beloved Panama City beaches are whiter but I've never seen an overall prettier tropical place than Varadero.

Roberto had arranged for me to be picked up at the Nacional by a car and driver. I was ushered into the back seat of an almost-new Buick, a more current version of the ones with Dynaflow Auntie and Uncle Reavis used to drive around Smithtown, Georgia. It was my first experience being *chauffeured* and, Angel, I just really didn't know quite how to act.

The beach house was named Casa la Concha or, in English, House of the Conch. It was aptly named because a nearby little grassy bay was a reliable source of fresh conch. The natives would either wade the shallow bay or pole themselves along in what looked to me like old wooden rowboats and simply reach down and grab the beautiful conch shells. They'd extract the meat from the shell and spend what seemed like hours pounding it to smithereens to tenderize it. Then they'd either pan fry or sauté it. It tasted *heavenly* and I loved looking at the pretty shells almost as much as eating what came from inside them.

Roberto changed his original schedule somewhat. He suggested that Dallis stay in Havana, base out of the Nacional, and travel to nearby locations to meet with the bureaucrats in charge of the school bus fleet. He would make presentations to them about his product and learn about the existing school buses so he could prepare a proposal for replacing a good portion of the aging fleet. Then he and Roberto would join me a couple of days later at Casa la Concha after my pampered time at what was surely one of the most luxurious spots in Cuba. I found myself wondering what I'd done to deserve this good fortune and came up with nothing.

On the ride to the coast in the back seat of that Buick, I couldn't help but think of the previous evening at the Havana Biltmore Yacht and Country Club. Dallis looked wonderful in his new white dinner jacket. As for me, I bought the cheapest gown I could find in downtown Havana, a strapless lavender organza thing that I *loathed*. And I found the cheapest black stilettos to go with it. But it was the best I could do with the few pesos Dallis had given me.

And speaking of how people looked, Roberto also wore a white dinner jacket and looked positively *luscious*. When Dallis and I walked in, Roberto's eyes locked on to mine and he didn't—wouldn't—look away. But I did. I had to because once again I was afraid I might faint. But Roberto wasn't the only gorgeous Cuban there that night. Honestly, it looked like some kind of Hollywood premiere; I've never seen as many handsome men and beautiful women. I paid plenty of attention to how the women presented themselves. All of them were glammed up so much more than I—with fancy hairdos and some with so much jewelry I don't see how they walked. And dresses? Lord, lord, some of them were elegant but so revealing I was embarrassed for them. But Dallis sure wasn't. I thought his eyeballs were going to fall out of their sockets.

I felt mortified by the dowdy way I knew I looked in my cheap outfit with just a smattering of almost ridiculous costume jewelry, but there was nothing I could do about it. Roberto didn't seem to agree with my self-assessment; he didn't leave my side, kept boring those eyes of his right through me, and paid more attention to me than any woman can expect from any man. I couldn't figure it out. What was he up to? If he was trying to get to my husband through me, that made little sense. After all, he'd already made a business arrangement with Dallis and surely he could see he was only annoying Dallis by fawning over me.

That next meeting with Meyer Lansky took place much sooner than Roberto had indicated–it was the surprise of the evening. It happened during the cocktail hour when we were all standing up. I had not realized that this powerful man was only five feet tall. Back in those days I was about five-three and he and I were eyeball to eyeball. I was wearing fairly high heels so I'm sure he must have been in some kind of elevator shoes. Even in his sleek dinner jacket, he looked just as weasely as before. I wondered if he had a wife. Later, I would learn he divorced his wife to marry his manicurist in New York City. I never liked him.

The meeting was pretty straightforward. Roberto started. "Mr. Duncan and I have come to an understanding on his representation in his effort to replace the aging, unsafe units of the government's school bus fleet with the Challenger line manufactured by the company he represents."

Lansky was stone-faced. "And tell me why this should be of interest to me?"

Roberto was unfazed. "I would be most grateful if you could mention this to El Presidente so Mr. Duncan's negotiations might go more smoothly."

Meyer looked sharply at Dallis and me. "And what makes you people think I even know President Batista?"

Roberto seemed not to even hear Lansky. "Mr. Duncan and I have come to an agreement regarding certain marketing expenses associated with this project. His company is ready to supply those funds as needed. We expect those marketing expenses to run somewhere around ten percent of the cost of the entire project."

I couldn't believe what I was hearing. It was a bunch of doubletalk to say that Dallis could sell lots of school buses as long as his company paid President Fulgencio Batista a bribe of ten percent of the value of the order, with Meyer Lansky as the apparent bag man, or at least the go-between. I later learned that that percentage was actually less than Batista's take from the Havana casinos he allowed Meyer Lansky to own and that the money was delivered to Batista in cash each day by a bag man who was sometimes Lansky himself. A courier was sent each morning on the Air Cubana flight to Miami to cash the high-rolling American losers' checks. The two men were not friends but rather partners who worked very closely together to amass lots of money.

But all that didn't stop Lansky from maintaining his curious charade. He studied us all carefully for a few moments, seeming to weigh things, and in his New York brogue finally said, "I barely know the president. But I will see if I can get an appointment with him and mention this. Nice to see you, Mr. and Mrs. Duncan." And he turned and walked away.

Roberto was smiling. "Mr. Lansky has become very adept at never admitting anything to anyone about anything. But the fact is he talks to Batista every day. And they see each other several times a week. Everything is going to work out. Now let us have some champagne, shall we?"

In the back seat of that Buick—it was red, by the way—I couldn't help but smile to myself at how confident and in control Roberto had seemed the night before. As I thought more about him, I remembered our dancing together that night. Your daddy seemed only a little jealous, partly because he was into the daiquiris pretty well and partly because Roberto had arranged for him to dance with the women who most seemed to be falling out of the tops of their gowns. It became clear to me that it was a diversionary tactic; when Roberto asked me to dance, he always guided me to the part of dance floor furthest from Dallis. He mostly asked me when there was a slow number being played, like "Besame Mucho" or something similar.

You don't speak Spanish, Angel, but even you know besame mucho means "kiss me a lot." Well, Roberto didn't try to kiss me on the dance floor but he tried just about everything else, if you know what I mean. I found myself trying to gently push him back to create a little more space between us. My success at this was very limited, partly because of his strength and obvious determination and partly because of my lack of will and my enjoyment of the whole experience. I swear, Angel, I can still remember the way he smelled that night. I can't describe it to you but it filled my senses with an essence of manliness that . . . well, it somehow suggested to me a classy fastidiousness he had combined with his basic carnality. It was a deadly combination for a woman still in her twenties to contend with. Sitting in that Buick, I found myself thankful that I would be away from Roberto for a couple days. I just needed to cool off and remember that I was married and that I loved your daddy very much.

But it didn't work out that way.

Chapter Thirteen

Hallie

It was a Thursday night and Hallie would be staying over at Rich's mansion. Late that afternoon, she took over everything she'd need, including her attire for the evening's affair Rich was hosting. Rich was in his den while Hallie, in the dressing room adjoining his bedroom, slipped into the outfit she'd chosen. It met the definition of the classic "little black dress" despite having some little rumply ruffles that she now smoothed with her freshly manicured hands as she did some mini-twirls in front of a massive antique mirror in Rodino's almost ballroom-sized bedroom. She had already "put her face on" and had fussed over her hair for what seemed like hours. She was reasonably satisfied with the result as she added some dangly earrings to complete the package.

As she wound up her primping process, she thought of her time at the ad agency earlier in the day. She and Grace Lamont had lunched at Mise en Place.

"Are you coming tonight?" she'd asked Grace.

Grace pursed her lips before replying and narrowed her eyes. "Yes, but I'm not sure why. I'm already an investor."

"He likes to have a few existing investors at these things. He says they're like living, breathing testimonials and, besides, they might invest more."

"I know, I know. But frankly, the main reason I'm going is you."

"Me?"

"In addition to being my professional colleague, you're one of my best friends in the world and I want to make sure Rich knows how much I value that."

"You're so sweet."

Grace Lamont showed a wry smile. "The fact that I'm a lonely divorcee whose current romantic prospects are zilch has absolutely nothing to do with it. Do you think there'll be any interesting men there?"

Hallie's right hand performed a perfect dismissive wave. "Listen to you. You'll probably be married before I will."

Grace Lamont's perceptiveness was in top form. "Hmm. Is there a reason you're saying that?"

"Um . . . yeah, probably."

"And?"

"Well . . . A, he's not asking me, and B, I don't know what I'd say if he did."

"Why not?"

"Well . . . I . . ."

"You in love with him?"

Hallie stared right into Grace's eyes for several long moments as if trying to divine the answer that way. "That's what I'm trying to figure out. I think I am. But . . ." She trailed off.

"There's something you can't put your finger on that's holding you back."

Hallie stared at her friend again, this time slack-jawed. "How did you know?"

Grace fell silent for a moment as a waiter appeared with an iced tea refill; she then held her hands high and looked to the ceiling as if praising God. "What else could it be? Duh."

"One thing I do know: I'm not moving in with him."

"Has he asked?"

"No, but if he does the answer's no."

"Good for you."

Hallie looked at her lap for a moment before looking up, wearing a slightly sheepish look. "Don't compliment me too much. Rich and I *are* sleeping together."

"I know that, silly, but there's a big difference and I'm still proud of you."

Both women sat back in their chairs as their lunch was delivered, curried chicken salad for Grace and a Nicoise salad for Hallie.

"Marrying Rich would solve a lot of problems, though. Mostly financial."

"So . . . ?"

"So, it would be sort of caving in. Throwing in the towel."

"You mean—"

"Yes, the book. I've started it. It isn't that I couldn't finish it if we got married; it's just that things would be different."

Hallie went on to explain to Grace that she had followed her professor's advice to begin her book as her mother's story was unfolding instead of waiting and outlining. When Grace begged for some details of the story, Hallie demurred, then relented slightly and revealed a sample of the "scandalous" stuff.

It made her recall the range of behavioral changes in her mother—all related to her stroke. Hallie knew that, pre-stroke, her mother would have never, ever been forthcoming with details of her youth and a budding extramarital affair with a handsome romantic Cuban. As Hallie had listened to the recordings, she'd felt a mix of the embarrassment she had experienced while listening to her mother (she'd had to look away at times, pretending to herself to be checking the digital recorder) and elation over her conviction that, damn, this is quite a story and, as a book, this could actually work.

She still wasn't sure she agreed with Ian's advice to go ahead and start. She felt frustrated by having to wait to learn what came next, almost as if she were transcribing testimony like a court reporter. But she was pleased that she was already doing extensive revisions to juice the story up and applying the storytelling and fiction writing techniques she had studied so carefully.

Hallie continued her explanation to her friend. "I kind of . . . need this book to work."

"You mean financially?" Grace asked.

"Yes, that, but I also need it for . . . well, for me, if you know what I mean."

Grace stopped her fork full of curried chicken salad mid-air so she could reflect a moment and then she replied. "Let me give this a try: You need it to define yourself—for yourself—instead of defining yourself by doing something like marrying Rich which would be like having *Rich* define you instead of *you* defining yourself. That's a mouthful but do I have it right?"

Hallie dropped her napkin to her lap, put both hands on the corners of their dining table, and looked down at her plate, smiling and shaking her head. When she looked up, she said, "You are just amazing. How do you do it?"

"Do what?"

"Just put your finger right on the heart of every matter."

Grace rolled her eyes and shrugged all in one motion, a pantomime for "who the heck knows" and said, "What I *can't* put my finger on is what to wear tonight. You never said if you think there might be anybody interesting there."

Later, while at the reception, Hallie would look around and think there were actually a lot of interesting men there. But it appeared that almost all of them were accompanied by either a wife or significant other.

Near Lutz, north of Tampa, Rich owned almost twenty acres that included a private lake; it was a mere twenty-minute drive from his office. Visitors, if admitted, would drive through his automatic gates and under the sign that bore the name of his estate. The sign read BIOYA. Rich told Hallie it was an old Seminole name he had chosen because it meant "strong and explosive" but she had never verified that. Every time Rich's male friends smirked when the name came up, it made her want to look it up but she never had.

It was party time. But for Rich, it wasn't a party; it was business. He'd invited about eighty people he had determined to be prime prospects to invest in his newest structured settlement fund. Hallie watched them come in, all professionally and cordially greeted by a couple of "Rodino & Ross Babes" checking them in and providing nametags. They were mostly dressed in business or even cocktail attire because they were expected to be able to invest a minimum of $250,000 with Rich, although a number of his present investors had written checks into the millions.

On her way from Rich's bedroom to his den, Hallie saw the first guests arriving. She waded through what seemed like an army of people that included the caterer's staff, the women checking the flower arrangements, the computer audio-visual people, and the piano and bass musicians starting to play cocktail music.

Rich didn't even look at her when she walked into the den. He was at his desk going over what appeared to be some lists–prospective investors, she assumed–with his chief financial officer. His name was Thomas Herring–not Tom, but Thomas. Hallie had met him a number of times at Rich's office and at other "investor receptions" and liked him. Rich was agitated and spewed some expletives she normally did not hear from him. He seemed to be upset that a particular prospective investor might not be attending.

"Tell me exactly what he said," Rich was glaring at Thomas Herring.

"He said he knows he agreed to come, but said our package raises more questions than it provides answers."

"Who is this guy again?"

"He's a big-time estate lawyer from New York who's also a real estate investor. He belongs to the Gilchrist Club quail plantation and keeps a condo and a sixty-foot Viking sportfish here in Tampa."

"So let's do a private meeting with him."

"That's what I suggested but he wouldn't commit. Said we might see him tonight but don't count on it."

"Dammit, my buddy Lee Snow said this guy could do ten million if he wanted to." Rodino leaned back in his chair, clasped his hands behind his head, and expelled air. It was only then that he noticed Hallie's presence in the room. Their eyes locked and Hallie knew that Rich read the expression of concern on her face.

"Is everything all right?" she asked.

Rodino broke out in a grin, his hands still locked behind his head. "Everything's perfect," he said. "These new settlement agreements are the best batch yet. We should bring in ten to fifteen million tonight, more if"—he glanced at his assistant—"a certain prospective investor stops being difficult."

"Is there anything I can do to help?" she asked.

Rodino turned to his assistant again. "What's his name again?"

"Albert Adams."

He looked back at Hallie. "If you see somebody with an Albert Adams nametag, just bat your gorgeous eyes at him and be nice to his wife; how about that?"

"I'll do my best."

Rodino stood now, walked to Hallie, and kissed her on the forehead. "Showtime!" he said, and strode into the part of the mansion where his guests were congregating. "Just do your mingling thing," he said to her over his shoulder.

Hallie tried to do just that but knew she wasn't very good at it. She even tried to find Mr. Albert Adams. She learned from one of the "Rodino Babes" that Adams had actually come, but by himself. She made a half-hearted effort to find him in the crowd but to no avail. She was relieved; what would she have said to him? She did see a few people she knew, including Grace Lamont, who looked shimmering in a green cocktail dress Hallie immediately coveted.

Hallie had just accepted her second glass of Veuve Clicquot champagne when the piano and bass suddenly increased their volume dramatically, playing some sort of fanfare, and Rich Rodino took a microphone connected to the mansion's sound system and asked for everyone's attention.

By then a large screen had been erected on which was displayed the Rodino & Ross firm logo, the artwork for which was sort of a bastardized version of the Rolls Royce car company logo. A jovial Rodino welcomed the crowd, thanked them for coming and particularly thanked his existing investors for their attendance and their support.

"Those of you have invested in our structured settlement funds these past six years need not be shy about answering any questions from those here tonight who are considering investing for the first time." His grin widened. "Of course, we all know there are two main questions: How much is the return? And do the checks come every month?"

A collective chuckle rippled through the assembled guests, accompanied by affirmative nods.

Hallie was standing next to a woman who edged closer to her, leaned in, and began whispering. "Isn't he wonderful?" she asked Hallie rhetorically. "When my husband died, my CPA gave me the best recommendation of my life; he said to invest everything with Rodino & Ross and, golly, I'm so glad I did." The woman nodded in Rodino's direction with an almost giddy smile. "He's right; those checks come every month and the return is way better than anything else people have shown me. This man is just such a blessing in my life!"

"I'm so glad," Hallie said.

"Are you already an investor or just considering it?" the woman asked, still whispering.

"Uh, yes, I'm already one," Hallie replied. "By the way, may I ask who your CPA is?" She wasn't sure why she asked but was somehow curious.

"Oh, certainly. It's Ben Lane of Lane & Company here in town."

Hallie nodded but didn't say anything else because she saw Rich was cranking up his presentation.

"Folks, I'm pleased to announce that we expect our newest fund to return at least the twelve percent most of you have been experiencing, possibly more," he said.

At that a few of the guests actually clapped their hands in applause.

"Now our new Silver Settlement Fund IV," Rodino, remote device in hand, turned to face the large screen which currently displayed a map, "has acquired a portfolio of structured settlements that satisfy claims brought by persons experiencing illness and death due to a series of faulty medical devices that, frankly, should never have been approved by the FDA and should never have been brought to market."

Rodino stopped, looked at the crowd, and grinned. "Anybody need any more champagne before I continue?" A few guests simply raised their full glasses toward Rodino and grinned back.

Rodino turned back to the screen. "Okay, once again we've hit a home run with these claims. Many of them were generated by our own law firm and we've been fortunate to acquire others at a steep discount from other law firms we have referral arrangements with. Now for you new investors, please allow me to explain how structured settlements work." The slides switched to a series of graphs and ultra-simple flow charts consisting of boxes, circle and arrows. "You see, most folks who win a legal claim for some kind of damages they have suffered do not receive a lump sum, but a payout over an extended time period. But a great percentage of these folks have immediate cash needs, so they are willing to take a substantially discounted lump sum amount immediately in lieu of a stream of payments over time. That's what we do with the money you invest with us: buy these settlements at a big discount, therefore allowing you to get the full amount of that money over time. It's how we can pay a twelve percent return."

Rodino then used the remote to advance to various screens depicting photos of the faulty medical device he had mentioned, columns of figures and diagrams using the laser on the remote to highlight certain ones as he reviewed them. Once again, Hallie marveled at Rich's smooth delivery, his grasp of the details, and his persuasive manner. But it was all Greek to her; she really had little idea of anything he was talking about. She just knew it must all work well. After all, she got her check every month from the large amount (for her) she'd invested and, God, did Rich spend money: on mansions (he had three of them altogether), cars, his yacht, trips, his jet.

When Rodino finished, he asked for questions. A distinguished, white-haired man wearing a navy blazer and a bow tie raised his hand and Rodino pointed to him. "Yes sir," he said.

"Yes, Albert Adams here," the man said. "Mr. Rodino, I decided at the last minute to come tonight. I'm an attorney myself. I looked at the package you sent me and I've followed your presentation tonight and find your documentation woefully lacking. All of your agreements have been redacted and are therefore incomplete. I see you provide something about a trust account where all this money resides, but do you plan to provide the actual files on these settlements to those who request them?"

Hallie did not remember anybody being so confrontational at one of these affairs so she watched Rich intently. His mouth never turned down, instead it maintained a hint of an I'll-patiently-humor-him smile. He replied:

"Mr. Adams, I thank you so much for deciding to come tonight and I also thank you for your excellent question. As a fellow attorney, I'm sure you can appreciate that all the documents relating to these settlements are confidential because they are the result of actual cases and are therefore subject to attorney-client privilege. To comply with your request would mean I would have to break the law and, of course, there is no way I would ever do that."

Albert Adams stood silent for a few moments. The entire room was silent with him. "Mr. Rodino, I don't agree with you and, without seeing the actual documents, I'll not be investing a penny with you. But thank you for the excellent champagne."

Now Hallie saw Rich's expression change as a little dark cloud seemed to cross his face. He gestured toward the crowd in the room before saying, "Mr. Adams, we're getting into technical legal details now that most of the folks here tonight do not understand. Why don't I have my assistant phone you and we'll set up a lunch meeting to discuss this further?"

Albert Adams just stared at Rodino.

"Mr. Adams?" Rich said.

Adams raised the champagne flute, drained the last of the Veuve Clicquot, and set it down gently on a marble-topped sideboard. "No thank you, Mr. Rodino. Good evening." And he walked out of the mansion.

Chapter Fourteen

Dimple

I adore the garden at The Meadows. Today, I take it all in as Ladasha wheels me out to get ready for Hallie's visit. It's a spectacularly pleasant morning in which bright sun and crisp air are combined with the scent of the nearby roses. But the sun angle is not quite right; it's hurting my eyes. I know Hallie will take care of it. I can't wait for her to get here but I wish we could sometimes talk about something besides my exploits in Cuba. I try to make those thoughts go away, however, because I know she's hell-bent on writing a book about it and it seems to mean everything to her. So, I'm going to keep doing my best to help. I love her so. She is *the* sweetest daughter.

I see her come toward me in the garden, with that bright sun reflecting off her mocha-colored, shoulder-length hair as it bounces slightly with every step she takes in her heels. She's smiling broadly and, in her face, I think I see genuine love for her withering old mother. At least I hope I do. When she reaches me, she notices the sun angle doesn't suit me and re-positions my wheelchair to fix it.

This is the first time she's used her recorder in the garden; I assume it has a battery. After asking how I'm feeling today, Hallie seems ready. On the edge of her chair, in fact. But it takes me a while to transition, to sort of gear up. I stare into space to gather my thoughts and, as before, I sense her anxiously wondering if my "mental motor" has suddenly misfired. When I open my mouth to speak, she seems to sigh with relief.

Angel, that beach house was a dream, just a dream.

As we drove up to it in that red Buick with the Dynaflow, we descended from a small mountain. That meant the house was in the foreground with the sea beyond. Angel, I almost couldn't breathe. You have to remember, growing up in Smithtown, Georgia we had no mountains, or oceans, or palm trees. In Miami, we had the ocean and palm trees and pretty tropical things, but we certainly didn't have mountains and rocky coasts just falling right into the sea like that.

The house was beige stucco with a red tile roof and the landscaping was gorgeous beyond words. We pulled in to a circular drive and, right away, a Negro man in a white guayabera appeared in the driveway. He wore the widest, whitest smile I've ever seen and, in very broken English, he said, "Señora Duncan! Señora Duncan! Hello."

I smiled back and, using one of the few words of Spanish I knew then, said, "Sí, Señora Duncan. Hello. I mean . . . hola."

He smiled wider now. "Hola, Señora Duncan. I am Miguel. Equipaje." He was still smiling. I had no clue and my face must have showed it because he pointed to the trunk of the Buick.

"Oh, my luggage," I said, then pointed to the trunk, too. "In there," I said, and the driver opened it. It was obvious that communication was going to be a challenge.

I tried to tip the driver but he held his hands up in refusal, so I bid him goodbye and turned to Miguel, who bowed and pointed to the elegant front door of Casa la Concha. Although he had both my suitcase and my train case in tow, he beat me to the front door and opened it for me.

I couldn't believe it. We entered a foyer with a floor of the most beautiful Carrara marble I've ever seen—and this was a beach house? Beyond that was a huge living room with some kind of tile floor and what I later learned were Cuban mahogany walls and beamed ceilings. The rugs were *lovely*, if you know what I mean.

Just when I thought my senses were filled, I looked out through the windows where I saw the swimming pool and the blue Caribbean beyond. I just stood in my tracks feeling paralyzed while I tried to take it all in. Then I noticed the vases of fresh-cut flowers every-where. I'd never been in a place so spectacular and I just couldn't get over it being a beach house. I was accustomed to boxy little Panama City beach cottages that weren't even *on* the beach. The ones my family rented, we had to walk hundreds of yards to get to the gulf.

Just then, I heard a female voice behind me. "Señora Duncan, welcome to Casa la Concha." I turned to see a smiling mulatto woman, small in stature and a little plump. "My name is Rosa. I am Miguel's wife," she said with a half bow.

"Hola, Rosa," I said. "Your English is so good."

Actually, it wasn't. I struggled to understand her. But it was way better than Miguel's. Rosa beamed at the compliment and said, "I show you room. Miguel bring baggage."

My room was just as spectacular as the rest of the house—also with fresh flowers—and was obviously the master. It was enormous and had a double bed, two chaise lounges, and incredibly fine fur-niture that simply had to have been imported from Spain. Miguel brought in my suitcase and train case. He knew enough to put the train case in the bathroom and the suitcase on a beautiful bench that was perfect for it. Rosa began to open my suitcase, then stopped and turned to me. "Me unpack?"

I couldn't help but smile. "Of course," I said.

Angel, I'd never been waited on like that in my life. Rosa hung my dresses on one side of what we used to call a chifforobe and put my other clothes in the drawers on the other side of the massive armoire-like piece.

"Maybe you like to swim; maybe you like to sleep?" A smiling Rosa asked. "Maybe you like a mojito?"

I was charmed by her and I'm sure my smile said so. "Oh, thank you, Rosa. Yes, I think I'd like to rest a bit; then yes, I would like to go for a swim." I had packed a bathing suit and bathing cap before I left Miami. We wore bathing caps back then, Angel. "We'll save the mojito for later," I told Rosa.

"Sí, Señora," she said. "Dinner nine o'clock on terrace."

I had already adjusted to the Cuban custom–same as Europe, I understood—of dining late. Nine o'clock was actually much earlier than what I'd been experiencing. "Rosa, would eight o'clock, or a little earlier be all right?" I asked.

Her smile seemed to fade. "No, Señora. Dinner nine o'clock. On terrace." Then she walked to one of the tables beside the four-poster double bed and pointed to the wall. "Señora, you need me, push this button *por favor*." I knew enough Spanish to know she had added "please" to the end of her request. I looked where she was pointing and, sure enough, there was a button. This was really starting to be fun.

I did just what I said and tried napping for perhaps thirty minutes or so. It didn't really work; so much was happening that it all replayed over in my mind like a movie. I rose and began to explore the house in more detail. I found the family photos particularly interesting. There were plenty of pictures of Roberto and of a couple who must be his parents. There was also a photo of a younger Roberto I found interesting. It was with a group of young men, one of whom had a mustache and, while not a full beard, the beginnings of one, and looked vaguely familiar to me. A Universidad de la Habana sign was in the background. On the coffee tables were books and magazines, mostly in Spanish. There was a copy of the *Havana Post*, obviously in Spanish, but also a copy of *Life* magazine.

I changed into my bathing suit and bathing cap. The suit was one of those flower-patterned mid-1950s one-piece jobs with a single strap that went around my neck. It was dreadful, really. I wasn't much of an ocean swimmer so I chose the pool over the Caribbean. I was amazed to find the pool was filled with salt water and not fresh. After my swim, I walked on the beach and gawked at some of the other homes. I couldn't believe there could be any more spectacular than Roberto's father's house but there were. The beach was beautiful and almost as white as my beloved Panama City beaches.

All of this made me tired so I did actually sleep for perhaps an hour. But that was after a luxurious bath Rosa drew for me. It delightfully laundered the salt water and sand from my skin which even then was very white. As you know, I was never an outdoorsy type.

As I anticipated the nine p.m. dinner, I wondered what it would be like to dine alone on a beautiful terrace and what the fare would be. I spent a fair amount of time arranging my hair in retaliation against the bathing cap but gave little thought to what I would wear. I figured that since I'd be dining alone it would make little difference. Well, apparently Rosa did not agree with me because she laid out one of my best dresses for me to wear. It was a yellow halter top that I usually wore with white pumps.

"Oh Rosa," I said. "I'll just wear—"

"You wear this," she said.

Hmmm, I thought. Wasn't I the one who was supposed to be the guest? Shouldn't I wear what I want? But I was so content in such a pleasant place that I didn't argue with her. By 8:45, I had finished dressing and Rosa brought me the coup de gras— a very small, white flower of a kind I had never seen before. She carefully arranged it in my hair.

"Oh, Rosa," I protested.

"You wear this," she said. "Señora very pretty."

She strode to the dressing table and picked up a bottle. "You wear this, too, Señora." She was holding a small bottle of Chanel No. 5. I'm not sure I'd ever *seen* a bottle of Chanel No. 5, much less worn it.

"Oh, Rosa . . ."

She opened the bottle and handed it to me, just smiling gently and nodding her encouragement. Our eyes met for short moment before I accepted the bottle and applied some to my wrist and some more to my neck. I tell you, it smelled *divine.*

So, here I was in this magical place, dressed to the nines, a flower in my hair, wearing Chanel No. 5, and all by my lonesome. It made me miss Dallis terribly and wish he could be with me. But work was work and it was why we were in Cuba in the first place. I was determined not to be the petulant wife.

By then it was almost nine, so I made my way out to the terrace. The house and its ambiance were even more enchanting at night, particularly with the sound of the waves from the Caribbean. There was very soft, recorded Cuban music coming from somewhere that was soothing, not chaotic. Rosa appeared again and started touching her fingers as if counting while she said, "Señora, you want mojito? Daiquiri? Cuba libre?

I smiled and said, "Rosa, I think I'll have that mojito now, please . . . uh, I mean por favor."

"Sí, Señora, un momento," she said and disappeared. And it indeed seemed barely a moment before she returned with my cocktail. I took it and sort of strolled toward the terrace, every step a visual treat just being in that place. The terrace was adjacent to the pool but it was covered and had the same lovely tile floor as the living room. It was slightly elevated and right on the Caribbean. When I reached it, I saw the dining table, beautifully set with flowers and burning candles that flickered in the pleasant breeze from the sea.

But something caught my eye. Something not quite right. It took a moment before I realized what I was looking at. In fact, I blinked my eyes a couple of times to make sure, then I felt myself quietly gasp.

The table was set for two.

In the next moment, I heard a now-familiar male voice with a Latin accent behind me. "Good evening, Mrs. Duncan. How is your mojito?"

Chapter Fifteen

Angel, I turned around and Roberto was standing right next to me. Just before I turned, I actually smelled him. He had that wonderful, manly smell that I could never put my finger on, could never describe. I just knew it drove me crazy like everything else about him. He was wearing a white sport coat and solid navy tie. Not a dinner jacket but a white sport coat—silk, I think. He was smiling and looked down at me. Although the light was low, I could see those dark eyes of his boring through me as they always did. Once again, I thought I was going to faint.

"Roberto," I said, trying not to sound as breathless as I was. "What in heaven's name are you doing here? You and Dallis are supposed to be in Havana working."

His smile grew wider as he swept an arm toward the dinner table then took the back of one of the chairs. "Let us sit down and I will explain," he said, and pulled out a chair for me.

"But Roberto . . . I . . ."

"What, my dear?"

"Roberto, I'm here alone at your parent's beach house. I'm married and my husband's not here. I can't just sit down and have dinner with you." I was flustered and knew I was sputtering the words.

His smile never wavered. "And why not?"

"Because it's not . . ."

"Not what?"

I hesitated a moment. "Well, it's not . . . *proper.*"

His smile sagged and he took his hand off the chair. "Not proper," he repeated flatly and then seemed to study me for several long moments. I found myself looking away while this was going on. Finally, he said, "All right then, as you wish. Rosa has prepared a wonderful dinner of roast suckling pig. But I suppose you can have yours here on the terrace by the sea and I will have mine in the kitchen with the servants." Then he drew the chair out again for me to sit. "After dinner, perhaps we can sit on opposite sides of the living room, supervised by Rosa and Miguel, and I can explain why I am here." The sarcasm was clear and it somehow made my heart sink.

"Oh, Roberto," I said. "Why are you making this difficult?"

He raised his eyebrows. "Who, exactly, is making this difficult?"

At that moment, my brain and my heart and my emotions were all tumbling inside me like dice in a cup at a craps table and I just didn't know what to do. I finally came around to the viewpoint that I was a guest at his family's house and did not want to be rude. At last, I took the chair he'd pulled for me and said, "Roberto, please have dinner here with me and not in the kitchen."

The smile was back and he sat. The place settings were not across from each other but more side by side so that we could both face the Caribbean. I momentarily felt his knee against mine when he situated himself. Almost immediately, Rosa appeared with a mojito for Roberto. He said "Gracias" and reached in his sport coat and withdrew a pack of Luckies. He shook a couple out in my direction; we each took one, and our eyes met as he held a light for me. I can't imagine why I did it but I steadied his hand that was holding his lighter with mine as our eye contact continued longer than it should have. I surprised myself more than I can tell you. I mean, who did I think I was, Lauren Bacall?

I took a quick drag on the cigarette and turned my head away from him and exhaled before saying, "All right, Señor Roberto. So what the heck are you doing here and where is my husband?" I picked a small flake of tobacco off my tongue as I waited for his answer.

He took a drink from his mojito. "Dallis is hard at work in Havana meeting with the people in charge of the Cuban school bus fleet. Things seem to be going very well. I am very impressed with your husband as a businessman. And he knows his products. After I arranged the meetings, there was nothing to prevent me from coming here. Dallis will be meeting with the fleet managers again tomorrow and perhaps the next day as well."

"But Roberto, why are you here?" As I asked the question, my heart pounded because I was terrified of the answer.

He looked at me more intensely than he had since he arrived. "My father has a safe in this house and there is something in it he needs quickly. He has a full schedule of surgery this week and he asked me to come and get it for him. I was too busy myself to get here sooner than now, so I thought we would have dinner together. That is all."

Our gazes were still locked as I tried to process what he had just said and figure out if I was happy or sad to hear it. I decided to take it at face value and simply enjoy his company over dinner, perhaps a wonderful Cuban coffee afterwards, then off to bed. I further figured I'd sleep in and not see him in the morning.

Well, guess what, Angel. It didn't quite work out that way.

The first mistake I made was saying yes to too many mojitos. Then, when the suckling pig came, Roberto insisted that we have a bottle of 1947 St. Emilion with it. I never was much of a wine drinker but this was different. So smooth and just the right amount of sweetness, and it somehow made the pork taste absolutely perfect. But, aside from the cocktails and wine, we just had a marvelous time together.

Roberto did most of the talking, which was fine with me. Once business with Dallis was no longer the main subject, he turned out to be a fascinating, yet very funny, man. He was an expert on wine, could dive to almost fifty feet without air tanks and shoot fish with a spear gun. And he had read *everything*. I had read *nothing* and was ashamed and intimidated by it. But he was gracious and in no way condescending or patronizing. Instead, he explained things he made reference to and would occasionally poke fun at himself in a charming way. I tell you, the whole thing was like the dreamiest dream date any girl could have. And remember, that's all I still was, really—just a girl. As this most romantic evening of my life continued, your dear father unfortunately became the furthest thing from my mind.

Dessert was something called a *flan*. Back in Smithtown, my mother used to fix pretty much the same thing in little glass custard cups. Brown sugar syrup was in the bottom and egg custard on top. The difference with a Cuban *flan* is that it's turned upside down on the plate so the syrup spreads out and it presents as a proper dessert.

By the time we finished the flan, there was a new development: the moon had risen on the Caribbean. It created a shimmering, cream-colored streak of light on the gently rolling sea that, combined with the balmy slight breeze, created a feeling I remember vividly to this very day. As I looked out through the rustling coconut palms, I was in a magical tropical tableau. Experiencing it for a few moments gave me a feeling of being lifted up and away. I felt like an aerial spectator, as though I were a movie director looking at the scene from a boom-mounted camera. Maybe having too much to drink had something to do with it, but it was one of the most languid, time-defying moments of my life.

Roberto seemed to feel it, too. I felt him move closer to me and gently take my arm. "The moon is beautiful. I suggest we take a walk on the beach and get a closer look." I looked at him. He was smiling but he had a different look in his eyes. It was a look any woman recognizes in a man. It made me shiver. I was at the same time frightened and filled with eager anticipation. I hesitated, not knowing what to do. Then I felt the gentlest pressure of his hand on my arm.

I nodded yes to his suggestion.

When we got to the beach, we both kicked our shoes off and then made directly for the gentle surf. We almost stepped on a large blue crab and I let out a girlish shriek. "We should catch him for crabmeat cocktail," Roberto said.

I hadn't realized it, but when I was startled by the crab I had reached for Roberto's arm. Somehow, as we continued to walk, we were now holding hands. His hand was large, dwarfing mine, and warm with a pleasing feel of being soft, yet very masculine. Ironically, a few moments later I found that his lips had exactly the same characteristics. That was because he stopped walking, released my hand, and took my shoulders so I was facing him. The lights from the beach houses shone on my face, the moonlight on his. I knew what was going to happen and I let it. The kiss was long, deep and accompanied by things happening between our bodies I should not be describing to my daughter. All I can tell you is that I had never felt that way before. Angel, it was . . . well, I don't know, it was . . ."

Chapter Sixteen

Angel, that man was *the* best kisser of all time. I just couldn't understand how a man's lips could be that lush and soft but still be . . . I don't know . . . manly and forceful, yet gentle and restrained when the moment called for it.

Well, anyway, we were kissing on the beach and the kissing part is not all of what was going on. In short order, we had dropped to the sand, the straps on my sun dress were down, my skirt was way higher than it should have been, and Roberto's hands . . . well, let's just say they were *wandering*.

Well, Angel, you may be disappointed because *nothing* happened. Somehow, I came to my senses and gently but firmly pushed Roberto's hands away, pulled my dress down, and got to my knees.

"Oh, Roberto," I said. "You're the most attractive man I've ever met in my life and I want to do this so badly, but I just can't." I think I was holding my hair up with both hands in frustration. "Roberto, I'm *married*. And on top of that, I love my husband."

Roberto was still for some long moments; then, he slowly stood and held his hands out to help me up. I took them, stood, and then just looked up at him, not knowing what was next. It was too dark to see his eyes very well but I've never felt as much *total* attention and empathy from a man as in that moment. His whole being seemed focused on me but in an understanding and caring way rather than an aggressive and still hoping for you-know-what way.

"I understand, Dorothy," Roberto said.

I swear, here was this man I almost had *sex* with and I think it was the first time he'd called me anything but Mrs. Duncan.

"I hope you will forgive me," he said. "I did not mean to offend you. On the contrary, the only reason I wish we could have continued is that I believe you are the most beautiful and desirable woman I have ever met in my life. Although I am a great admirer of your husband, at this moment I find myself wishing you were not married."

"But I *am* married," I said. "And Dallis—"

"Let me remind you that I just said Dallis is a fine man. But our customs are different here in Cuba. It is possible for men and women to have happy, loving marriages and raise fine children, but not give up unique and wonderful opportunities to experience passion and romance with someone else when it is truly special and when the person is truly special. Dorothy, it has been a long time since I have met anyone as special as you." He was standing closer now and drew my hands up in his so they were just under our chins. "All I ask is that you take your time and think about how you and I could have something so special together. Of course, to be polite we would not tell your fine husband about it but it would show no disrespect to him. It would be our special thing and, after you leave Cuba, would provide us both with lasting, wonderful memories."

I was losing control again, looking up at him and wanting to say yes, yes, let's get started right now! But I didn't.

"Roberto, I think I'd better go to my room now," I said softly. "Thank you for a wonderful dinner and a wonderful evening." Then I brushed his lips with a soft, quick kiss before walking briskly back to my shoes, then to the house.

The next morning came late for me. The combination of replaying the evening's events, the mojitos and wine, and the guilt I felt, had ganged up on me and produced maybe only two hours of credible sleep. I was a wreck and knew I must look like it, but when I awoke, I was sure it was Roberto's voice I heard speaking Spanish with Rosa.

I couldn't just hide in the bedroom; they might think I'd died. And I was, after all, a guest. And of one thing I was more sure than anything: I wasn't venturing out of that room looking the way I did after just rolling out of bed. So I flew into action, did the best I could, and emerged wearing my best pink satin robe, fluffed and lipsticked to the greatest extent possible under the circumstances.

I found him on the terrace where we had dined the night before. It was a sunny day and the Caribbean looked glorious, a moderate breeze making the occasional whitecap peek out above the blue water. He was wearing a business suit and was finishing up the *Havana Post* and a cup of Cuban coffee. When he saw me, he sprung to his feet and came to me. He took my shoulders and kissed me softly and quickly on my forehead.

"Buenos dias, Señora," he said, with a broad smile.

"Buenos dias to you too, Señor." My reply was spoken in what I now know was a dreadful Spanish accent.

"Rosa!" he called. "Café con leche para la señora."

Then looked at me. "What would you like to eat?"

"Nothing, thank you," I said, patting my tummy. "Still recovering from last night."

Then he looked at me intently. There was no mistaking what was in his eyes now as his voice dropped. "Speaking of last night, for me it was very nice."

I felt myself drop my eyes for few moments in an embarrassing recall of the previous evening's frankly delicious naughtiness. When I forced myself to look up and meet his eyes I said, "Roberto, I confess I enjoyed it too, but that has to be the end of it because—"

He put his first two fingers gently on my lips to shush me and smiled his devilish smile. "Just remember what I explained last night. And think about it. It is all I ask."

I didn't say anything; I just looked down again. What I really wanted to do was say that I'd thought about it all I needed to and let's rush into my bedroom immediately.

"Are you sure you do not want some breakfast?" he asked.

By now, I was holding the coffee Rosa had brought. "You know what I'd really like? A quick tour of the house."

He brightened. "Yes, we will do that. But it will indeed have to be quick because I must be at my law office in Havana. You will have the day here to relax by yourself and I am sorry, but you will have to dine alone tonight. Tomorrow a car will come for you and take you back to Havana."

"What happens when I get to Havana?" I asked.

He didn't answer, instead saying, "Come, we will start our quick tour in the living room. I expect you would like to know which of my family is in all the photographs."

I told him that was precisely what I was hoping to learn. As we went through the dozens of pictures, I learned that most of my guesses were correct. I had pegged his parents perfectly. When we arrived at one of the pictures I had noticed the previous evening, I asked him about it. It was the one of a much-younger Roberto with some other young men with the Universidad sign in the background. I pointed to the young man next to him in the picture whose image had seemed vaguely familiar to me the night before.

"Who is that" I asked.

"One of my classmates in law school. All of them are."

"But this one looks somehow familiar."

His eyebrows shot up. "I am impressed. You are very observant; he has been in the news lately."

"Oh? What's his name?"

Roberto paused for a long moment, almost as if he was somehow considering how to answer me.

"His name is Fidel Castro."

Chapter Seventeen

Hallie

Ian Lightbourne's house was in the older Beach Park section of Tampa and was a roomy, two-story salt box with a living room on one side of its staircase-graced foyer and a dining room on the other. The living room extended back into an "L" that became a large kitchen and breakfast room, and behind that was a sunroom that ran laterally across the rear of the house. Sporting a swimming pool, it was more house than a college professor's salary might support, but with the lucrative income of a successful lawyer spouse, it was no problem.

The house lent itself to the kind of critique-group sessions Ian Lightbourne occasionally hosted for his creative writing students in the University of South Florida's MFA program. Hallie lingered after this evening's session so that she became the last student there. When they had arranged it, Lightbourne said, "I've read your pages. Stay after the critique group, if you'd like, and we'll go over them."

Ian Lightbourne closed the door on the last of Hallie's fellow students and turned to look at her. "Glass of wine?" he asked.

She answered his question with one of her own. "Where's your wife?"

She thought he wore a look that was almost sheepish. "Spending the night in Orlando. Three straight days of depositions." His British accent pronounced it "Or-lahn-do."

His answer made a shiver run through her. She wasn't sure if it was her keen anticipation over hearing her professor's reaction to her work or something else. She knew she had found herself looking at Ian as he conducted the session. She could not help but compare him to Rich. They were polar opposites in the way they carried themselves, spoke—everything really. While Rich was gregarious, flashy, and manifested little that seemed cerebral, Ian's thoughts and concerns seemed to always be devoted to Hallie when they were together. In fact, he seemed to anticipate her feelings. His mind was nothing less than imposing and it was a force that was a counterpoint to the power of Rich's wealth.

Hallie realized she was also physically attracted to Ian. She found his unique blue eyes particularly captivating. While they were languid, they were still stalwart and penetrating in a restrained way that was both inviting and a source of safety and assurance. As she had studied him during the session, she imagined what it might feel like to run her hands through the somewhat lengthy salt-and-pepper hair on his neck.

"So. Glass of wine?" he repeated his question.

She remained silent as she pursed her lips and thought about the situation she was in.

"Ian, I didn't know your wife was out of town. You and I here alone? Drinking wine?" But as she said it, she could feel herself getting lost in those eyes.

"What's wrong with that?" he asked.

"Well," she said. "It's just not . . ."

"Not what?"

"Not . . . proper." As she said it, she was jolted by recalling her mother using the exact same words at Roberto's beach house when she realized there were two places set for dinner.

Ian Lightbourne took a step toward her so they were close enough to embrace or kiss, but he left his hands at his sides as he smiled and said, "Hallie, my dear, it will only be improper if we *do* something improper." His smile broadened and his eyebrow arched as he added, "I'm just wondering what you had in mind."

She absorbed the quip but was nonetheless flustered. "I didn't have *anything* in mind. Other than going over my pages." Of course, she knew that was not true as she recalled daydreaming about running her hands through his hair.

He moved an inch or two closer and now gently touched her cheek with the back of his fingers. "I confess I *have* had some other things in mind, actually," he said. Hallie noted his use of the typical British syntax of adding "actually" to the end of declarative sentences. "But I suppose I've been too . . . oh, I don't know, *British* to act on them."

Hallie had almost shivered when his hand had touched her cheek and now they were so close, their eyes almost creating an unctuous pool of communication revealing feelings and urges to each other. Their lips touched as Ian took her shoulders.

But that's as far as it went. Hallie gently backed away and looked down. "Ian, I . . . I will confess I have some of the same feelings, but . . . I just can't." She looked up at him again. "What about your wife?"

He dropped his hands from her shoulders and stepped back. He smiled again. "You never did answer me on that glass of wine. I think I could use one."

"Sure, sure," she said. "A glass of wine."

In a few minutes, they were seated on the sofa in the sunroom, each with a glass of Syrah he had poured. Hallie curled her legs beneath her while Ian Lightbourne sat facing her with his arm on the back of the couch.

"I'm not going to say something as boorish as 'my wife doesn't understand me,'" he said. "I believe we understand each other very well. She is totally, I mean totally, absorbed in her work and fiercely competitive. When even a motion in court doesn't go her way she's like a female bear whose cubs have been threatened. I can tell you, it's not much fun. The fact is we've drifted pretty far apart; we're more like roommates than anything else. She's rarely here in the house. Particularly when some election campaign she's interested in is under way. And I know for a fact that she's not always faithful to me."

He looked down in sadness and Hallie felt a wave of nurturing feelings washing over her. Implausibly, she somehow felt *responsible* for his circumstances. She wanted to hug and console him but restrained herself. At that moment, going over her pages was the furthest thing from her mind.

"So, what does the future hold for you two?" she asked.

"You mean are we going to get a divorce? Probably someday. It's more like we just haven't gotten around to it than anything else. How about you? You're probably getting ready to do the opposite."

"What do you mean?"

"Aren't you and that Rodino chap figuring on getting hitched?" He tried to force a smile as he said it but he looked more anxious than anything.

"I'll tell you, Ian; this book project is the most important thing to me right now. I just . . . I just *need* it, if you know what I mean. Need to be successful at it. Does that make any sense?"

"Perfect sense."

She laughed. "Now watch, Rich will propose and I'll cave in and say yes."

Ian slid a little closer to her on the couch and the back of his fingers were on her cheek once again, his Gulfstream blues ensconced in hers. "I certainly hope not," he said. His hand then went to her hair, her ear, and he drew her closer. This time, the kiss happened and Hallie was a hungry participant. In moments, she was on her back on the couch, Ian on top, and she realized where things were going, where she very much wanted them to go. But she stopped and gently pushed him away.

"Ian, I like this very much but I think I like it a little too much, if you know what I mean. And it's something I just can't process this quickly." She realized she was breathing rapidly.

"Right," he said. "Of course." All very British-y.

"Maybe we should go over my pages now," Hallie said.

"Right. The pages. Yes, of course."

And they did go over them. It was a productive session resulting in suggestions—a few structural, most stylistic—that struck Hallie as very well conceived. Standing at the door as she was leaving, their bodies came together again as did their lips. Hallie knew her breath came in short bursts when she became sexually aroused and she was still panting when she answered Ian's final question.

"When can I see you again? And I'm not talking about in class."

She knew her answer would not please him. "I don't know; I'm leaving day after tomorrow on Rich's plane for the Bahamas. We'll be on his yacht for five days."

Chapter Eighteen

Hallie was always amused by the name of the fixed-base operator that operated the private plane terminal at the Tampa airport. She knew it was a chain but the name still struck her as either clever or tacky; she wasn't sure which. The name was Million Air. She wondered if, in Rich's case, it shouldn't be called Billion Air, although she really had no clue how much money Rich had. As she pulled in the parking lot at Million Air, she mentally tallied a few of his earthly toys: The jet they were about to fly on, his yacht they'd be sailing on, a garage full of cars ranging from Bentleys to Ferraris, and . . . let's see, she thought, how many homes? She counted the Tampa mansion, the place on the water at Islamorada, the condominium at Steamboat, and his New York apartment. Actually, she did know that he only leased the New York apartment, but it was right on Fifth Avenue overlooking Central Park.

As she considered his consumption, she immediately thought of what balanced it. Rich was always Tampa's top supporter of charitable causes. He even had a building named for him at the university. The community's admiration for Rich Rodino might be more aptly described as idolatry.

It was early May, so Hallie had thrown in a wet suit in case the water was still chilly. Rich and Hallie loved diving together. He was an avid saltwater fly-fishing angler but she had never gotten into that. The motor yacht was waiting for them in Marsh Harbour, Abaco, Bahamas. She loved the yacht, but who wouldn't? It was a custom-built 130-foot Westbury, very similar to golfer Jack Nicklaus's *Sea Bear* and luxurious beyond anything she thought she would experience in her life. Rich had given the craft the lawyerly, metaphorical name of *Just Cause* which Hallie really didn't care for. But it was his boat.

She pulled up to an automatic sliding gate at Million Air and into the keypad entered a code Rich had given her. The gate slid open and she drove through it onto the tarmac and right up beside Rich's corporate jet. It was a Cessna CJ2+, a model designed and approved for single pilot operation. Rich had over 2000 hours of flight time and was certified to fly the plane alone but—thankfully, Hallie thought—he always took another pilot with him in the right seat. It was usually a former airline captain named Chris; when Hallie drove up, he was waiting for her. Chris sprang into action, unloading her car and transferring everything to the plane. Hallie then parked her car and walked into the Million Air terminal to see Rich coming out of the little room where pilots check weather.

"Well, if it's not Angel!" He boomed it. Although there was no one around, it still embarrassed Hallie. He took her in his arms for a rousing kiss on the lips. "We're going to have *so* much fun," he said, obvious joy spreading over his face. "Weather forecast is like I wrote it." Then, still holding her, his smile left and he looked at her as earnestly as he ever had. "Baby, I've really been looking forward to this trip and it just being the two of us. I know I haven't told you this when we're not in bed, but . . .," he paused and she waited. "I'm really in love with you. I should have been telling you that all along and I'm sorry—"

Hallie put two fingers to his lips. "Baby, don't apologize, you do your best. But I'm glad to hear you say it this way."

"Well?" he said, looking somewhat anxious.

She smiled. "Of course. I love you, too."

He beamed, kissed her again firmly but quickly, and said, "Want to ride in my beautiful balloon?"

She laughed. "Up, up and away? You bet."

Hallie rode alone in the seven-seat passenger cabin of the jet while Rich and Chris got them to Marsh Harbour in just under an hour. She spent the entire time with her laptop doing revisions and self-editing on the book. On arrival, they cleared customs at the Cherokee FBO and were taken by taxi to the Boat Harbour Marina at the Great Abaco Beach Club where *Just Cause* was moored. Chris flew the plane back to Tampa.

Hallie wasn't even sure how many crew the yacht had. She knew there to be at least a captain, a mate, a chef, and maybe somebody else, but she also knew she and Rich were the only ones on the boat and had plenty of privacy. She unpacked in the massive master stateroom that featured the most beautiful wood paneling she'd seen anywhere. She figured it was either teak or mahogany but never could remember to ask Rich. She had forgotten that the bathroom fixtures were gold.

The weather was grand and, after a superb lunch of Bahamian lobster salad on the aft deck, they got underway, bound for some reefs between Marsh Harbour and Green Turtle Cay. They anchored where they would dive and spend the night. The water was as clear as the weather was good and their dive was spectacular—several huge grouper, a kaleidoscope of tropical fish, and a motionless, staring four-foot-long barracuda. They also saw many beautiful but nuisance lion fish, killing as many as possible, as encouraged by the Bahamian government.

After diving, they showered and changed into tropical clothes. With the weather so nice, they chose the aft deck for cocktails and a dinner of fresh sautéed hogfish with beurre blanc sauce accompanied by a 2006 Puligny-Montrachet. By the time the dessert came, darkness had fallen. The chef had made a fresh chocolate soufflé and Rich unveiled a bottle of Dom Perignon to go with it.

"Leave us for a while, please, Eddie," Rich said pleasantly to the mate after the soufflé was served and the champagne poured.

"Yes, sir," Eddie said, withdrawing quickly.

"Wow, Dom Perignon for just the two of us?" Hallie said.

She saw Rich smiling and, if she didn't know him better, she would have thought it a nervous smile.

"It's a special occasion," he said.

"Oh?"

"Yeah."

She waited him out.

"Remember what I told you at the airport before we left?"

"You mean when you said . . . ?"

"Yes. When I told you I love you. I've been thinking about it a lot and I want to back it up."

He reached in his pocket, pulled out a small box, and opened it. Hallie was almost blinded by the largest diamond she'd ever seen except maybe when she saw the Hope Diamond.

"Rich . . .," she was speechless as she held her palm to her chest. "I . . . I don't know what to say." She couldn't help but stare at the ring and not look at him.

"Well, let me give you a hint. How about yes?"

She looked at him now and reached for his hands, looking at him earnestly. "Rich, I love you, too. But I'm going to need to think about changing our lives in such a drastic way. I know my life would be one of utter luxury if we got married but I just feel like I have to prove something to myself . . . with this book. I—"

"Baby, why can't you write your book as my wife? What difference does it make?"

She was silent for long moment. "That's an excellent question and I just need a little time to figure out the answer." She squeezed his hands. "Will you give it to me?"

He looked at her and nodded but with such devotion in his eyes that she almost changed her mind and said yes right then. Instead, she drew his hands closer to her. "I understand there's a very nice master stateroom on this tub," she said. "Any truth to that?"

He broke out in a smile as he took her hand and helped her to her feet.

Much later, back on the aft deck, each with a glass of vintage port, they watched what Hallie had always called "heat lightning" way in the distance over the Atlantic, while they listened to the gentle hum of the yacht's generators and the mesmerizing sound of the water near the reef slapping the hull. Way in the background, soft jazz piano played on the yacht's sound system.

"I've been meaning to ask you a question," Hallie said.

"Fire away," Rodino said.

"Remember that last investor reception? Remember that old guy in the bow tie that asked those questions you didn't like?"

"Sure, I remember him. Why?"

"Well, I was just wondering why you didn't like his questions. I say that not remembering exactly what they were right now."

Rodino reached for the coffee table on the deck and popped a crumble of Stilton cheese in his mouth before taking a sip of his port. "He wanted to see the confidential files of the cases, and I can't do that. It's illegal."

"Now I remember," Hallie said. "He seemed to think it wasn't."

He leaned forward to answer her. "Well, he's wrong, but I still believe he'll invest ten million. Maybe more."

"Really?" she said, surprised and puzzled.

"I was going to tell you this tomorrow. I'm not going home with you. Chris is bringing Mr. Albert Adams himself down on the plane and deadheading you back. Turns out Mr. Adams is a fanatical fly-fishing angler. He and I will bonefish for a couple of days and go back in the plane together when Chris brings it back down." Hallie saw a confident smile on Rich's face. "Mr. Albert Adams *will* become an investor."

Chapter Nineteen

Dimple

I'm agitated when Hallie walks in this morning because I haven't seen her in days. I fuss at her about it, saying something ugly like they could have rolled me out of here with a tag on my toe and she wouldn't have known it. Then she reminds me she's been in the Bahamas with Rich and I feel terrible. I assume they're sleeping together. I don't like that but, after Roberto, who am I to talk? I apologize for fussing at her, reminding her that I don't remember much of anything these days. Then she reminds me of how well my long-term memory from the Cuba days is working. I assume she's prodding me to start talking again. So I do.

Well, Angel, I think I left off at the beach house when Roberto and I were doing all that kissing and he'd had my dress up around my neck. He left the beach house right after he gave me a tour of the house and showed me Fidel Castro's picture which, at that time, didn't mean much of anything to me. Well, I had a *wonderful* day at that *marvelous* beach house all by myself. Except it wasn't exactly all by myself because that dear Rosa was there attending to my every whim. I walked on the beach forever, swam some more, snooped around the house a *lot*, and tried to get all I could out of Rosa about Roberto and his family. It wasn't a great deal: she said Roberto was a lawyer in Havana but didn't know what kinds of cases he did. Not surprisingly, Rosa said he likes the *muchahas* . . . uh, that's girls. And his father was a hard-working surgeon. No juicy stuff at all. I even asked about Fidel Castro. She didn't even realize Roberto went to law school with him, but her eyes seemed to light up when I mentioned his name.

And I'll tell you what I spent *lots* of time on that day: Spanish. I had this little English to Spanish pocket guide and I spent *hours* going over it with Rosa. It was just what's called "kitchen Spanish," really, but I can't tell you how much it helped and it was the kickoff to my learning the language. Sort of got me into it, if you know what I mean. Her help in pronunciations was particularly helpful and I couldn't wait to try out a few of my best words and phrases.

Late morning the next day, the same driver with the same red Buick showed up. I tried some of my newly discovered Spanish on him. The result was an appreciative grin and some replies that were absolutely unintelligible to me. I tell you, it was totally deflating. I had understood Rosa so well. I remember thinking: oh well, I'll just have to work harder at it.

It was a glorious day for the ride back to Havana and I took in the Cuban countryside, the cane fields, and people-watched like crazy. As I recalled the boliche Rosa fixed last night, which was *marvelous*, I realized I was feeling so much at home in Cuba it was scary, and I found myself dreading the day Dallis and I had to go back to Miami. And I had no idea when that day was.

The Buick took me directly to a restaurant to meet Dallis and Roberto for lunch. It was almost two o'clock but that was the norm for Cuba. My nice, smiley-faced driver assured me he would take my luggage to the hotel and that it would be waiting for me. At least I think that's what he said. With my new linguistic skills, I thought I'd picked up the word equipaje, and, of course, "hotel" is "hotel", and he threw an "okay" in there for good measure. When I got out of the car and faced the restaurant, I saw its name: Pacifico. I'd noticed we'd ended up right in the middle of Havana's Chinatown but I hoped the Pacifico restaurant was maybe a seafood place. I was wrong; I later found out it was Havana's finest Chinese restaurant. Your daddy and I both *loathed* Chinese food so I knew it had to be Roberto that chose the place. I knew Dallis and I would be testing our ability to tell white lies.

I can't *tell* you how nervous I was. How could I even look at your daddy after what I'd done the night before last? For that matter, how could I look at Roberto? I was embarrassed, ashamed, and felt nauseated. I knew my tummy wouldn't hold anything down. Even if it was one of my favorites like a tomato sandwich with homemade mayonnaise or fresh-made fudge, much less any of that Chinese mess.

They were waiting for me at a dining table and both rose. I made myself put on a big smile but I just knew my lips were trembling uncontrollably. I went to Dallis first and gave him the briefest of hugs as he held my chair for me. I felt myself mumble, "Hello, Roberto." I said it almost under my breath and without looking at him. Then I stole a glance at your daddy to see if he picked up on it. Thankfully, he was gazing at the cute behind of a Chinese waitress. That allowed me to sneak a peek at Roberto who was simply staring right at me in unabashed amusement at my obvious discomfort. I could have killed him.

With no more bottoms or bosoms in sight at the moment, Dallis turned to me and asked pleasantly, "Well, how was the beach?"

I forced the biggest smile I could and just said, "Oh, it was wonderful."

Dallis just looked at me. "That's it? What did you do?"

I rattled off swimming, walking, eating roast suckling pig. Nothing about Roberto showing up.

Dallis looked at Roberto. "Sounds like quite a place. Wouldn't mind seeing it myself sometime when we get things really rolling."

Roberto smiled broadly. "You may count on it, Señor."

Then there was a lull in the conversation and I felt like I should say something. "So, how did it go with the bus people?"

I directed the question at Dallis but he looked at Roberto and said, "What do you think, Roberto?"

We were going around in a circle because Roberto then looked at me and said, "Your husband has been working very hard and he is very good at what he does. I talked with several of El Presidente's transportation executives and they were all impressed with Dallis and the way he handled himself. I think we have an excellent chance of receiving an order for many school buses. I believe the only detail that remains is . . ."

Dallis was silent, so I broke the pause. "What?"

"Well, Dallis has to go to Illinois and convince Challenger to come up with the cash for the marketing fees."

I looked at Dallis. He looked worried. "We've talked about this and we're both okay with it," I said. "What do you think Challenger will do?"

"I don't know but I've got to go find out. You and I will be leaving tomorrow, Dimple."

"Okay," I said, but with a strange sinking feeling in my stomach. I couldn't believe he called me by my nickname "Dimple." It was the first time it had slipped out during the trip. I took a peek at Roberto and saw he picked up on it.

Roberto raised his index finger in the air. "Dallis, may I offer a suggestion that I believe may be helpful to all concerned and may be pleasing to your wife?"

Dallis shrugged. "Sure."

"First, may I assume Dorothy will not be accompanying you to meet with the Challenger Company in Illinois?" (Thankfully, he said, "Dorothy," not "Dimple.")

"That's right."

"And you two have no children to tend to in Miami?"

"Right. What are you getting at?"

Roberto spread his hands and smiled. "Your wife could be very helpful if she stayed here while you are in Illinois. Many wives of El Presidente's transportation executives play canasta at the Havana Yacht Club in the afternoons. Sometimes they even have tea afterwards. Occasionally, they will have dinner at a restaurant with or without their husbands. Everyone who meets Dorothy seems to like her, so I believe she could be a valuable asset in making this business opportunity come together."

Dallis shook his head. "Maybe so, Roberto, but I can't afford to put her up at the Nacional for another week or whatever and I damn sure can't get Challenger to spring for it." Then he looked me.

"Besides . . . I'd . . . miss her." And he took my hand. I thought I would simply roll up and die right then and there I was so ashamed about the other night.

Roberto was still smiling as usual. "But you will miss her anyway, my friend, because you would be in Illinois and she would be in Miami. Why not have her here enjoying Cuba and helping you with your business?"

"Like I said, I can't afford the hotel bills."

"May I suggest you let me worry about that?" the smiling Roberto said.

"You mean pay my hotel bills?"

Roberto laughed. "No, I am not making enough fees on this deal for that. You see, I own condominiums. It is the new thing. They are apartments, really. You may not know this, but about three-quarters of the people in Havana rent their homes from more wealthy Cubans as they cannot afford to own or build one. So apartments have been a very good investment. This new condominium concept is a way to get around the Cuban government's 1939 version of the rent controls you have in some American cities. My father and I own these units together and we actually sell them on an installment plan over a period of years and, if the "buyer" does not pay, we can now legally evict them and start over with a new "buyer." I happen to have a vacancy right now; it is a very nice, furnished place in an excellent neighborhood right in Vedado. It is on the fifth floor and has a beautiful view of the Malecon."

Dallis and I looked at each other but said nothing.

"Please let me suggest this: Check out of the Nacional this afternoon and both of you stay in the condominium tonight. See how it feels, then decide in the morning about leaving Dorothy here to help with your deal. What do you say?"

I took another look at Dallis and knew instantly he was going to do it. I felt like I was going to pass out. At that moment, the waitress with the cute bottom came and asked for our order.

"I . . . I'm not hungry," I said.

"But you must have *something*," Roberto said.

I looked up at the waitress and forced a smile. "Just bring me a fortune cookie, please."

The lunch was served and Dallis and Roberto dove into plates of some kind of stir-fried Chinese mystery meal that came from a wok. The waitress brought me a single plate with a single fortune cookie in the middle of it. With nothing else to do with my hands, I decided to crack it open and eat it. I read the message inside on the little piece of paper. It said, "There is romance in your immediate future."

I made a fist around the wadded paper and hurriedly excused myself for the ladies' room.

Chapter Twenty

Roberto was right. The apartment was lovely and it did have a wonderful view of the Malecon. By the time Dallis and I checked out of the Nacional and got to the apartment, it was pushing cocktail hour. Leave it to Roberto: he'd had a bottle of chilled champagne delivered and it was waiting on us. As you know, I *adore* champagne. Even though your daddy hated it, he opened the bottle and joined me on the balcony while we sipped and watched the boats in Havana Harbor.

We sat side by side and he reached for my hand. "I'm going to miss you," he said, giving me the full brunt of his baby blues.

I melted. "I'll miss you, too, honey," I said, praying that he wasn't looking into my eyes and seeing something I didn't want him to. My heart screamed silently for him to tell me that I should go home with him, maybe to Illinois with him, or just stay in Miami and come back to Cuba when he did. But he didn't. Instead, he said, "I think Roberto's come up with a good idea. You staying here, I mean. It sounds like those canasta-playing women could really help us."

I was staring at the harbor. "Yes, I suppose so," I sort of mumbled.

He squeezed my hand. "You don't sound very enthusiastic."

I looked at him, this time without shame. "It's just that I'll miss you terribly." And I meant it with all my heart.

He laughed. "That's my girl. Well, I'm sure between the ladies and Roberto you'll be plenty busy and have a good time. Just watch out for Roberto, though; sometimes I think he pays a little too much attention to you."

I just stared right back at him for several long moments, thinking about how to respond. Finally, I said, "You know something? I think you're right. Why don't you say something to him about it?"

That stopped him for only a moment before he replied, "Maybe I should. But I probably won't. One, I don't want to mess up our deal, and, two, I think he's harmless. Anyway, he's probably in bed with some Cuban gal as we speak." He grinned and added, "Maybe two of them."

"Yeah, probably," I said, as I drained my champagne and stared at the harbor. Definitely not the answer I was looking for. Dallis filled my glass and I think I downed half of it in one gulp. Realizing that it was his last night in Cuba for a while, I turned to him and looked at him in a totally different way as I tilted my head in the direction of the interior of the apartment.

"Speaking of beds, my dear, I do believe I saw one in there."

Your sweet daddy broke into his best crinkly-eyed grin. "Now you're talking," he said, as he took me by the hand and led me inside.

Dallis flew back to Miami on the late morning Air Cubana Constellation and I decided to set out on my own in Havana. I had not yet been able to visit the famous El Encanto department store, Havana's version of Saks Fifth Avenue. It actually wasn't far from the apartment and it was a pretty day, so I walked. The store was on the corner of Galiano and San Rafael, which I later learned was known to Cubans as "La esquina del pecado." It means "The Sin's Corner" because of all the beautiful women walking there on their way to El Encanto. But I didn't feel very beautiful that day, Angel.

I knew one thing that would change that: buying a pretty dress at El Encanto. So I decided to go to the fine dresses department. Oh, I knew I couldn't actually buy one; we couldn't afford it. But I was thinking of trying a couple on and saying to myself what Momma used to: "It's mine while I'm trying it on, at least for a few min-utes." When she did that, I always felt bad for the sales people who would get nothing for their efforts. Recalling it, I wondered why I was about to do the very same thing. But I knew the answer. I just wanted to *feel* a really fine dress on my body in Havana, if only for a few moments. And, although I didn't like myself for it, I was willing to take advantage of the sales people for that brief feeling.

So I asked a clerk in the cosmetics department where fine dresses were and when I said the word "fine" her eyes seemed to light up and she gave me the floor they were on. When I got there, I saw the most beautiful, tasteful sign bearing the logo of Christian Dior. Well, Angel, what I didn't know at the time was that El Encanto's Christian Dior department was way closer to Florida and the southern U. S. than New York or Paris and that wealthy women from there, Latin America, and the Caribbean came to Havana just to shop. So, your daffy, oblivious mother marched into the Christian Dior department like she owned the place and started trying on designer dresses. The ladies all spoke excellent English and I tried a few of my new Spanish words just to try to be polite. I had *the* best time and had already decided on my excuse for not buying: "My husband is arriving from Miami in a few days and I'd like him to see some of these before I decide."

I knew it would work, and it did, but you'll never guess what happened when I came out of the dressing room in my third dress to look in the mirror and twirl around a bit. I looked not three feet from me and guess who was also twirling in a *fabulous* Christian Dior dress she was trying on: Lana Turner! Angel, I thought I was going to fall over right there on the expensive carpet. And she was just *gorgeous*.

I know you'll ask what I said, and the answer is nothing. I was tongue-tied and my mouth suddenly went cotton dry. But guess what? She looked at me—mainly at my dress—smiled, and said, "That's lovely." I somehow mumbled a thank you as she turned toward her dressing room. Seeing Lana Turner and knowing I was a fraud made me suddenly want to just *flee*. And when I learned the price of some of the dresses I'd been trying on, I thought I was going to throw up. So I quickly put my own clothes back on and left, never seeing Lana Turner again.

After I left, I calmed down and reflected on how exciting that had been. It made me hungry so I walked to the Malecon and a wonderful place for lunch called Salon Miami—I just found it by accident. I had fresh lobster salad and it was divine. Then it was back to the apartment where I found what I pretty much expected: a note from Roberto asking me to call him.

Chapter Twenty-One

Roberto was his usual jovial self on the phone. "Well," he said. "Is Mrs. Duncan—or perhaps I should say, Dimple—ready to go to work to help with her husband's business deal?"

I'd forgotten that Dallis had let my college nickname slip. "Nobody calls me Dimple anymore," I lied, "and yes, I'm ready to go to work."

"Excellent. We will begin tonight with a social event involving El Presidente's top fleet executive and his wife. There may also be one or two of what Dallis calls the "canasta ladies" there; I am not sure yet. We will be dining at a famous place I have, unfortunately, not yet taken you and Dallis: La Tropicana. And, of course, we will see the show."

It seemed that things were looking up, because I'd been hoping to make it to the Tropicana. When I was last in Havana with my girlfriends, we couldn't get a reservation and were almost relieved because we'd figured we couldn't afford it anyway. Going there meant wearing the dressiest thing I had. It also meant wearing something Roberto had already seen because my travel wardrobe was paper thin. Ha, what am I saying? My *entire* wardrobe was paper thin. In fact, even calling it a wardrobe was a stretch. But I had actually bought something that afternoon at El Encanto. It was an ice blue shawl with little sparkle things on it that made it look kind of dressy. I decided Roberto and La Tropicana would see it tonight and that it might make Roberto forget that he'd already seen my dress.

"What time?" I asked Roberto, expecting him to name an hour when most folks in Miami would already be asleep. Instead he surprised me.

"I will pick you up at eight. We will first go to another place you have not been, El Floridita. We will have a daiquiri while we discuss strategy for dealing with the fleet executive and his wife and discuss how the canasta should go at the Yacht Club. Afterwards, we will meet our guests. Sound okay?"

"Yes, I suppose so," I said, and rang off so I could begin to get ready.

Well, Angel, "have a daiquiri" was a joke because I found out our reservation at Tropicana wasn't until ten. But, on the other hand, Roberto didn't arrive to pick me up until almost 8:30. I was beginning to learn about CST. That stands for Cuban Standard Time. I was learning that when Cubans decide on a time it's more of a suggestion than an agreement.

I had heard of El Floridita. It's a famous seafood restaurant on the corner of Obispo and Monserrate dating from around 1900. But, as we settled in at the bar with our daiquiris, Roberto explained to me that where we were sitting was El Floridita's main attraction.

"A fellow named Constantino Ribalagua Vert started working here as a bartender but in 1918 became the owner. In the 1930s, he was the one who invented what you are drinking. In fact, this place is also known as "La cuna del daiquiri" which means "cradle of the daiquiri".

By the time the second round of daiquiris came, I decided I might like them better than mojitos, if that was possible. As I sipped that second one, out of the corner of my eye I caught Roberto looking at me with one of his dreamy stares. "My dear Dorothy," he said, " . . . uh . . . notice I did not say Dimple—"

"Thank you," I said.

"Dorothy, I must tell you that you look *marvelous* tonight."

You know, Angel, I can remember almost everything about every minute I ever spent with Roberto. It was many years later when I saw that TV character imitating Fernando Lamas saying "mahhvelous" that this particular comment of Roberto's came flooding back like Niagara Falls.

"I particularly like that shawl," he said. "That blue is very good on you." He was edging closer to me, our forearms touching, and he was trying to literally burn a hole in my soul with his eyes.

He was having good success at it.

We never got around to the so-called "strategizing;" we just talked the same way we had at the beach house. I, of course, told him about my exciting encounter with Lana Turner. We talked about *everything*, and the time flew by. He wanted to know everything about me, what I liked and why, what I didn't and why. What my life in Miami was like. I usually felt like I was probably the most uninteresting person in the world but he somehow made me feel just the opposite. He actually *listened* to everything I said and made me feel like I was occupying every thought passing through his head at that moment. It was something I had frankly never experienced with *any* man, including your sweet daddy. By the time the third daiquiri came, my head was swimming, Roberto had edged even closer, and I knew I was in trouble.

At one point he said, "I hope you will forgive me, but I must visit the gentlemen's room," and left me alone at the bar.

He'd been gone less than a minute when I saw a heavy man with a whitish, grayish, full beard walk in the place, perhaps a little unsteadily, wearing a guayabera. To my horror, he made a bee line for me and slid onto the bar stool Roberto had just vacated. To my further horror, he actually put his arm around me and leaned close. He spoke pure American English with no accent.

"I'm going to go out on a limb and say I'll buy everybody in the bar a daiquiri if I'm wrong about this. You're an American."

"Yes I am, but—"

"I'll tell you what, let's have a drink together first, then enjoy a little piece of sautéed yellowtail, and then . . ." He paused and grinned the most lecherous one I'd ever seen. The man was obviously pretty drunk but he looked strangely familiar.

At that moment, Roberto's hand appeared on the man's shoulder and partially separated him from me.

"Not tonight, Hem," Roberto said sternly. "On your way."

The man shot Roberto the most malevolent look I'd ever seen, even in the movies, and snarled at him. "Kiss my ass, Cubano," he said.

Excuse me for saying that, Angel, but that's what he said.

The man continued snarling at Roberto, "Look, Alvarez, you Cubanos don't get to have all the pretty American ones. You don't even know what to do with them; it takes an American like me to know." The words were slurred.

Roberto increased the pressure on the man's shoulder trying to separate him from me but the man turned away from him. "Leave the pretty lady and me alone, Alvarez; this is for a *real* man."

"I know you are a real man, Hem, but your time is up. Do not make me do what I do not want to do."

At that, the man turned, slowly stood, and faced Roberto. "Oh? And what might that be, Cubano?" I could feel waves of testosterone pulsating as the man stared at Roberto, their chins not that far apart.

Roberto didn't answer him. At least not verbally. Instead, he looked away and raised his left hand as if to call for a waiter. The man looked away with him, and when he did, Roberto suddenly punched this rather portly man maybe three or four times in a row, not in the face, but in his stomach. It was the most *violent* thing I'd ever seen but it was so fast that I could barely see it.

The man didn't have a chance; he simply collapsed in a heap right in front of us, gasping for air and holding his stomach. Waiters rushed toward us and began trying to help the man to his feet. They succeeded and guided the man, still gasping, moaning, and cursing down to end of the bar. Roberto called after the waiters loudly in English, "Please make Señor Hemingway a daiquiri and put it on my bill."

I just stared at Roberto. "Hemingway?" I said, more rhetorically than anything else. "Was that . . . ?"

Roberto adjusted the white dinner jacket he was wearing. "Yes, I am afraid so. He has a bit of a drinking problem and he likes the ladies—not a good combination. And tonight is not the first time. Well, it is at least the first time *I* have had to do that but he has had similar problems with others." He took a long drink from his dai-quiri. "He is quite the boxer, you know. He would have wanted me to step outside; we would have drawn a crowd; it would have been in the paper, and who knows what the outcome would have been?" Roberto grinned. "The quick bolo punch was the answer."

If I hadn't been swept off my feet before that, I certainly was now. "Well, thank you for saving me, my prince," I said. And I meant it because I had been genuinely frightened. As I thought about it, I realized I'd had an encounter with Lana Turner and Ernest Hemingway in the same day, the former most pleasant, the latter anything but. Quite a day already and La Tropicana was yet to come.

Chapter Twenty-Two

By the time Roberto and I arrived at La Tropicana, I had lost track of how many daiquiris I'd had. I knew that wasn't good, but I was having a *wonderful* time on what was easily the best date I'd ever had in high school, college, or after. The only problem was I wasn't supposed to be on a date in the first place, because I was married. However, I knew my little reverie would end when the business people joined us. I found myself dreading it.

Well, you'll never guess what happened. Or maybe you will. We'd just been seated at our table for six when the maître d' approached with a telephone attached to the longest cord I'd ever seen. He told Roberto, in Spanish, that he had a phone call. Roberto took the receiver and I listened to his half of the conversation, picking up almost nothing because it was in rapid Spanish. I did hear "lo siento" frequently, which I later learned was an expression of sympathy. As Roberto was concluding the conversation, he began looking at me and then held his hand over the mouthpiece.

"Unfortunately, our guests will not be joining us. Sergio was on his way home to pick up his wife and had a minor automobile accident. No serious injuries but Sergio has a rather painful bruise on his knee and his wife is upset. And the other ladies did not want to come without Sergio's wife. He wants to speak with you." And he handed the phone to me.

I heard a voice speaking fairly good English but with a heavier Cuban accent than Roberto. "Señora Duncan," the man said, "this is Sergio. I am in charge of fleet operations for El Presidente and I have been having business discussions with your husband. I want you to know I like your husband. He is a very smart man. A good businessman."

"Thank you," I said.

"Did Roberto explain what has happened?" He rolled the "R's" in Roberto so much it sounded like when, as children, we used to put playing cards in the wheel spokes of our American Flyer bicycles.

"Yes, he did," I answered. "I'm so sorry."

"Yes, we are too. But we must reschedule. My wife will be calling you soon about playing canasta at the Yacht Club."

"Yes, good," I said. "Yes, that will be fine; I'll look forward to it." I handed the phone back to Roberto who traded goodbyes with Sergio. The maître d' had been standing at a discreet distance and, as he approached to retrieve the phone, asked Roberto a question. When I heard the Spanish word "dos," I knew we were heading for a table for two. So there I was at La Tropicana, a married woman alone with the sexiest man I'd ever met in my life.

A few moments after we were seated at our table for two, an attractive couple approached. She was wearing a classy, cream-colored, halter top dress. He was wearing a white sport coat with a necktie and holding a highball glass with what appeared to be a whiskey. Roberto recognized the couple and immediately stood. He effusively embraced the woman and shook hands with the man as he embraced him as well. They jabbered in rapid Spanish for a few minutes before I saw Roberto looking at me out of the corner of his eye. He directed their attention to me.

"Señora Dorothy Duncan, please meet Martín and Ofelia Fox."

"How do you do?" I said, remaining seated, by this time holding a lighted Lucky.

The couple wore broad smiles. "Señora, please allow me to welcome you to La Tropicana. My wife and I hope you will enjoy your evening."

I said thank you but I wasn't looking at them when I said it; I was looking at Roberto with a quizzical expression.

Roberto was grinning. "Yes, Dorothy. Martín and Ofelia own La Tropicana."

I was duly impressed and said something that so indicated, although I can't remember exactly what.

Martín Fox then addressed Roberto but spoke English this time. "Roberto, we have a surprise for you and Señora Duncan tonight." His expression was that of the proverbial cat that had just polished off the canary.

Roberto cut a glance at me before saying, "What would that be, Martín?" He pronounced his name Mar-TEEN.

Martín gestured broadly in the direction of the center of nightclub. "Perhaps you would follow me."

Roberto helped me out my chair and we followed the owners. The place is huge and it took a few moments to reach the center of the table area where there was an intensified hubbub of people. We made our way through them to something that astonished Roberto and me. In front of us was a huge table that could accommodate perhaps thirty people, a little more elevated than a dining table. Its top was in the exact shape of a grand piano and it had extremely oversized piano keys painted all along one side of it. There were three *gorgeous* candelabras on top. But, Angel, listen to this: Sitting at the table, sporting his trademark wall-to-wall grin, and chatting with other guests, was Liberace! He wasn't performing that night as it was his birthday. The Foxes were honoring him, which included having the special table built for the evening. He chatted us up a bit and was just exactly like he was on TV: big smile, cracking jokes. For me it was surreal.

Angel, I can't tell you how spectacular La Tropicana was. First of all, it wasn't in central Havana. Instead, it was on six acres in a suburban area, the Marianao District. It was *enormous* and lived up to its name by having real live tall palm and fruit trees in situ. They were all over the place, in between the tables and growing up through the roof, which I noticed was only partial as I looked up and saw the stars.

I'll tell you, Angel, this was my kind of place. We switched from daiquiris to mojitos and the service and food were indescribably good. But the visual effect of the place that night is something I can remember like it was just *last* night. Xavier Cugat was playing and had a *forty-piece* orchestra. And there were *fifty* girls in the chorus. They were dancing all over the place, including on these amazing decorated catwalks above the dance floor and all around the place. As good a time as I was having without your daddy, I couldn't help but think of him because those girls were wearing next to nothing. He would have *loved* it. This was the place Las Vegas copied. Showgirls with the most spectacular costumes I'd ever seen: just a strip of cloth here and there, and more feathers and sequins than anything else. And so many of them with multiple changes. The headdresses were simply amazing. I'll never forget when all the chorus girls came out wearing royal palm trees on their heads that must have been three feet tall. And they danced with them like crazy, moving everything *but* their heads.

Speaking of dancing, Roberto and I did our share. I became rather good at the rhumba. It's a very sensual dance involving a lot of hip movement. Roberto, in his Cuban accent, would tell me "it's all in the *heeps.*" Well, let me tell you, he knew how to move his "heeps." And he also knew how to move them when we were pressed together dancing slowly to ballads. I found myself moving mine along with him and thinking thoughts a married woman shouldn't. But I had had very much to drink, and the entire evening was enveloping me in way that gave me a helpless feeling of floating weightlessness. I felt as if I were floating down a long, round, pleasantly decorated tunnel toward something mostly unknown but something I knew I wanted very much.

Later I found that "tunnel" ended at the apartment. Roberto was not exactly sober either and, when we arrived, he said with a grin, "I had best come up and make sure Señor Hemingway is not propped up in your bed waiting for you."

As much as I'd had to drink, I still knew this was the moment of truth. We looked at each other intensely for several long moments as I wrestled with my moral dilemma. The more he looked at me with "that look," the more I melted and, sadly, what little resolve I had left melted too.

"Maybe you'd better," I said.

Well, Angel, I'm not going to sit here in front of my sweet daughter and spell out the details of what happened next.

But I'll tell you that at almost the moment I awoke the next morning, Roberto appeared at my bedside wearing nothing but his underdrawers and holding a tray with a sumptuous breakfast he'd fixed for me. Dallis and I had noticed the food in the pantry and fridge when we "checked in." I subsequently learned that Roberto fixing my breakfast was very un-Cuban, as Cuban men are not accustomed to doing *anything* domestic.

So I propped myself up in bed, looking at this nice breakfast in bed on the tray and all I could think of was diving into the fresh orange juice and coffee because my head was pounding from the night before. Roberto climbed in beside me and I turned to him. "Is this all for me?" I asked. "What about you?"

He leaned on one elbow and looked at me, smiling. "You looked so pretty sleeping I did not want to disturb you. I had my breakfast a while ago."

At that moment, as I looked over at this amazingly handsome man in bed with me, a married woman wearing nothing but a sheet and him wearing only his underdrawers, a little tuft of black hair on his chest, the recollection of the previous evening all started hurtling at me like a locomotive. The memory of what I had done billowed inside me like a rising tide filled with sordid moral flotsam. It disgusted me. The guilt that surged inside me at that moment was every bit as intense as the previous evening's sensations that caused it. I was overcome and began sobbing. Roberto put his hands on me to comfort me. I didn't fling them off but removed them firmly.

"What is wrong, amorcito?" Roberto asked, lapsing into a mixture of English and Spanish when faced with the dilemma of a girl crying.

"*Everything's* wrong," I sobbed. "I'm wrong; you're wrong for even being here, and . . . I don't know . . . I'm just so ashamed!"

"Amorcito, there is nothing to be ashamed of. Last night was the most wonderful, beautiful night of my life. I mean that."

Well, that only made my sobs intensify. And just at the wrong moment because the telephone on the bedside table began to ring. I couldn't possibly answer; I was sobbing too intensely. As the phone continued its ringing, Roberto reached for it.

"No!" I said. "It might be Dallis." Then I sat up straighter in bed as it hit me: My God, it *might* be Dallis! I had no choice but to answer. When I did, I was still sobbing. It was Dallis.

"Honey, you're crying; what's the matter?" he asked.

Between stifled sobs, I squeaked out a tiny, "Nothing."

"Come on now," he said.

"It's nothing really. I guess I just miss you."

Saying that while I glanced over at the almost-naked man in my bed nauseated me, but I gathered myself enough to say, "Look, I'm just upset right now. I miss you and I just stubbed my toe on the coffee table and it hurts. Why don't you call me back in about thirty minutes and we'll talk, okay?"

He agreed, we hung up, and I turned to Roberto and spoke quietly to him.

"Roberto, you must leave now and I must move into a hotel. A cheaper one than the Nacional. That's if I can't talk Dallis into letting me fly back to Miami today." I started crying again. "I'm so ashamed. I have this wonderful husband I love and here I am in bed with you." I was holding my hair up with both hands as I resumed my sobbing and the sheet fell below my bare bosom. I noticed it and quickly pulled the sheet back up.

Roberto reached for me.

"Roberto, please don't touch me. I already feel . . . dirty. Our little fling is over; it should never have begun in the first place."

Roberto was sitting up in the bed now, facing me. "Dorothy, you are the most special, beautiful woman I have ever met in my life. What we have together has nothing to do with your fine husband; it is *ours*." He put both his hands to his chest as he said "ours." "You can still love Dallis; that has nothing to do with us, just as the love we share has nothing to do with Dallis."

I looked up at him curiously, my sobs abating somewhat. "What did you just say? Something about our . . . love?"

"Yes, yes I did. Of course . . . I love you. How could I not fall in love with someone like you? And I pray you love me, too. But that should not affect your love for Dallis. He is a fine man and we are going to do some excellent business together. And, by the way, men can love each other too. I am not talking about sexually; I mean, for example, that I love Dallis too as my new good friend. You see, God is love and he made us capable of loving each other in so many ways. Why not take advantage of that?"

I had to think about that one a minute. "Well, Roberto, you certainly know how to put a spin on things. What about the little matter of the vows I took? You know, love, honor, and obey?"

Roberto was kneeling on the bed now and spread his hands in defense of his position. "But of course, my dear. You should do that. Dallis deserves that and you love him. And you *are* honoring and obeying him. But right now Dallis is there; you are here, and you and I are in love as well. My darling, even if you never see me again after this moment, I will always treasure you." Then he gave me one of his looks. "But I pray that you will get over your unnecessary guilt and I will see much of you. I do love you."

It was all too much for me and Niagara Falls erupted again. Roberto could see what he needed to do and he began looking for his clothes. "I will call you later," he said with a smile, and blew me a kiss as he retreated from the bedroom. At that moment I was struck by one of my more foolish thoughts: the embarrassment of Roberto leaving "my" apartment in the morning in his dinner jacket. Then I realized it was really his apartment and that I didn't really know anybody in Havana anyway. Then I had another crazy thought: I realized to my horror that I had become just like my mother—out drinkin' and smokin' and then coming back and . . . well, you know.

Before Dallis called back, I ate the breakfast Roberto had fixed, felt better, and managed to get through my conversation with Dallis without cracking. But he told me something I didn't want to hear: his meetings in Illinois would take place a week later than he thought. I asked him if I could come home to Miami. He said he didn't want to risk not doing everything remotely possible to make sure the deal happened. "Do you think Roberto will let you have the apartment a little longer?" he asked.

The question unleashed a range of emotions that tumbled inside me like clothes in a dryer. "Dimple?" he said, when I didn't answer.

"Yes, I suppose he would," I finally said, and hated myself for the thoughts that accompanied my answer.

After hanging up with Dallis, I tried to combat my raging hangover with a nap. It mostly worked and I was sitting on the balcony overlooking the Malecon when the phone rang again. I thought it might be Dallis calling again. It was Roberto.

"How are you doing now, my darling?" he asked.

"Better," I said in a tiny voice.

He was jovial as usual. "Well, I have a nice surprise for you. I would like to invite you to accompany me to the polo matches today."

"Polo?" I said.

"Have you ever been to a match?"

"Of course not; that's what rich people do."

He laughed. "Yes, that is true. Well, the chief executive of United Fruit Company is a friend of mine and we will take a nice, long drive through the countryside out to their polo field for their Sunday matches. They have their own teams, the jerseys, the good horses, everything. We will take a picnic lunch, a blanket, and bottle of champagne. Pick you up in about an hour?"

"Roberto, you must not have been listening earlier; I can't do this with you."

He laughed again. "Do not be silly, my darling. After all, I hear your good friend Lana Turner may be at the matches. And anyway, the ladies wear grand hats and I have already borrowed one for you from my mother. It is blue like your shawl last night."

Chapter Twenty-Three

Hallie

Ian Lightbourne's office at the University was in one of the older buildings on campus and was its own cliché: small, cluttered, musty, and loaded with way too much Victorian furniture for the space and way too many books for the shelves. One small window let the late afternoon light stream in and the oak floor creaked when walked upon.

Lightbourne sat with Hallie on his small, high-backed sofa. An antique silver tea service was on the coffee table and they each were working on a cup. She had come to his office to hear his review of her latest pages of the novel. He was her primary reader, support group, and editor all wrapped up into one person. He would never do all those things for any other student; but for him, Hallie was different. They sat side by side on the small sofa, almost touching, but there were no romantic charges invading the air's molecules. On the contrary, it was all professional, and Hallie was on edge with anxiety waiting to hear his comments.

"Well, I have some very good news but I'm afraid I also have some not-so-good news."

Hallie's spirits soared at his opening words then sank. "Tell me," she said.

"I'll give you the good news first which is that I absolutely love the work. I'm suggesting a few changes but they're mostly stylistic. We'll go over them in detail in a few minutes. And, structurally, the book is as sound as Raymond James Stadium."

"The bad news?" she asked, her heart now in her throat.

He leaned toward the coffee table, picked up his cup and saucer, and held it with both hands while he spoke. "I did something I probably shouldn't have. I haven't told you this until now, but I am casually acquainted with two or three New York literary agents."

"That's good," Hallie said.

"But there is one I know quite well. We met at a conference. She's British and we learned that our families are both from the Hampshire area just west of London. We've kept in pretty good touch and seen each other at other conferences."

"And?"

"As I said, I probably shouldn't have, but I like the book so much thus far and I—"

"You sent it to her."

"Yes. I should have asked your permission. I'm terribly sorry."

Hallie let out a great sigh as she put her hands together in her lap and looked down at them. "She didn't like it," she said very softly.

"No, that's not true. She liked it; she just commented that it might be too . . ." His voice trailed off.

She looked up. "Too *what*, Ian?" she asked, almost too sharply.

He put his cup back down on the coffee table and began shaking his head. "I can't really believe she said this. She said it might be too 'namby pamby.'"

"Namby pamby?" Hallie rose from the sofa and began pacing the room to the extent its small size permitted. "What the hell does that mean?"

"Good question. The upshot of it was that it's perhaps too . . . goody two shoes. The impact of *Fifty Shades of Grey* in the marketplace seems to have changed things. I think she thinks your mother should have been more explicit about her sex with Roberto. And . . . I hate to tell you this . . . but she said it could use a little more spice, like possibly your mother being also romantically interested in a new character who might be another woman.

"Oh my God!" Hallie said.

"And she said it would be more interesting if Roberto were black. Like so many Cubans are now."

Hallie stopped pacing. "How old is this agent?"

"Very young, actually. Far younger than I. Perhaps in her twenties."

"That figures," Hallie said. "Ian, with all due respect to your friend, what she said is absurd. You know me well enough to know I have no problem with a lesbian character or characters of African descent, but I have a huge problem with throwing verisimilitude out the window in the name of political correctness or marketing trends or whatever her reasons are.

"I'm sorry, but through my mother I know how Southern women of that era thought, behaved, and operated in social and romantic situations. And I've characterized all of that with utmost accuracy. Ian, our population is aging. All the non-millennial readers out there would hoot with laughter if I implemented some of her suggestions."

She continued pacing, getting more and more upset. She stopped and turned to him again.

"I just can't believe this. My mother was born in 1928. In her day, interracial romance was right up there with pedophilia. I mean, like everybody then, she called African-Americans Negroes. In her Georgia accent, it even came out 'nigra,' which is not saying the 'N' word; it's just a pronunciation. Now all that is unfortunate, but it happens to be the way things were and I'm sorry but I'm just not into revisionism. I mean, what happened happened. And we shouldn't forget that stuff or we can't learn from it. Anyway, most of the Cubans doing anything other than manual labor or subsistence farming in the fifties were white. And a lesbian romance in the fifties? I'm sorry. Way too low on the plausibility scale."

He rose and went to her. "My dear Hallie, I couldn't agree with you more. I urge you to put this out of your mind and continue. But I simply had to tell you; I would have been remiss not to. But you must be prepared in case there are similar critiques. As I've stressed to you many times, fiction is highly subjective. And the landscape has changed in New York. The legacy publishers are waging a mighty battle against digital self-publishing and it seems that anything new they buy must be totally unique and somehow edgy. And most of the editors are young females who think the edgier the better."

"How am I going to get through this?" she asked.

"Two ways. One is continuing to work your very attractive derriere off, and the other is to continue to rely on me. Now let's go over those revisions, shall we?"

"Sure," she said. "And, Ian . . ."

"Yes?"

"Thanks. I don't know what I'd do without you; I really don't."

He seemed to think that one over for a moment before saying, "Frankly, I wish you didn't *have* to do without me. By the way, after we finish, how about dinner?"

It killed her to have to turn him down. "I would but I can't. Have to go to that banquet to dedicate the new YMCA tonight. Excuse me, I mean the new *Richard Rodino YMCA*. He gave five million."

He smiled, almost sheepishly. "I could buy you a five-dollar cheeseburger."

She wrinkled her nose. "Tell you the truth: I'd rather be having a cheeseburger with you than eating rubber chicken and listening to all the phony speeches about how great Rich is. I mean, he is great, but you know what I mean."

He deadpanned a few beats before saying, "Yes, I suppose I do."

Chapter Twenty-Four

The banquet was in the huge ballroom of the Civic Center near Tampa's tony Harbor Island waterfront area and the Amalie Arena. Everybody who was anybody in Tampa was there.

Hallie was pleasantly surprised by the food; nevertheless, she picked at hers while seated next to Rich at the head table. She had worn a sea foam green wrap to protect her shoulders from the ferocity of the center's air conditioning outlets. She was still upset by Ian's news of the literary agent's comments. The whole business kept playing over and over in her mind and she found herself nodding to people without having the slightest idea what they had just said. It was after dinner when she came out of her fog and realized someone was speaking at the dais.

" . . . was just a dream until Tampa's favorite son stepped up to the plate. Rich Rodino and Rodino & Ross are always there for our community. When things really get tough, when we're facing possible defeat, Rich Rodino always comes through for this community and gives generously and often. I know God is smiling on him tonight . . ."

Hallie had heard it all before and, despite her efforts to focus, she zoned out and went back to thoughts of her book. The speaker was the president of the YMCA board of directors and Hallie heard, " . . . and Rodino & Ross . . ." At that moment, she realized that she'd never met Rich's partner, David Ross. Finally, Rich was introduced and she stood along with the hundreds of others in the room and applauded long and hard. Hallie smiled the entire time and gazed devotedly at Rich while trying not to look like Pat Nixon, that is to say, she at least tried to show some teeth. Finally, it was time for Rodino to approach the podium and speak.

"It wasn't that many years ago that a poor Italian kid who grew up on the second floor over a meatball restaurant in a rough section of Miami came to this town to try to get an education. When it came time to earn my law degree—which my now-dearly departed parents sacrificed *everything* for—I didn't see any reason to leave. And when it came time to start my career, I still didn't see any reason to leave. Folks, those were, hands down, the best decisions I ever made in my life!"

Thunderous applause ensued as the crowd rose again. Then, to Hallie's shock, when the applause subsided, he turned to face her and smiled. "I have very recently made another decision that is just as good as those others. All I'm waiting for is the right answer before I can announce that one to you all."

Hallie turned crimson and looked for a hole to crawl into as the crowd erupted again. Then Rodino launched into the YMCA and why it was important to him to contribute to the new building. He even threw in the verse from Ecclesiastes about casting your bread upon the water and you will find it in many days. Hallie, her embarrassment having subsided, found her mind wandering again as she had heard the speech before at similar functions.

Rodino was concluding. " . . . love this Y, I love Tampa Bay, and I love all of you!"

The crowd leapt to their feet once again and applauded furiously and long. Hallie, of course, joined them.

Much later, Hallie and Rich were the last ones seated at the Palma Ceia Club. They were at a table in the bar having a Warre's 1983 vintage port and some Stilton cheese.

"Well, how'd I do?" he asked.

"Great, as usual, with one exception."

"And what might that be?" He was grinning.

"You know exactly what I'm talking about."

He stroked his chin. "Hmmm. Maybe I do." And he took her hands in his. "You know, right now would be as good a time as any for you to just say something about that. Something like maybe . . . yes?"

Hallie just looked at him and said nothing. But after the report from the literary agent, she'd been thinking a lot about Rich's proposal. It would solve many issues in her life and make things so much easier. Maybe she owed it to herself, she thought. She scooped up a piece of Stilton with a half of a ginger snap. "I'm getting closer to saying yes, but if you ever embarrass me like that again, I won't even speak to you again, much less marry you."

He said nothing but gave her a little deferential bow.

"By the way," Hallie said, "I realized tonight I've never met David Ross. How's he doing?"

"Getting older and older. Just about ready for a nursing home." He brightened. "He could start dating your mom."

She laughed. "Speaking of old guys, that reminds me. You never told me how it went with that old guy in the bow tie you invited to the Bahamas."

"How do you *think* it went?" He answered the question with one of his own.

"Knowing you, he's now probably an investor."

He touched his temple with his index finger and smiled. "Smart girl."

Chapter Twenty-Five

Dimple

When I first started talking to Hallie about Cuba, I was worried I would run out of gas early into it. But now, with some of my shameful sexual escapades with Roberto out in the open with her, I find myself warming to the task. Today I'm anxious for Hallie to arrive so I can pick things up where I left off, at the polo matches.

When she arrives, I see something in her face that doesn't look quite right but she urges me to start, so I do.

Well, Angel, Roberto picked me up at the apartment and I wore kind of a cream-colored sun dress I thought would match the blue hat he was bringing me. And Lord, what a hat it was.

It was the biggest, floppiest thing you've ever seen. It was more baby blue than the ice blue Roberto had said, but it had tiny little navy blue polo horses needlepointed around it. It was truly a polo hat and it was just *darling*. Don't ask me how, but somehow that hat cheered me up and made me temporarily forget my shame. I know that doesn't make a lick of sense but it did. And Roberto kept his distance. To make me more comfortable, I guess.

Roberto was driving a red and white Chevrolet convertible and had the top down. It was kind of cloudy and I was worried it might rain. I kept the hat on to keep my hair from going too crazy and had to hold my hand on it most of the way. We drove for forty forevers out in the country to the United Fruit Company town and, my heavens, did they have a layout. Polo fields, tennis courts, swimming pools, even their own golf course. It was a strange place in one way because all the houses and buildings were painted exactly the same color: ochre yellow.

We settled in beside the polo field after some sort of security person Roberto knew seemed to approve of us. We spread our blanket and opened our champagne as did others near us who seemed to be mostly families. They worked for United Fruit, I assumed. And yes, all the ladies wore large hats. Roberto had brought empanadas stuffed with pork and a wonderful rum cake called panetela borracha which means "drunken cake."

The matches were *so* exciting I just can't tell you. And frightening. There was really nothing to keep those horses from trampling us except the players riding them and keeping them on the field of play. And they came *very* close. The noise was so unique—the thundering of those hoofs. I'll tell you, Angel, I loved everything about it, including the jodhpurs, boots, and colored shirts they wore. It made my guilt over the night before fade a little further but it still smoldered inside me.

Between matches, a man wearing a white suit and white shoes came striding up to us. Roberto got to his feet. As a lady, I didn't. They greeted each other very cordially in Spanish with a hearty handshake, then immediately began speaking English. Roberto introduced the man to me as the chief executive officer of the United Fruit Company. Please don't ask me his name—I've forgotten it—but he was as American as could be, and *very* nice. When Roberto explained why I was there, the executive said, "Well, Mrs. Duncan, I hope you are enjoying your stay in Cuba. And I hope you and your husband can get your business concluded as promptly as possible."

"Oh? Why is that?" I asked.

The man cut a glance at Roberto. "You haven't told her about your law school classmate?"

Roberto laughed. "You mean Fidel?" Roberto used a dismissive tone. "I believe Fidel may be harmless."

The man suddenly drew himself up taller in what appeared to be indignation and the volume of his voice increased. "Harmless? Roberto, I can take you to hundreds of acres of our sugar cane fields Fidel and his rebels have burned to a crisp and you say he's harmless? The son of a bitch has . . . uh, excuse me, Mrs. Duncan . . . the man has only succeeded in contributing to the starvation of hundreds and hundreds of the peasants. He claims to represent them because we've had no choice but to lay them off. And besides that, he can't be very smart."

"Why do you say that?" Roberto asked.

"Because his rebels even burned his own *father's* cane fields. That's why I say that." The chief executive, still worked up, was shaking his head in bewilderment.

"Ah," Roberto said. "The fields Angel leased from United Fruit. I see what you mean; that was not smart. But I doubt Fidel knows it."

"He most certainly *does* know it. In fact, he was quoted as saying he was 'forced' to make the terrible decision to burn the cane fields to make Batista capitulate and that he gave instructions that his family's crop had to be the first to burn as an example to the rest of the nation."

I later learned from Roberto that this Angel person—they pronounced it "Ahn-Hell"—was Fidel Castro's father and, ironically, quite the entrepreneur and capitalist as he had leased large quantities of land from United Fruit and successfully grown sugar cane on it. He was, in fact, a moderately wealthy man and his son Fidel was a beneficiary, having had a comfortable life growing up and a law school education.

As the conversation continued, the man's face was getting redder and I was getting uncomfortable. "Do you ever talk to him?" the CEO asked Roberto. "Can't you drum some sense in to him?"

Roberto smiled softly. "No, I am afraid not. I have no contact with Fidel. I only went to law school with him; I have not seen him in many years. From the newspaper, I understand he is living in the mountains with his soldiers, sleeping on the ground."

The man pulled out a pack of Chesterfields and offered them. Roberto and I both took one and we all lit up. "Well," the man continued. "I *know* you have some connection to Batista, so make sure he gets serious with this Castro guy. I obviously have a connection too, but El Presidente is not inspiring very much confidence in me that he's on top of the situation. My country has sent Batista planes and tanks and machine guns, but I'm not sure he even knows what to do with them. And I still can't believe that *New York Times* boner his people pulled."

Roberto looked puzzled and stroked his chin. "Please remind me."

"You didn't read the article? That fellow Matthews? He embedded himself with Fidel and his rebels in the mountains for days, interviewed Castro extensively, and then wrote about it in the *Times*. Made the son of a bitch a hero . . . uh, excuse me again, Mrs. Duncan but this really is a bad man . . . made him a hero with all the peasants who don't know how *anything* on this island actually works. They just think Fidel might steal something from the hard-working people and give it to the peasants for nothing. Unfortunately, I'm afraid that's exactly what may happen."

"What was the . . . what did you say? Boner?" Roberto asked.

"Yeah, a big one. Batista's idiot defense minister, that Verdeja guy, issues a statement saying Matthews had simply written a fantastic novel, had never interviewed Castro, and that Castro is actually dead as a doornail. Next day, the *Times* publishes a photo of Matthews and Castro side by side up in the Sierra Maestra and then the brilliant El Presidente says he *still* doesn't believe it. I'll tell you, Roberto, we're in big trouble and nobody realizes it."

"My friend, I am sorry about your cane fields, but I believe Batista will prevail and everything will be good for you and your fine company." He smiled. "Take heart. Be optimistic."

The CEO took a long drag on his smoke, exhaled, and looked off toward a distant mountain. Across the field, the next polo game was being announced. "I hope you're right." Then he looked at me and bowed ever so slightly. "A pleasure to meet you, Mrs. Duncan." And he left.

I waited for Roberto to say something but he was silent. "Well," I said. "That was certainly interesting. You really believe what you told him or were you just trying to make him feel better?"

Roberto blew smoke toward the grass he was standing on before answering. "Good question, my darling." He looked right at me then. "I am not sure."

When he called me "my darling" it brought a potpourri of feelings back that I'll not try to describe, but I think you know what I mean. "So you're *not* still in touch with Fidel Castro?"

The question really seemed to stop him. He looked at me a long time before he answered. "Yes, I am in touch with him. But I cannot tell everyone that, particularly the man who is Batista's greatest ally. It might not be good for my health."

I gulped when he said that. It had never occurred to me that Dallis and I might be walking in on a real live revolution about to take place in this Latin-American country we maybe didn't have any business going to in the first place. At that point, I had not yet become aware of Batista's mass executions. I took a last drag on my Chesterfield—they were not my favorite brand at all. My legs were tucked underneath me and I used both hands to rearrange my skirt which was sort of spread in a circle like a lady's bamboo fan. "So you're in touch with both President Batista and the man who is trying to overthrow him?"

He smiled a slow smile. "Yes, Dorothy, that is exactly correct."

That one made me go for my champagne glass. "So . . . can you explain why and how that is?"

He dropped to the blanket now and took his own champagne glass. He had to speak louder because the next polo match had begun. "It is just the way it is in Cuba. Everybody of any importance knows everybody else. And you are quite correct. The outcome of Fidel's attempted revolution is unknown. He may very well succeed. For that reason, it is in my interest to stay in touch with him, in case he becomes our new dictator. Because I am a lawyer and can do legal work no matter who is power, I must make Batista and Castro both believe I support them. It is a delicate task, like walking a tight rope in a circus, and one that is being attempted by many Cubans right now. All over the country, even *declared* loyalties are changing faster than the customers of the prostitutes in Havana. It is a difficult situation."

"You said Castro will be your new *dictator?*"

"Of course he will be a dictator. What? Did you think that he would be like Eisenhower?" He laughed.

I felt foolish. "Well . . . no, I guess not. So what kind of man is this Castro?"

He seemed to consider his answer carefully and then he looked at me in a strange way. "Perhaps you would like to find out for yourself."

Chapter Twenty-Six

The combination of the champagne, the country air, and that wonderful cake had pretty much taken care of my hangover from the night before. A little dozing on the very long ride back to Havana helped, too. It was after dark when we arrived at the apartment where I morally struggled with another moment of truth. Was my fling with Roberto going to continue until your daddy returned to Havana or would I cut it off right then and there?

Well, if you want the answer, all I can tell you is that Roberto brought me breakfast in bed again the next morning. This time he was only wearing a fluffy white towel around his waist as he had just showered. He smelled *wonderful* and, Angel, he had muscles in all the right places, just enough body hair to be exciting and . . . well, I shouldn't be going into those details with my sweet daughter. I'll just say I propped myself up in bed, tried to fluff my hair a bit, and smiled my thanks for his thoughtfulness. I'll tell you, I was in pretty deep now.

The night before, we both had said we loved each other. And he emphasized to me again that I could love both him and Dallis. I actually believed him, never mind that I'd known him barely over a week. But Angel, knowing and feeling that I loved this man was the only way and the only reason I was in bed with him. I was not into promiscuous sex and never *dreamed* I would ever be involved in *extramarital* sex. Come to think of it, I was never even involved in *premarital* sex. Well, unless you count that one time with Bugs

Berigan after the Auburn-Georgia game, and I guess you have to count it. But I certainly did not view this thing with Roberto as anything close to promiscuous; I viewed it as a serious love affair with a man who, unfortunately, was not my husband.

So, did that make my guilt dissolve? Ha! Anything but. I called Dallis that night (before he could call me) and launched into my first foray of lying to him. I had never thought I was very good at lying but, after that call, I decided I might be wrong and that fact disturbed me as much as anything. I told him I'd played canasta that day and walked around the city. When I hung up, I started crying and Roberto had to sort of "nurse" my composure back over a period of about an hour. His patience and attentiveness just made me fall for him even harder.

I didn't know *what* I was going to do when your father returned. I certainly wasn't leaving him for Roberto. I loved your father; I took my vows with him; I wanted to have a child with him. That was you, of course, eventually. It would have been easier if your daddy would come back to Cuba to pick me up; we both would wave goodbye to Roberto, and that would be that. But no, I knew the *three* of us would have to be together a lot before we left. Lord, Lord, I was thinking, how has this happened to me? I was just figuring on going to Cuba with Dallis on a lark. Well, Angel, I sure got one. And then some.

The night before, between our lovemaking, I couldn't help myself. It's one of the things we women do, I guess. I started asking him questions.

"You've never married?" I asked.

"No." (Well, that was a lot of detail, wasn't it?)

"Ever come close?"

"Mmmm, not really."

I snuggled up really close before asking my next one in kind of a little voice. "Roberto, you have other girlfriends, don't you?"

He was cradling me in his arm and looked down at me with a very serious expression. "Yes, I have what you might call 'girlfriends', but, my darling, you are not a 'girlfriend.' In all my life, I have never met anyone like you."

"Well, Angel, that made me . . . my goodness, there I go with details again. Let's just say we picked up where we'd left off only twenty minutes earlier and I initiated it."

After breakfast, Roberto assumed a more urgent and pre-occupied attitude as he dressed and gathered himself. "It is Monday and I have clients to see so, unfortunately, I must say goodbye for now."

I pushed out my lower lip in a mock pout but I wasn't mocking all that much because I was going to miss him. And what was I to do with my time? It could be another week before Dallis returned. He answered my question as though he'd been reading my thoughts.

"So what are you to do, my darling?" He said it rhetorically in advance of providing the answer. I loved it when he called me "my darling." "I plan to arrange for you to play canasta with Sergio's wife and a few ladies. I will call you in a while and tell you the time. It will be this afternoon at the Havana Yacht Club. You should dress nicely; I am sure they will serve tea later in the afternoon, perhaps play some more cards and then likely start on the daiquiris. It is a daily ritual with these women whose husbands are very well paid by Batista, and bribed by others, to keep the country running and who have many servants at their homes. But most of them are not very happy and many are on their way to becoming alcoholics. At daiquiri time, it would be helpful for you to see what you can find out about our deal."

Our deal. That sounded so strange. But it was true. What bizarre triangles I was caught up in: one was business, the other love. I found myself shaking my head contemplating it all.

Roberto noticed. "What is the matter?" he asked.

I looked up, smiling. "Not a thing. I'm pretty good at canasta. Should I play 'customer canasta' or try to win?"

His grin was wide. "To win, of course. But not by too much. You have some money to play with, do you not?"

"Yes."

"Good. Now, let us talk about what will happen later in the week."

I said okay but what I really wanted him to talk about was what would happen tonight. I didn't want to be drinking daiquiris with a bunch of Cuban women if I could be with this wonderful Cuban man I'd fallen in love with in parallel with my dear husband.

"Were you serious about wanting to meet Fidel Castro?"

That perked me up. But I tried to figure if it was in a positive or negative way. It both intrigued and frightened me. I didn't know what to say, so I said nothing.

"If you are, let me tell you what we would do," he said. "Fidel is embedded with his men—and some women—in the Sierra Maestra Mountains. It is an all-day drive to the city of Santiago de Cuba where we would stay in a hotel—"

"Did you say some women?" Fascinated by that, I had interrupted him. "Are they . . . ?"

He laughed. "Prostitutes? Of course not. The primary one is Celia Sanchez, who is Fidel's most trusted advisor. Even more than his brother Raul or Che Guevara. But they are there, too. Anyway, after spending the night in Santiago, we would take a jeep, at least part way, up into the mountains. Then we would walk the rest of the way. Were you a . . . what did they call it . . . a Girl Scout?

"No, I wasn't. Why?"

"Have you ever been camping?"

"Actually, no, I haven't. Why?"

"Well, it could be a problem for you. You are a very delicate and refined lady who likes to be taken care of. This visit would be physically taxing as there is much hiking up rugged mountain terrain."

I remembered going over a little mountain to get to the beach house but, until that moment, it hadn't dawned on me that Cuba was mountainous. Most of what I'd seen had been palm trees and beaches. I would later learn that the Sierra Maestra had peaks over 6000 feet.

"We would stay in the mountains with Fidel and his rebels," he said.

After he said it, he just looked at me, waiting. Slowly I began to grasp what was coming and I asked, "Uh . . . where exactly would we stay?"

He kept staring at me for several moments without saying anything. Finally, the corner of his mouth turned up into more of a smirk than anything else. "As I said, we would stay with Fidel and his rebels. And his ladies, of course." He paused again.

"And . . . ?"

"And, yes, we would sleep on the ground." Then he added, "I say that, but there may be the possibility of sleeping in a peasant's house. I frankly prefer the ground. That way the mice are not a problem."

At that moment, I know I visibly shuddered and then hated myself for it. It's true I played golf with your daddy but, Angel, beyond that, my idea of the outdoors was going out to get the newspaper in the morning. I had never done anything like what Roberto was talking about. Not only did I stand on the sofa if a mouse put in an appearance, I did the same for spiders and roaches. I knew enough to know Roberto was talking about two days without a bath and going to the bathroom in the woods. A tomboy I was not.

"So," he said, "do you want to meet Fidel or not? I must go anyway, with or without you, as I have something to discuss with him."

My heart sank. The thought of being apart from him for that time was unbearable. Especially when there were very few nights we would ever be together again. I didn't have to think very long. I took a deep breath, squared my shoulders, and said, "Roberto, I would *love* to meet Fidel Castro."

He broke out in a wide grin. "Excelente, my darling." For some reason, he slipped in a Spanish word. I chose to think it was because he was genuinely pleased. "We will leave first thing Wednesday morning. As I said, it is an all-day drive. We could fly and reduce the travel time, but we will need my car. Tomorrow, we will go shopping for some boots and socks for you and some fatigues. Maybe a cap, too." He grinned. "When we finish, you may look like one of Castro's rebels—a genuine *Fidelista*."

Chapter Twenty-Seven

So for Roberto, it was off to work. As he left, I kissed and embraced him as if he were my husband. You may not remember it, but a popular television show in those days was *I Love Lucy*. Roberto's accented, stilted English reminded me of Desi Arnaz's character Ricky Ricardo, and I could visualize Roberto as Desi returning at the end of the day announcing, "Lucy, I'm home!"

The moment Roberto disappeared behind the door, I had the emptiest feeling. I slowly walked around the apartment, pausing at the places Roberto and I had been and remembering and savoring *every detail* of what had happened during our time together. This behavior of mine may have been because, as I was kissing him good-bye, I asked, "Will I see you tonight?"

"No, I am afraid not." He smiled. "I am sorry, my darling, but all play and no work makes Roberto a poor boy."

I nodded my understanding as I forced a smile and wondered where he'd picked up the American cliché and reversed it so cleverly.

"I will call you soon about the canasta and give you the ladies' names." And he was gone.

He did call and my spirits soared when he surprised me.

"Do not stay too long at the club with the ladies. I remembered there is a reception tonight at the U. S. Embassy. Would you like to go?"

That wasn't hard. "Of course!" I almost blurted it.

I mean, Angel, how exciting—the Embassy?

My melancholy had turned into joy. In fact, everything was working out perfectly because the cards were not to be played until the afternoon and I was able to do something I had been thinking about. I went ahead and dressed for canasta but took a taxi to the national library of Cuba. It's in an area that today is called the Plaza de la Revolución and in Spanish it's called La Biblioteca Nacional José Martí. Hmmm, I thought. There was that José Martí fellow's name again. First the airport, now the library named for him. He was one of the reasons I was going to the library, but the main one was Fidel Castro. And I had a special interest in learning about this Celia Sanchez person who was Castro's advisor, mainly because she was a woman.

Angel, I was never much of a scholar. I majored in parties, lipstick, bridge, and which fork went where. But when I found out I would be meeting an actual revolutionary who could very well take over the country your daddy and I were counting on to save our financial skins . . . well, I had to learn *something*. Until now, I was willing to be blissfully ignorant of Cuban politics so long as the taxis ran, the mojitos flowed, and that marvelous Cuban music didn't stop. But no more. If I was going to meet Fidel Castro and this Sanchez woman, I was going to do more than just bat my eyelashes.

The library was in a brand new, massive, twelve-story building. Surely, I prayed, there would be archives of English-language newspapers and maybe some books written in English that could tell me what was going on. Thankfully, there were.

I won't bore you with a lecture on Castro because you can go to the library yourself, but I will tell you that he was an enigmatic figure in many ways. First, although Fidel Alejandro Castro Ruz was illegitimate (his mother was his father's servant after a divorce) he was a bit of an aristocrat because his father, Angel, was a rather wealthy sugar cane grower, leasing land from United Fruit Company. So Fidel had a comfortable childhood and was well educated, even attending boarding school. That said, certain things he was denied as a youth may have influenced his revolutionary, socialistic and anti-American proclivities. I'm talking about the fact that he was never allowed on the grounds of United Fruit Company's town or access to their wonderful amenities, or allowed to mix with the powerful Americans that ran that industry, or even their children. He never really got over it.

Although he wasn't a particularly good student, he still got his law degree and became engrossed in politics as a young man. He married, had a child, but divorced, and went to some other Caribbean islands on political escapades. But his homeland and his view of its lack of social justice is what consumed him. He was an activist, a frequent rabble-rousing public speaker, and he ended up leading an almost absurd failed attack on Batista's Moncado army barracks on July 26, 1953. The results were a prison sentence for him and a name for his group: The 26th of July Movement.

That name stuck but so did the prison sentence. At least for two years until Batista, who had no problem ordering the summary execution of anyone who even looked at him the wrong way, inexplicably granted Fidel's release and amnesty. Castro exiled himself in Mexico with his brother, Raul, and the Marxist, Che Guevara. But a year later, they returned with a small band of rebels on a rickety old yacht, oddly named *The Granma,* and landed near the Sierra Maestra. Narrowly escaping Batista's soldiers, they made their way up into the mountains and established themselves there.

They were still in that general area and it's where Roberto and I were to meet them later in the week.

I found it fascinating that Roberto was somehow in touch with Castro and knew how to find him when Batista obviously didn't. Particularly since, in parallel with that, Roberto was working our business deal with Batista and taking me to the embassy of a country that was sending Batista weapons and tanks in opposition to Castro. It was an obvious bit of duplicitous tightrope-walking Roberto was doing. I prayed he would be successful at it for a variety of reasons. I didn't want anything to happen to him because I'd fallen in love with him. I wanted him to get our business deal done so Dallis and I wouldn't starve. And finally, I wanted the best for Cuba because I had come to adore the country and its people.

Canasta with the Cuban ladies was quite an experience. Some of them spoke excellent English but I tried my best to use as many Spanish words as I could—the collection of them I was building in my head grew daily. The ladies seemed to appreciate my efforts. Angel, these women were dressed to the nines and were just as sweet to me as they could be. And talk? Lord, could they talk. The wife of the apparent boss of the school buses—all the fleets, actually—was named Maria and she knew why I was there.

"My husband really likes your husband," she told me privately and I thanked her as profusely as I could, adding that Dallis just thought the *world* of Sergio. I was lying through my teeth because Dallis had never mentioned a *word* about any of the people he'd met.

"What do Americans think of Castro?" one of the women asked. I hit my lying button again and answered, "Most of the ones I talk to don't care for him. He appears to be a socialist, maybe even a communist." The fact was I had never had a single conversation with anyone in Miami about Fidel Castro. I had only been vaguely aware of him before I got to Cuba—just enough that his law school photo at the beach house struck me as someone I'd seen before. But after my hours at the library I knew a lot more. Maybe more than I wanted.

I wasn't kidding when I told Roberto I was pretty good at canasta. But I did play a little "customer golf" and managed to lose just a few pesos. I begged off the end-of-day daiquiris, saying I had a phone call arranged with my husband. I thought it best not to volunteer that I was going to the Embassy reception.

So it was back to the apartment to put on the best dress I had for the Embassy. It was a green taffeta thing Roberto had seen twice already but it was the only option. I had no idea what was in store at the Embassy because Roberto had been in a rush when he told me we were going—all I knew was the time.

I fully expected the United States Embassy to be in a stately old Spanish-style mansion built perhaps around the turn of the century or earlier and surrounded by palm trees, gumbo limbo and bougainvillea. But, boy howdy, was I wrong. The embassy was a brand new, sparsely landscaped, seven-story building of modern architecture on a beautiful site on the Malecon overlooking the harbor. Many said it was supposed to resemble the United Nations building in New York and I could see that. Roberto and I arrived just before dark. The breeze off the water was gentle and the view was magnificent.

As we walked in, it occurred to me to ask Roberto a question. "So, what are you going to say about why we're out together? That you're dating a married woman, or what?"

He smiled. "I will simply tell them the truth. That you are the wife of a Norte Americano client of mine who has been here on business but had to briefly return to Miami."

The reception was actually an art auction fundraiser to benefit last year's hurricane victims in the Dominican Republic. "I can't buy anything," I whispered to Roberto. "Dallis and I are almost broke."

He smiled again. "You do not have to buy anything. Neither do I, but I may anyway. If you see something you really like, let me know. It will be my gift to you and Dallis."

Angel, it was almost beyond my conception that any man could be this sweet and charming. I felt my eyes get moist. "It will be fun to see what's here," is all I said. I hadn't the slightest intention of having him buy anything.

"So, will we meet the ambassador?" I asked.

He looked at me seriously before replying. "You probably would except for one thing."

"Oh?"

"There is no ambassador."

"What?"

"He was recalled by Eisenhower. 'Recalled' is an elegant way to say he was fired."

"Who was he?"

"His name is Arthur Gardner. He was a big Batista supporter and largely responsible for all the weapons the United States has been supplying to the Cuban government to use against Castro. But with the outcome of the revolution up in the air, he was thought to be a little too pro-Batista and a possible political liability, depending on how things go. He was not at all happy about it. Even flew to Washington to beg Eisenhower not to do it. The new ambassador, a man named Earl E. T. Smith, arrives soon."

I thought about what Roberto had said and tried to merge it with all I'd learned at the library and process it. I didn't get very far. I looked around at all the nicely dressed people and, of course, didn't know a soul. "So who *will* we meet? Anybody?"

"Well, you will probably see your friend from the polo matches."

"The Fruit man."

"Right. And I'm sure we'll see Hawk."

"Hawk?"

Roberto sort of smirked. "E. Hawkins McHenry III. But most people call him Hawk. He's temporarily the chargé d'affaires, but when Ambassador Smith gets here, Hawk will go back to what he was doing which, frankly, no one has ever figured out. He seems to mostly play golf with the United Fruit people and with a few Cuban businessmen."

At that moment, I noticed Roberto's glance was diverted over my shoulder at the same moment I heard a booming, American male voice. "Roberto, old chap. You don't even have a drink yet." The man, dressed in a business suit, was holding a glass of champagne. As he joined us, he looked at me for the first time and his eyes got wide. "My God, man, where have you been keeping *her*?"

I thought it was terribly rude. This man was referring to me as if I were a different car Roberto had decided to drive that evening—one this man had never seen. I'd never met him before but he seemed a little drunk to me. But maybe that was because I'd always heard those embassy types end up with drinking problems because of all the functions they must attend. He had some kind of Bostonian accent that annoyed me as much as his rude remark.

Roberto put on a big smile and, bowing slightly toward me, said, "Let me introduce you to Mrs. Dallis Duncan from Miami.

Dorothy, this is Hawkins McHenry and I think he is from Hell or somewhere like that."

"Very funny, old chap," the man said with good-natured sarcasm.

With the "old chap" routine, it was almost as if he was affecting a British style of speaking. "Old" England instead of New England. Whatever . . . I just knew I didn't like him.

"Mrs. Duncan's husband is a client of mine," Roberto said in his typical formal way of speaking English. "He was called to Miami briefly, so I thought Mrs. Duncan might enjoy the auction."

Hawkins McHenry seemed to hit "reset" and looked at me in a serious way with a pleasant expression. "Well, Mrs. Duncan, as a fellow American, may I welcome you to Havana and say that I hope you enjoy your stay. If there is anything you believe our embassy can assist you with, please do not hesitate to contact me." He reached in his breast pocket, pulled out a gold business card case, and gave me one of his cards. Sure enough, it said E. Hawkins McHenry III.

He was smiling very politely now. "My name is Hawkins but almost everybody calls me Hawk and I hope you will, too."

What an instant metamorphosis. I put the card in my purse and said, "Thank you, Hawk. Please call me Dorothy." Just like that, we'd made up.

Roberto threw out some banter. "Hawk, if there is anything Dorothy needs in Havana, do you not think I can take care of it?"

But McHenry didn't hear him. He was too busy furiously waving at a waiter in a tuxedo passing trays of champagne. He succeeded in getting his attention and soon Roberto and I were holding full champagne stems.

"So, Dorothy, may I ask what business brings your husband to Cuba to consort with the likes of this circling shark?" He nodded at Roberto.

I didn't know exactly what to say but Roberto beat me to it. "May I assume you do not have American relatives in the school bus business?" he asked McHenry.

"Safe assumption," Hawk said.

"Well, that is Mr. Duncan's business. We are trying to get a large order to replace much of the government fleet. We are hoping El Presidente will approve it very soon."

Hawk raised his glass to me. "Well, I hope it happens for you." He took a large swig of champagne. "Actually, I hope it happens very quickly."

He was sounding like the United Fruit CEO. "Why is that?" I asked.

He snorted and said, "Because El Presidente may not be El Presidente much longer." He threw his head in Roberto's direction. "His law school buddy may be perched in the palace sooner than we all think."

"You mean Fidel Castro?" I asked.

He drained his champagne glass and seemed to sway a little. "Yes, the great bearded one." He raised his now-empty glass. "I'm trying to drink all the Embassy's champagne before he arrives in Havana."

Hearing Castro's name made me brighten with excitement and I proceeded to do the dumbest thing since arriving in Cuba. "Funny you should mention Fidel Castro," I said. "Why, Roberto and I—"

"Do not ever speak of him as my law school classmate again." Roberto had sharply interrupted me and was speaking directly to Hawk. "I have only seen him perhaps twice since then and even that was many years ago." Roberto was looking daggers at Hawk and grabbed him almost roughly by the arm as he spoke through clenched teeth. "Do you understand what I am saying to you, amigo? I am not very interested in wearing a blindfold anytime soon."

McHenry seemed embarrassed. He looked down at his empty glass. "I need to find a waiter. Excuse me a moment." Roberto released his arm and he walked away.

"What were you saying about a blindfold?" I asked.

Roberto gave me a long deadpan. "You do not understand how serious all of this is, do you?"

"You mean—"

"If you did, you would not have almost told him where we are going day after tomorrow."

"I—"

"To their credit, Batista's thugs have the decency to blindfold Castro sympathizers before they murder them by shooting them in the head."

Angel, at that moment I could feel the color drain from my face and was sure I was going to drop in a heap with my green taffeta piled up around me. What on earth have I gotten myself into, I was thinking. And how *stupid* of me to almost say Roberto and I were going to visit Fidel Castro in his mountain hideout.

Roberto must have seen all of this playing itself out in my revolving facial expressions. He gently took my arm. "Do not be too hard on yourself. It is my fault for not emphasizing the importance of not even breathing Fidel's name around Havana. For your own safety as well as mine."

McHenry reappeared with a full champagne glass. Roberto and I had plenty left in ours. "So, Dorothy, what do you and your husband enjoy doing? Are you golfers by chance?

I gave Roberto a look that signaled asking for permission. He smiled and nodded. "Well, we're not very good, but we do play occasionally and enjoy it."

"Splendid." He was using the British affectation again. "When your husband returns, have Roberto let me know and we'll give it a go at the club."

"Why certainly," I said. "That sounds wonderful. Thank you."

McHenry raised his glass to me and bowed slightly. "Now, if you two will excuse me, I have an embassy to run. At least until the next rich, old bastard gets here and screws everything up."

Chapter Twenty-Eight

Hallie

"Well," Ian Lightbourne said, lifting his glass of lunchtime New Zealand sauvignon blanc, "as they say . . . the plot thickens."

Hallie raised her glass in response. "You said in class once that a good story is like a rising tide; it lifts all boats."

"Indeed I did. Of course, that was a metaphor for 'overcomes mediocre, lazy writing.' But in the case of your work, we have the treasured combination of story and talent." He smiled broadly as he said it.

Hallie glowed at the compliment from the attractive man who was her professor, her mentor, her friend. At that point, she wasn't sure what else he was to her and what he might become. A lot of that depended on her response to Rich's marriage proposal. But Ian made no effort to hide his romantic interest in her. She suddenly had a jolting thought: My God, what if he's only complimenting my work because he just wants to get in my britches!

She knew a cloud must have come over her facial expression because he said, "What's wrong, my dear? You look like you just saw a ghost."

She forced a smile and a nervous laugh involuntarily accompanied it. "Nothing. Nothing at all." She put her palm to her chest and looked skyward. "For some reason, I suddenly thought I might have left the stove on but now I'm sure I didn't."

They were lunching at Palma Ceia to talk about the book. "You may also recall another of my profound academic declarations," he said. "That no matter how good the story is, it's really not about the story but the characters. If the reader doesn't truly *care* about the characters, even a good story will experience limited success."

She was smiling almost gaily. "Indeed I do, kind professor."

"Well, speaking of characterization, I really love what you're doing with your mother. You've given her a certain innocent insouciance that's endearing and vulnerable." He held up his right index finger. "But I have a strong sense that she's not to be underestimated."

Her eyes were dancing. "You may be right but you'll have to wait and see."

The waiter placed menus in front of them and they both studied them. "What's the latest with your boyfriend?" he asked, without looking up.

Hallie did look up. "He and Thomas are in New York right now. Seeing a potential huge investor. Maybe fifty million, Rich says."

Lightbourne did look up now. "Hmmph. At the rate your Mr. Rodino spends and gives away money, that's hardly enough to fly to New York for. Who's Thomas?"

"Thomas Herring. His chief financial officer. He's nice."

Lightbourne looked back down at his menu. "So?" he asked. "What's the answer going to be?"

"Well," Hallie said, looking back at her menu, "I was sort of thinking about the walnut chicken salad."

His head jerked up this time and his look was reproachful. "That was *not* my question."

She looked up again. "I'm sorry?"

"What answer are you going to give Mr. Rich Rodino? You know, his proposal?"

That sent Hallie's head and eyes back to the refuge of the menu. She didn't know what to say because she didn't know the answer. She did know she'd been wavering. Things were *so* tight financially and, beyond dinners and trips, she would never accept anything from Rich unless they were married. Several times over the past week or so, she'd actually made up her mind to say yes. But she couldn't put her finger on why she hadn't. Could it be Ian? She had the feeling that telling Ian she was marrying Rich would crush him and the thought of that made her die inside. How did she really feel about Ian? She felt that if she could get the book finished she could focus on that more.

"Well?" Lightbourne was waiting for an answer.

"I . . . I'm still thinking about it."

He looked up and smiled. "Good. *Keep* thinking about it. The longer the better. I'm still a relatively young man so time is on my side. Shall we order?"

"Yes, let's do," Hallie said. "I actually think I *will* have that walnut chicken with . . ." She trailed off mid-sentence as her eyes followed two diners being seated a few tables away from them.

"Hallie?"

She smiled. "Sorry. Yes, the walnut chicken salad with no dressing, please. But would you excuse me a moment?"

The combination of the British in him and living in the southern United States for a long time made Lightbourne spring to his feet to help Hallie out of her chair. She made her way over to the table where two male diners had just been seated.

"Excuse me," she said. "My name is Hallie Duncan and I believe we met at Rich Rodino's reception at his home a few weeks ago."

She was addressing a stately, dignified man with white hair and glasses who was wearing a natty bow tie with his navy blazer and grey slacks. The other diner was a young man, perhaps in his twenties, wearing a golf shirt. The older man rose and the young one eventually followed his lead.

"Why yes, I was there. I believe I remember you. I'm Albert Adams."

Hallie was convinced the man had zero recollection of her but was only being polite.

The man continued. "This is my grandson, Alston Adams. He's a junior here at USF."

"Yes, I remember your name, Mr. Adams, and it's nice to see you again. Forgive me for barging up to your table like this but I was just wondering if you enjoyed your bonefishing trip with Rich in Marsh Harbour."

Albert Adams face lit up now. "Now I really *do* remember you," he confessed. "You got on the plane when I got off. You were coming back here to Tampa."

Hallie just nodded. "So. Good fishing?"

Adams closed his eyes momentarily as if recalling. "Superb fishing. Just outstanding. Are you an angler?"

"Diver," she said. "Well, you certainly must have enjoyed it because Rich says you're now one of his investors and I know he appreciates it. I just thought I'd say hi and—"

"Miss Duncan, I'm afraid you are mistaken." His face went deadpan.

"I'm sorry?"

"I had a delightful time fishing with your friend and carefully considered his investment opportunity. But I ultimately passed."

"You . . . you didn't invest with Rich?"

"Why no, I'm afraid I didn't."

At that moment, Hallie felt as if she'd chartered one of those thrill-seeker airplane flights that soar high enough to produce outer space-like weightlessness. She stood speechless for several long moments trying to wrestle her composure under control. Just as Adams opened his mouth to speak, Hallie said, "Mr. Adams, I'm so sorry to bother you. It was nice to see you again and nice to meet your grandson." She blurted the words through a mouth that was suddenly devoid of saliva and she turned to leave.

Hallie already had her back to them when Adams said, "Miss Duncan, just a moment please."

She turned back to face him.

"May I just ask you if you are an investor yourself?" Concern was plastered over his face.

She nodded.

"Well, I have a fair amount of experience in these matters and I would suggest you get a good lawyer and a good accountant to review your investment. And I further suggest you liquidate your position in it, if possible."

Hallie felt her lower lip trembling and her eyes filling with water. "Thank you, Mr. Adams," she managed to squeak out. "Could you just please tell me why you say that?"

He paused several long moments just looking at her. "I've probably already said more than I should. It was nice to see you. Enjoy your lunch."

Chapter Twenty-Nine

The morning after Rich Rodino returned from his trip to New York, Hallie called and asked if she could drop by his office.

"Sure," he said. "What's up?"

"I just want to talk. Are you sure you have the time?"

"Angel, I will *make* time for you."

On her arrival, she went through the usual drill of greeting the staff, and she never tired of admiring the objets d'art in all their copiousness. When she was seated across from Rodino's desk, he was sitting in his high-backed chair beaming at her. He reached in his desk drawer and pulled out the small jewelry box he'd had with him on the yacht in the Bahamas and placed it in the middle of his desk.

"I'm hoping you've come to talk about this," he said, still beaming.

Hallie smiled nervously. "Maybe indirectly."

His eyebrows shot up. "Hmmm. What does that mean?" Then, before she could answer, he seemed to think of something. "Ah, how's your mom? Is it about her? She didn't . . ."

"No, she didn't die; she's fine for the moment." She put her hands in front of her and motioned them back and forth as if to call off what she'd said. "Oh, I don't know what I meant by that. How was your trip? Land the fifty million?"

He maintained his smile but she thought she detected a slight chink in it. She couldn't be sure. "Won't know for a week or so."

"Thomas go with you?"

"Yeah, but Hallie, you knew that. What's up? What's going on here?"

"Nothing, just interested in you and how things are going. I meant to ask you if that fellow who wears bow ties who came down to bonefish with you ever invested. What was his name, Adams?"

Rodino leaned forward in his chair and put his elbows on his massive antique Italian desk. "Hallie, you *did* ask me about Albert Adams and I told you he *did* invest." He spread his hands and took on a quizzical expression.

Hallie rose from her chair and began slowly pacing the enormous room, looking at the Persian rug under her. She stopped and, still looking at the rug, said, "Rich, I ran into Mr. Albert Adams yesterday. He remembered me from when we switched places on the plane. He said he had a very good fishing trip but he specifically said he did *not* invest with you." She looked up now and met his eyes. "Rich, why did you lie to me?" Her voice was shaking with emotion.

He immediately stood and went to her, taking her by the shoulders. "So that's what this is about. Baby, I didn't lie to you. Yes, I answered your question incorrectly but, when you asked it and I answered it, I believed he *was* going to invest. It was later that I found out he'd reconsidered."

She realized a tear was making its way down one cheek and she used her little finger to deal with it. "Well, why *didn't* he invest?"

He released her shoulders now and returned to his chair. "Oh, I'm not really sure. Just said it wasn't for him after all. Thomas and I have found that, once they say that, there's no use arguing; best to just move on to the next prospect."

She emitted a small sniffle. "Well, can you think of any reason why he would tell me that, as an investor myself, I should hire a lawyer and an accountant to review my investment and that I should get out of it as quickly as possible?"

Rodino came out of the chair again and retook her shoulders. He was agitated and his voice increased in volume. "Yeah, I can think of a reason. The old fart is angling for a slander lawsuit and I know just the law firm to file it. In fact, you happen to be in their offices right now." He dropped her shoulders and found his chair again. "That old bastard," he said.

"Rich, if anything ever happened to that money I have with you . . . I . . . I don't know what I'd do." She started crying again.

Rodino was wearing out his chair getting out of it to comfort Hallie then plopping down in it again. But he went to her again, this time more gently. "Now, now," he said. "You've always gotten your checks, right?"

"Yes, but what about the capital?"

He stood away from her. "The capital? You're worried about the capital?" He laughed. "All right, tell you what. I'll cut you a check for the entire amount right this second. You can put it in your purse and walk out of here with it." He walked to his office door, opened it, and called, "Karen, get Thomas in here, please."

Hallie struggled for what to say, but before she could come up with anything, Thomas Herring came in the room. Rich's chief financial officer was his usual nice, clean-cut self, today sporting a crisp, starched white dress shirt and a natty club tie. Hallie had always thought Herring had kind eyes.

He wore a big smile as he said, "Hello, Hallie, how's it going?"

"Good to see you, Thomas."

"Thomas, we need to cut Hallie a check for—"

"Thomas, never mind," Hallie interrupted with a smile. "I answered my own question."

"You sure?" Rodino asked.

She smiled and nodded. "I'm sure." Thomas Herring shrugged and left the room, closing the door behind him.

Rodino gave Hallie one of his most earnest looks. "You know, babe, there's a very simple way to solve all your financial worries. As you know, I got nobody. So you don't even have to worry about a pre-nup. The next day you're worth half what I am." He took her in his arms. "But that's not why I want you to do it. I want you to do it because you love me as much as I love you."

She was looking at his chest as he loosely held her but when he said that, she sneaked a peek at his eyes and smiled a little smile. She was trying to hold back another round of tears.

"All you have to do is utter one simple word," he said.

Despite her best efforts, a couple of wandering tears escaped. She dabbed them as she said quietly, "I know. And I'm getting closer to saying that word." She put her arms around his neck and kissed him gently. "Please just be patient with me, okay?"

Chapter Thirty

Dimple

Lunch is late today. I wish lunch didn't have to happen at all because it's all so depressing. For one thing, I can't use my left arm. And sitting at the table with wheelchair-bound ladies in their nineties who either babble or stare into space is anything but uplifting. Today, one of my lunch partners is a white-haired lady who constantly dips her napkin in her water glass and strokes her hair with it while mumbling incoherently.

But who am I to talk? For a while after the stroke I did well just to mumble. It makes me wonder again how long my current relative eloquence will last. For Hallie's sake, and for her book project, I hope it continues. She should be here any minute.

Today's dessert is some kind of red Jell-o. After the second bite, I hear Hallie's voice and put my spoon down. I don't like it anyway, and I'm trying to remember exactly where I left off talking about Cuba last time. Yes, I have it. I was about to meet Castro. Hallie wheels me to the solarium and I begin.

Angel, the first thing I had to face about the trip to see Castro was what to tell your daddy. I was getting better and better at the lying but hating it more and more. I discussed with Roberto my current dilemma over going to Santiago de Cuba and the Sierra Maestra

Mountains with him and, to my amazement, he said he'd take care of it.

"Take care of it?" I said, incredulous. "So, let me get this straight. You're going to call up my husband—your client—and tell him you're taking his wife on a little trip and that we're going to stay in a hotel and you're going to have your way with her. Is that it?"

This conversation took place at El Encanto shopping for appropriate clothes for me to wear in the mountains but we were far enough away from customers or sales clerks so that it was private. He smiled at what I said and replied, "I will not speak with your husband about it—you will do that. As for me, I will speak with Sergio. He will tell Maria that he will be accompanying you and me to Santiago de Cuba to meet a fleet manager and his wife who are based there. It is a small story but will work nicely and keep everyone happy." He continued wearing his maddening, yet irresistible smile.

I was furious. "Roberto, are you saying you're going to tell Maria's husband that you're having an affair with me and that he needs to lie to his wife, and to my husband when he sees him, so you can hustle me down to Santiago or wherever for some hanky panky?"

He stood very, very close to me then. So close I could smell that wonderful smell of his. I hated it when he did that. Except I loved it.

"Now, now, my darling, calm down. First, we are not going to Santiago for—what did you say?—hanky panky. We are going there on our way to see Fidel Castro. But I cannot tell Sergio that for obvious reasons." He put on a mischievous expression. "But, if you are interested in that hanky panky, I might be persuaded."

I playfully punched him in the arm.

"But here is the main point," he continued. "I will not be telling Sergio I am having an affair with you; I will be telling him I *wish* to have an affair with you and that a trip to see the fleet manager is a means to that end. He will understand that his accompanying us on the trip is something he will cancel at the last minute."

"You're just a devious bastard, aren't you?" The instant I said it I regretted it. It just popped out. He immediately looked hurt and I wanted to hold him and tell him I hadn't meant it. I ended up doing the latter but not the former. "I'm sorry," I added for good measure.

"It is fine," he said. "Just a difference in the culture of North America and here. Frankly, I know enough of your culture to have been disappointed if you had not said what you said." Now I really did want to hold him, but we were in the middle of a large department store and that wouldn't have worked, even as affectionate as Cubans are.

So that was that. I now knew what I would tell your daddy but I was still overcome with an array of feelings about calling him that included fear, guilt, shame, self-loathing, and a few others I can't remember now. I only knew I dreaded making the call that night and kept checking the time until I knew I could get him on the phone.

The call went better than I expected because I was getting better at being a scheming, lying adulteress. One thing I learned from Dallis during that call is that his meeting in Indiana had been postponed several more days. That news introduced me to a new batch of conflicting emotions. I remembered to tell him to bring our golf clubs when he came back as we'd been invited to play at the country club by the Embassy's chargé d'affaires, that man everybody calls Hawk. He was impressed and pleased, which made me feel better.

Roberto said he wouldn't see me until he picked me up the next morning for the trip. He instructed me on how to pack—a few city clothes for Santiago and a list of everything I'd need for the mountain wilderness. I can't tell you how excited and terrified I was all at the same time. Roberto assured me we would be safe from harm from either Castro's guerrillas or Batista's soldiers, but I was *petrified* at the thought of sleeping on the ground with God-knows-what crawling all over me. And that's not to mention going to the bathroom in the woods while wondering if some Cuban guerilla was hiding and watching. Oh well, I thought. I trusted Roberto and this was the opportunity of a lifetime. A chance to experience history.

So I used the rest of the day to do something I'd been wanting to: go back to the library and learn about this Sanchez woman who was supposed to be Fidel Castro's right hand. And I wanted to read more about Castro himself.

I found out Celia Sanchez was thirty-six years old when she and Castro, five years her junior, actually met. It happened in the middle of a mountain pasture only months before Roberto and I were heading out to meet them both. Remember, this is the woman who was to become the most important person in Fidel's life. I learned that Celia Sanchez Manduley was one of five daughters of a physician from Manzanillo near the Sierra Maestra. She was drawn to concerns over social justice in an honest way—she got it from her father who would typically treat peasant farmers and cane cutters without charging them. Never having met Castro, Celia was nonetheless solidly connected with his movement and was active in it even while he and Raul Castro and Che Guevara were in exile in Mexico. In fact, it was Celia Sanchez who selected the landing spot for Castro and eighty of his revolutionaries who made their way from Mexico to the eastern portion of Cuba aboard the decrepit old *Granma* in December of 1956. It was a natural, really, because she was intimately familiar with the entire area, including the Sierra Maestra Mountains, and knew so many of the area's peasants.

Angel, the more I began to read about this woman, the more intrigued I became. Apparently she was smart as a whip and, at ninety-nine pounds, toted some kind of rifle and was actually fighting with the rebels. I'm talking about shooting Batista's soldiers! A *woman*, for Pete's sake! But she was a master organizer, thinker, and administrator. In fact, if you decide to read about post-revolution Cuba, you'll find that she made most of the major policy decisions that Castro announced. And here I was, about to meet a woman like this when I was just a glorified sorority girl masquerading as a housewife who knew nothing about nothing. To say I felt intimidated would be the understatement of the century. Especially when my reading told me there were other women up in the mountains carrying rifles and fighting as rebels alongside Celia Sanchez. And they had the prettiest names. One was named Vilma Espin. She would marry Raul Castro. And another was Haydee Santamaria. Thinking about it all, I just couldn't fathom a woman feeling passionate enough about a *cause*— as opposed to a *man*—to put on fatigues and boots and become an actual soldier. I hoped I would meet these women just to see what they were like. At least that was my hope on a sort of grand level. On a more petty level, I hoped maybe they'd like me and somehow keep creatures from crawling over me while I slept on the ground. And if they could keep the men soldiers from watching me tinkle in the woods that would be nice too.

Roberto picked me up at the apartment early the next morning. I had barely slept the night before. For one thing I was journey-proud, to use an old Georgia expression. Another was that I'd missed Roberto being next to me for the first night in a few.

Stupid me, I actually had my new fatigues on before I realized we were spending the night in a city before heading up into the mountains. I changed into a sun dress, some medium-high heels, and spent a lot of time on my hair. But I was on time.

That was *the* longest drive I've ever taken. All day. But it gave Roberto and me a chance to talk. I tried not to be a question box but it was hard. There was so much I wanted to know. About him, about his family, about his love life apart from me. And I realized he never had said how he and Dallis connected. I asked him.

"Very simple, really. I became aware that the school bus fleet was dilapidated and much of it needed replacing. I knew I could collect a handsome fee for being an intermediary, so I identified several companies and Challenger looked like the best." He turned to me and smiled. "Your husband Dallis was the Caribbean representative."

Well, that made sense to me but I had also become so curious about his relationship with Fidel. Why was he going to see him? Why was he taking me? Whose side was Roberto *really* on?

"I told you," he said, his eyes back on the road. "I am impartial. Similar to Eisenhower."

"What do you mean?" I asked. "He's my president but, now that you mention it, I'm not sure I know which side he's on, Batista or Castro."

He looked over and smiled. "I am not sure he knows himself. He is probably on the side of whoever wins but, of course, that is unknown. That is why he is supplying arms to Batista on the one hand, and on the other, money to Fidel's 26th of July Movement through the CIA. Fifty thousand dollars, so far."

I was amazed. "How do you know all this?"

He kept looking at the road. "I have clients; I have contacts; I have friends. And I have them on both sides. And as a lawyer, I cannot reveal anything more or it would violate my code of confidentiality. That is not to mention putting myself in physical danger."

"Hmmph," I said. His remark about danger certainly got my attention but I still thought I'd try him again. "So why are we going to see Castro?"

He cut a glance at me. "You never give up; do you, my darling? I cannot tell you other than he is an old friend and classmate and it is time for a visit. And it is a chance for you to have an unusual and interesting experience in your life."

Well, honey, even this partying, canasta-playing housewife knew there was more to it than that, but it was obvious that that was all I was getting out of Roberto. So I decided to just try to enjoy the experience and take what came.

And what came next was Santiago de Cuba. I had no idea what a large Cuban city it was; later learning that it was second only to Havana in size. It was dark when we arrived at our hotel, the Casa Grande. Built in 1914, it was brightly lit and a unique-looking place from afar—all white and sort of stacked on itself like layers of a cake with lots of meringue. But it was as lovely and charming as any place I've ever been to. I *loved* the marble terrace that opened onto gardens. After we checked in, we started on that terrace with our mojitos then took dinner in the hotel dining room, which was *divine*. After that, it was on to our room for what I had missed the night before. I couldn't believe I was ready again because Dallis and I never were that . . . well . . . frequent. But with Roberto . . . I don't know; it was just different.

Later, when I was cradled in his arms in our room's huge bed, and when I felt myself drifting into sleep, I sort of murmured, "So what time tomorrow do we go to the mountains and see Señor Fidel Castro?"

Roberto was silent so I looked up at him. His expression was deadpan. "It already is tomorrow. It is almost one."

I hadn't realized it was so late. It's the way it was with him. "So what time do we go in the morning?" I felt myself drifting off again.

He was silent again but this time I didn't open my eyes or look up at him; I just waited for his answer. It came. "One o'clock *is* the morning," he said. "We will go now."

Chapter Thirty-One

When Roberto said "we will go now" my eyes clicked wide open as if a switch had been thrown. But I otherwise remained motionless because I assumed I must have misunderstood. "Did you just say—"

"Yes, I did. We will go now. Would you like me to have room service send up some strong Cuban coffee?"

As I began to stir, I couldn't help but note Roberto's redundancy in saying "*strong* Cuban coffee." "But Roberto, it's the middle of the night. How will we even know where we're going and how—"

"Leave that to me, my darling. Right now, you need to get dressed."

Now I was sitting up in bed and for some reason was holding the sheet over my body which, I must admit, was sans nightgown. It was almost as if the notion of being yanked out of bed at that hour to hike in the woods made me feel somehow *violated.*

"But Roberto, you told me to leave my suitcase with the mountain clothes in the car. Will you please go down and get them for—"

"In the car is where they will remain."

"But I thought we were leaving now to go—"

"We are, but do you want the whole world to know it? Including the SIM?"

"SIM?"

"Servicio de Inteligencia Militar. Batista's secret police. It is led in Santiago by a delightful fellow named Captain Manuel Lavastida who has two specialties. One is gouging out the eyes of the rebels he captures. The other is hanging them from a tree and setting a bonfire under them. So if you do not want to draw the attention of the SIM, please put your dress and high heels back on so it will appear we are going to a nightclub."

I thought about that a moment and understood. "Oh, I see," I said. But I don't know *how* I said it because my mouth felt like it was full of cotton and it was trembling with fear.

"Roberto, are you sure we—"

"Do not worry, my darling." He could read my face and now held me gently and added a reassuring smile. "We will be safe, I promise. Now get that dress on. We must go; the jeep is waiting on us."

So I dressed just as I had been for cocktails and dinner. I tried to do something with my hair but it didn't work very well. Roberto did order the coffee for me and, realizing we would get little if any sleep that night, I quaffed every drop.

"We will go down and get in the car now," he said. "We wish to create the impression that, after some romance in our room we are now in search of perhaps a glass of straight Anejo rum and a good rhumba. So it would be advisable to remove the fear from your face and give me some laughter as we go out to the car. Can you do that?"

He was holding the bottom of my chin with his thumb and forefinger, gazing at me and waiting for my reaction. Although I was still scared silly, I forced a smile and nodded.

"What about my city clothes?" I asked.

"Leave them here. As far as anybody knows, we are staying here at the hotel. We will just be gone for a while."

That was my fear, I thought silently. That we would be gone a *long* while. Like gone, gone. But I gathered myself, straightened my shoulders, and told Roberto I was ready. Off to the car we went as I forced laughter at absolutely nothing. I'd always toyed with the idea of taking drama in college, so I pretended I was an actress as I grabbed Roberto's arm and put on my best girlish giggles.

We drove straight to a nightclub called Casa de la Trova and parked as if to get out and go in. Then Roberto started demonstrably shaking his head, indicating he'd decided against the place and we got back in the car. We drove to another nightclub and slowed but didn't stop, then drove literally in circles while Roberto kept his eyes more on the rear-view mirror than the road. It was obvious even to me that he was trying to make sure we weren't followed. Angel, I kept looking around for Humphrey Bogart because I felt like I was in a movie. My fear had, for the moment, turned to excitement.

Roberto, seemingly satisfied that no one was following us, drove past the outskirts of Santiago, continued for some number of miles, and eventually turned off the road through an open gate into what to me, in the darkness, appeared to be a finca. (I knew by then that that was the word for a very large "farm.") We made our way down a dirt road and came to a small shed beside which was an army-style jeep with a young bearded man wearing horn-rimmed glasses and military fatigues sitting behind the steering wheel. (No, it wasn't Castro.) Without even looking at the man or the jeep, Roberto pulled our car into the shed and turned off the headlights. He got out and headed for the jeep and I followed.

"Faustino!" Roberto called to the man, who climbed out of the jeep and in turn called Roberto's name. My Spanish was getting better but their exchange was way too fast and complicated for me so I just kind of tuned out and waited until their conversation was complete. Finally, Roberto turned to me and said, "Meet my friend, Emilio." Well, that wasn't the name he'd called him; it was obvious that Roberto thought the fewer real names I knew, the safer I'd be. Years later, I learned the man's name was Faustino Hernandez Perez, one of Castro's closest confidants.

The man stuck out his hand to shake. Angel, I was horrified. In those days in the South, a man didn't shake hands with a lady. Unless she extended her hand first, which was rare. I didn't know what else to do, especially since he had this humongous rifle over his shoulder, so I shook his hand. His palm felt like steel wool. The more time I spent in Cuba, the more I was learning that Cubans are perhaps the warmest, touchiest people on earth and better to join them because you'll never beat them.

Roberto retrieved our suitcases from the trunk of his car and motioned for me to follow him inside a shack that was near the shed where his car was now parked. "Un momento," he said to the man he had introduced as Emilio. In the shack, we changed into our mountain clothes, put our city clothes in the suitcases, and put everything else of mine into a backpack he'd bought me at El Encanto. He put the rest of his things in a well-used backpack he obviously already owned.

That was a horrible moment. Because it was then that I realized something: there were *two* backpacks. At the store, I had assumed the backpack purchase was for the one *he* would carry with *all* our supplies in it. But I now realized that I would be toting my own backpack. Ye Gods, I thought, how was I going to do *that*? I picked it up and tried to sling it over my back and almost fell with it in a heap it was so heavy. Roberto was laughing his head off at me.

"What's so damn funny?" I said in a blend of playfulness, genuine anger, and sheer panic over having to carry that pack. I had a vision of myself coming back three inches shorter and with curvature of the spine. That's if I came back at all instead of just collapsing under the weight of the pack and waiting for the buzzards. "Roberto, you dirty dog, why didn't you tell me I was going to have to carry this stupid backpack?"

He was still laughing. "Because you did not ask me, my darling. I can assure you that you will be happy to have everything that is in that pack once we get up in the Sierra Maestra."

Well, I *was* thankful that one of the supply items he'd put in my pack was johnny paper; never mind that the woods would be my johnny. Roberto helped me organize my backpack and distribute the weight of its contents more efficiently. Then he helped me put it on my back and tightened the straps so it rode higher and didn't feel so heavy. Now properly adjusted, I took the pack off before climbing into the jeep. Roberto was in the front; I was in the back seat by myself, and off we went down a dirt road in the middle of the blackest night I've ever experienced. There was no moon at all and a cloud cover must have rolled in because there was no reflection of any light whatsoever. I tell you, it was eerie.

The dirt road was actually pretty smooth and comfortable. But that didn't last long because we soon reached the *real* dirt road. Angel,

I didn't know if I was more worried about the fillings getting jarred out of my teeth or my entire body getting tossed out of the back of that jeep like a ragdoll. In those days, seatbelts were only in airplanes. "Make sure you hold on to the grab rails," Roberto had said when he'd showed them to me. If I hadn't, I would have bounced out soon after we hit the real dirt road. Roberto and this Emilio character were talking up a storm and would never have noticed. That would have been it for me and you would never have come into this world.

It was becoming quite apparent to me that, in order to go on this adventure with this man I loved in addition to your daddy, I was going to experience a lot of something I unfortunately had very little tolerance for: pain. The only thing that didn't already hurt were my feet and I knew they would be joining the party because I'd not taken Roberto's advice to do some advance walking in my hiking boots. So here we went, caroming down this so-called road in this guided missile of a jeep with my derriere spending precious little time in contact with the back seat of said jeep.

This ride, if you could call it that, seemed interminable in the same way as a drilling by a dentist. I found myself praying and praying that it would end. And it suddenly did because the "road" did.

"Well, this is the end of the road. It will be on foot from here. Are you all right?" Roberto had rotated in his front seat and was looking at me.

I opened my mouth to speak but nothing came out. On the third try I managed, "Yes, I'm just wonderful. What a lovely ride. So pleasant."

That drew a grin and a hand squeeze from Roberto which I appreciated more than I can tell you. Somehow, my bruised and creaky body made it out of the jeep and onto my feet. Then it was getting that damn backpack mounted on my already sore female frame. Off we went on a trail that seemed to go straight up the side of the mountain. When I say "trail" that's almost as generous as calling where we'd been a "road." It was rocky and muddy with huge tree roots and actually required a little climbing at times. There was no doubt we were in the mountains. And when I say straight up, I mean I was huffing and puffing like a pack mule. Which is what I guess I was at that moment. I wanted to stop and have a cigarette but Roberto wouldn't let me. Honey, the extent of my physical activity until then had been vacuuming and sweeping the house and my lungs hurt so bad I wish I could have stuck a fire extinguisher down my throat and turned it on. But on we went.

Then the rain came. We had heard no thunder; it just started with little drops that appeared on the leaves of the guaguasi trees and then turned into a steady, soaking drizzle. The tree canopy over us simply made it take a little longer for us to get drenched.

"What time is it?" I called to Roberto.

"A little after three."

"Are we almost there?" I didn't add "daddy"—I was past being clever.

He didn't answer.

"Roberto, are we getting close?" I repeated.

Still no answer.

"Roberto."

He and Emilio had been speaking rapidly in Spanish but now he stopped and turned to me. "My darling, I am afraid we are lost."

Chapter Thirty-Two

When Roberto told me we were lost, I slipped out of my backpack straps, let the pack hit the ground, and sat on it. Then I proceeded to cry my eyes out, holding my head in my hands. Roberto came to me and did his best. "Do not worry, my darling; we will find the proper way."

I responded with sobs and a modest amount of not-very-becoming ranting about why he allowed this to happen and why he thought I would want to do this in the first place. He piled on the comfort and assurance and I responded with more sobbing—it was a stalemate. Finally, my sobs subsided about the same time he ran out of comfort and assurance. "We will try to sleep a bit, let the rain stop, and if necessary, find our way at dawn," he said. "Believe me, everything will be fine."

So Roberto and I tried to sleep while Emilio served as the guard or sentry or whatever you call it. Of course, the sleeping didn't work. Have you ever tried sleeping on a rock in the rain? *Lots* of fun. We tried it anyway; at least it was better than trying to bust a gusset climbing that damn mountain. After we'd been sort of just resting, not sleeping, for thirty minutes or so we all heard it. Two soft, low, toneless whistles. They repeated. Then Emilio whistled in the exact same way and it was answered in kind. At that, a rebel scout emerged from the mountain woods and greeted us. I can't tell you what his name was. I could not have cared less about that. I only cared that he said he would lead us to our destination. I felt my eyes well up with tears of joy.

And lead us he did. At first it was more of the same sort of hiking but then the terrain began to be less severe. Finally, we came to a pasture-like flat place in the middle of these huge mountains and there were other rebels waiting for us with saddled horses. Angel, I went horseback riding one time in college and *hated* it. I hear those animals have a brain the size of a thimble and will throw you if you don't know what you're doing. Which, of course, I didn't. But as far as we'd hiked, and as exhausted as I was—not to mention the pounding from the jeep—that horse and saddle looked *wonderful.* Thirty minutes after we mounted those nags, we arrived at Castro's camp at a place known as Los Chorros.

The camp was in a clearing and consisted of a campfire and two thatched huts that had been built, a makeshift cistern, and three shacks that had obviously pre-dated the camp by a long time. There were a few more horses tied to trees. The only way I could see anything was due to the light from a small campfire that was surrounded by thatched "walls" to keep it less visible from afar, thus deterring detection.

Angel, the guerillas looked just exactly like what you'd expect. They all wore green fatigues and most wore caps like Fidel. But they obviously were short on these uniforms because many of them were tattered and torn. In fact, one soldier's shirt didn't have a back. I'm still not sure how it stayed on. And it was obviously his only one, a fact that was confirmed when I found myself a little too close to one of the guerillas and downwind of him. Almost all had Fidel-like beards and absolutely all were heavily armed with the biggest, baddest-looking guns I've ever seen, in the movies or anywhere else. Some even had hand grenades hanging from their shirts. The whole thing gave me chills and I found myself shrinking away from these smelly, battle-toughened men.

Roberto had an animated conversation in Spanish with one of the soldiers who kept pointing in the distance and looking at his wristwatch. It was now pushing five a.m. and still boo dark, as we said in Georgia. When Roberto concluded his conversation with the rebel soldier, he came over to me.

"Fidel is at another camp nearby. By the way, he never sleeps more than four hours at night; he has probably only been sleeping for an hour now. This man says Castro has a meeting with the liaison from his Column Number Two at ten and he will see us here after that for some lunch and conversation. He says we should try to get some sleep until then. How does that sound?"

How did that sound? Well, I was out on my feet. Maybe even swaying a little bit. I could probably have slept standing up. "Sleep," I said, and just began nodding. I was too tired to say anything else.

The next thing I remember was Roberto shaking me awake to bright sunlight. I was in one of the old shacks and lay on some kind of bedding that, in the absence of my exhaustion at the time I lay on it, I would have run from. Lord only knows who or what had been sleeping on it. I sat up and grabbed one of my boots to put it on but Roberto's hand shot out and grabbed my wrist.

"What?" I said.

He looked at me earnestly. "Always check for scorpions. Turn your boots upside down and shake them. Like this." He did it for me and Angel, damned if one didn't fall out of one of my boots. I had never seen a scorpion before. This one was huge and kind of curly-cued in shape with its two menacing-looking pincher things. It was the most hideous creature I had ever seen in my life. Roberto squashed it with his boot.

I held my hair up with both hands and almost screamed. "Roberto, how do I know that . . . *thing* . . . wasn't crawling all over me while I was sleeping? Horrors!"

He smiled his usual patient, loving smile. "You do not know if they have crawled over you. But when you are asleep, you are still and not aggressive. They only bite when they are threatened."

"Oh," I said. "Well, that explains everything. Maybe I should order one for a pet!"

"Now, now," he said. "We must calm down; it is almost time to meet Fidel."

"Well, I can't meet anybody on an empty stomach. When will breakfast be ready?"

Roberto literally snorted with laughter in a way I'd never seen. "My darling, that is part of your charm."

"What are you talking about? I'm hungry."

"Remember? We are to eat with Fidel. But I suggest that right now you eat one or more of the apples we brought because there is very little food in these camps and what is here is not the cuisine you are accustomed to."

At that, I dove into the backpack. I was halfway through an apple when something happened. It was a sudden change in the molecules in the air, a subtle electrical charge I could feel, almost as if a violent thunderstorm was close. In the camp, steps quickened and the velocity of the conversations in Spanish accelerated. In a moment I found out why. A group of a dozen or so men on horseback came riding into the clearing that was the camp. Leading the way was a heavily bearded one with horn-rimmed glasses and a telescopic sight rifle slung over his shoulder. A large man anyway, he was sitting very tall in his saddle. He drew the horse up and dismounted, handing his gun to some underling person who came running up. But I noticed he was not unarmed as he still wore a holster with some sort of pistol in it. Roberto approached him and they shook hands warmly using both hands but did not hug or anything like that. I didn't need confirmation that it was Fidel Castro; I recognized him from his pictures in *The Havana Post*.

I had thought Roberto was tall but this Castro seemed to tower over Roberto as I looked at them standing together talking. Roberto was talking rapidly in Spanish, so much so that I had little chance of picking any of it up even if they'd been close enough for me to hear them well, which they weren't. I stared at them as I stood there in my fatigues, boots, and cap. I had one hand on my hip and with the other I was holding the apple I was munching. The whole thing struck me as bizarre. Roberto kept talking rapidly and occasionally gesturing in my direction. Each time he did so, Fidel Castro would look over at me and nod.

Finally Roberto concluded his conversation with Castro and came over to me. Fidel did not. "Here is what will happen," Roberto said. "I must have some discussions with Fidel for a little while. You should eat another apple, drink some water, and rest. When I finish talking with Fidel, he will meet you and talk."

I thought about that a moment. "Okay," I said. "I assume you'll translate because, as you know, my Español is somewhere between *muy poquito* and *no existo*."

"There will be no problem," he said, and turned to walk away.

"Roberto, wait," I said. "Is Celia Sanchez here?"

He stopped and pointed way across the clearing and I saw her. She had dismounted. She was a wisp of a woman—the ninety-nine pounds may have been generous—and was lighting one cigarette with another one. She looked attractive, but not beautiful, and had her own huge gun over her shoulder.

"You will meet her and Che Guevara as well."

Chapter Thirty-Three

Roberto was right. When he came back, I did meet Celia Sanchez and Che Guevara. But it was rather disappointing. She proffered her hand, smiled, and said, "I am Celia. How are you?"

"Oh, just fine, thank you," I said with a wide smile. "I'm so happy to be here and meet you because I went to the library in Havana and read about you and I was so impressed."

Well, at that her eyes glazed over and I realized she had just disgorged her entire vocabulary of English words. She turned to Roberto for help and he translated after which she smiled broadly. She was a paradox; despite having just laid down her very heavy rifle, she sat on one of the old ammunition boxes we were all using as chairs, crossed her legs and was very feminine, warm and cordial. At least to the extent she could be as she worked with our translator—Roberto.

Our ultimate moment of bonding was when she seemed to have difficulty finding a cigarette in her fatigues and I quickly produced a Lucky Strike. I'm not sure what brand she was smoking but she seemed so thrilled with the Lucky that I gave her the rest of the pack. She initially objected with great profusion but, in the end, accepted with another of her warm smiles. I had no way to know that in a little over twenty years she would be dead from lung cancer.

Che Guevara didn't speak a single word of English either. But even if he had, I doubt if he would have uttered a syllable because he looked like he was about to die. I mean literally. His chest was heaving mightily up and down with every breath; his eyes looked buggy, and his wheezing was so loud I thought somebody was trying to tune an old violin. I learned he had severe asthma. But I must say he was a dashing fellow. The beard on his moon-shaped young face was more cultivated than the rest and he wore a smart beret instead of the cap worn by Fidel and the others. After a few minutes of mainly listening to my translated conversation with Celia Sanchez, he excused himself. I had the impression that he was just fulfilling a promise made to Fidel to speak to me. Che—that's what everyone, including the press, called him—was a doctor from Argentina who was an inveterate Marxist revolutionary. I obviously wasn't into any of that but I still hoped his asthma got better and, through Roberto, I told him so. He gave me a hint of an appreciative smile as he walked away.

Meanwhile, Celia Sanchez and I continued our visit with Roberto as translator. I asked her how it was that she learned to become a soldier, to manage such a big gun herself, and fight alongside men. Her reply was that no task was too challenging for the cause of the revolution. I certainly wasn't buying into anybody's revolution—in fact your daddy and I were counting on the man they were revolting against to buy a lot of school buses—but I was certainly impressed with her passion, her conviction, and the way she handled herself. I told her I had read about her in the library and her eyes brightened. I told her I knew she had become active in the revolution before even meeting Fidel and asked why. She replied that her dedication to the revolution came from her time as a young girl helping her physician father on his rounds caring for the region's peasants and often not charging them. She said she came to the conclusion that the revolution would be the only hope for those people. By then I hadn't learned as much I would have liked but I knew enough to know I didn't agree with her. But I obviously kept my silence, smiled and nodded politely.

When Celia and Che had both excused themselves, it was just Roberto and me sitting on the ammunition boxes.

"Those apples were good but I'm still hungry," I said, and could have added that I was also exhausted. "I thought he was going to feed us."

"He is, but I suggest you not discard the apples."

Then we waited. I dozed while sitting on the box, every now and then feeling my chin hit my chest and then bounce up as I scanned the camp for Castro. I was so hungry but I was too tired and sleepy to get up and go to the shack for another apple from my backpack. During one of my dozes, I was jarred awake when I felt something cold and metallic placed in my hands. No, it wasn't a gun, but a bowl of food. Roberto had one too, and I looked across to see Fidel Castro with a bowl of his own sitting on an ammunition box right across from us. I saw him negotiate a huge spoonful of food past his beard and into his mouth.

Now, here's where I got a shock: Fidel Castro spoke English. Almost as good as Roberto but with a somewhat heavier accent. Many never knew he did because so many of his interviews—like with Barbara Walters—were in Spanish with a translator. But in later years, I watched a replay of a New York press conference he conducted in English. It was more like a mini-speech.

"You are Señora Duncan," he said with a mouthful. He made no effort to cover his mouth, but then, he was on a battlefield. It was a statement not a question, made while looking me right in the eye.

Angel, first of all, this man was physically huge. I later found out he was six foot three, which in those days was gigantic. And knowing what he'd done and been through thus far, and that he might end up in control of the country, I was frankly intimidated. As you know, I've never been at a loss for words but I struggled a bit and finally got out, "Yes, I'm Dorothy Duncan. How do you do, General Castro?"

Castro erupted in laughter so suddenly that he involuntarily spit food out of his mouth. Roberto joined his mirth. At that moment, I felt about as small as one of the black beans in our dishes.

"I'm sorry," I said in a tiny voice, but not knowing for what.

"Señora Duncan, I am not a general; I am a rebel. A leader of a great revolution that will soon overthrow an evil man who *is* a general. As for you, you are an American housewife who plays canasta all day and does not even know who I am talking about."

Well, I didn't care who this Castro was, I wasn't going to take that. "I know *exactly* who you're talking about," I said. "Batista. El Presidente." I thought I'd throw in a little Spanish.

"That is correct, Señora Duncan. Batista. *He* is a general. And *he* is the man who continues to murder our citizens daily. He is also the man who steals from Cubans. The man who is an oppressive tyrant who deprives Cubans of what is rightfully theirs. When I am in power, peasants like these who are now my soldiers will own their land and farm it. Workers and employees will get thirty percent of the profits of their employers. Sugar planters, instead of being slaves, will get fifty-five percent of all the production. My government will take control of all that is suffering under Batista. I am talking about education, housing, health, and employment. We will change everything. We only have 200 brave men and women but we will prevail in this fight. A revolution is a struggle to the death between the future and the past."

I had read that Castro is known for giving impromptu speeches and that he once gave a formal speech that lasted seven hours. I wondered if he was out to break his record today. I prayed not. He continued.

"Cuba is in a state of war but Batista is hiding it. A dictatorship must show that it is omnipotent or it will fail. We are showing that Batista's dictatorship is impotent. Batista is using arms furnished by your president. Not only against my soldiers but against all the Cuban people. Batista is a murderer. He has bazookas, machine guns, planes, and bombs but we are safe here in the Sierra Maestra. They must come and get us but they cannot find us and we are winning the battle. Time is on our side. We have many weapons we have captured from Batista's troops, such as Browning automatic rifles, Thompson sub-machine guns, even a few mortars, but what we lack is ammunition. I only wish the boxes we are sitting on were full."

I didn't know what to say so I said nothing.

"We have had *The New York Times* here to interview us. Señor Matthews wrote the column; did you read it?"

"Uh, no, I'm afraid I didn't."

"And CBS television is bringing their cameras here. Perhaps you will watch that."

"I . . . I'll try."

"Señora, when you go back to Norte America, it is necessary for you to tell your friends about the important work we are doing here and that we are winning. Will you do that, Señora?"

"Why, yes, of course." What else was I going to say?

"Roberto tells me you and your husband are trying to sell school buses to Batista."

I cut a glance at Roberto for guidance and he nodded approval. "Yes, that's right," I said.

"I hope you are successful because, as I said before, education is very important to me. I would prefer that Batista acquire the school buses before I run him out of Cuba so he can spend money on the buses he would otherwise steal. Do you understand?"

"Yes, I do."

"Señora Duncan, do you and your husband know what is required to do business with the Batista government?

Before I could answer, Roberto jumped in and said something in Spanish. Castro cut him off by saying in English, "I know, but I want to hear what she says. So, Señora, do you know what is required?"

"I . . . I assume you're talking about what Roberto calls the marketing fees?"

Fidel Castro chuckled. "So, marketing fees is what they are calling it now. Of course, that is what I am talking about. Do you believe your husband can raise the bribe money from his company?"

I thought a moment and decided to do something that I couldn't believe later I did. I said, "Señor Castro, may I ask why you want to know?"

He didn't miss a beat. "I already told you. I wish for the buses to be purchased with the money of the Batista government so my government will not have to spend its money. But also, Batista is my enemy. I owe it to myself, my people, and my soldiers to know everything I can about my enemy."

"I believe my husband will be successful getting the money. He's the best salesman in the entire world. A fine man."

Castro was chewing his black beans and rice along with something else that was in the bowl. As hungry as I was, I had not touched my food; I was too involved in the conversation with this soon-to-be world figure. Smacking his lips, he said, "Señora, do not take too long with this bus business with Batista or it may be too late. Do you understand that?"

I nodded vigorously. And also appreciatively because it sounded like, if Dallis and Roberto got busy and pushed the deal through, we could get paid before Castro pulled off his revolution. Castro had wolfed down his food and was stirring to rise, I assumed to get to his next task. But before he stood, he slapped his hand on Roberto's knee, looked at me with a wry smile, and said, "My law school classmate. I am still angry with him for embarrassing me by making better grades. But I was always thinking about justice for the people of Cuba. Even then."

Roberto looked at me and said, "It is true. If he had concentrated, he would have done much better than me."

Castro then stood. And I did something out of character for my ladylike upbringing: I did, too. In a battlefield camp with a guerilla leader, all of us wearing fatigues, it sort of seemed the right thing to do. Then I noticed Castro looking me up and down. "Well, Señora, I will let you get back to your canasta." Then he looked at Roberto with a sly grin. "Amigo, she is very beautiful. I would not let her out of your sight or I might move in."

Roberto grinned back at him. "Do not worry, Fidel."

As for me, I stood there trying to figure out if Fidel Castro, a known skirt chaser before he'd hunkered down in the mountains, had just made a pass at me. I'd have to think about that one but, in the meantime, I had to say *something*.

"Señor Castro, thank you for having us in your camp. I have been reading at the library about you and Celia Sanchez and it is very impressive. You are a very interesting and important man." It was the best I could come up with.

He studied me for a moment. "The only way I will be an important man is if I follow the words of José Martí. He said, 'A true man does not seek the path where advantage lies, but rather where duty lies.' That is something that worm Batista has never understood and never will." And he turned and walked away.

Roberto and I just looked at each other for several long moments as we felt the air in the camp decompress after the bearded one no longer seemed to fill up the entire clearing with his presence.

"Wow," I said.

"You can see why the people are following him," Roberto said.

I suddenly remembered how hungry I was and sat down to dive into my black beans. "What's this other stuff?" I asked Roberto.

"Malanga root," he said.

I looked up at him for a moment then decided not to ask for more detail; I was too hungry. I guess I had become combat-zone hardened after only a few hours in the Sierra Maestra. Roberto and I ate in silence. At least I ate as much I could because it was dreadful–tasteless black beans and rice with that disgusting root. But we were fortunate that day because lack of food in the mountains was a serious issue for Castro's rebels. I later found out that when they were really desperate, the number of horses in camp would go down by one. It made me gag when I heard it. Anyway, I was glad there were some more apples waiting for me in the backpack. And not covered by scorpions, I prayed.

As I ate, I reflected on the extraordinary meeting with Castro and tried to remember anyone I'd met that had more raw charisma and magnetism. I couldn't. But I'd met few politicians. As a result of meeting Fidel Castro that day, I simply *knew* he would overthrow Fulgencio Batista and rule Cuba. This man was too smart and too determined for it not to happen. So that gave me a sense of urgency for Dallis to get the bus business done quickly. In thinking about that, it occurred to me that Roberto also had an in with Castro, but assuming Castro did prevail, who knew how long it would take to start over with the bus deal? Dallis needed to get it done now.

Having those thoughts triggered other ones: What "discussions" were Roberto and Castro having? And what exactly *was* Roberto's current relationship with Fidel? I decided to ask him.

Roberto smiled one of his smiles at me. I melted, as usual. "All that curiosity inside such a beautiful head," he said. Before I could bristle at that, he added, "Those are smart questions but then you are smart, so I should not be surprised. So here is the situation. Fidel and I have kept in touch but no one in the Batista regime must know that or my life will be in danger. However, Fidel knows I am in touch with the Batista people and the mafia people like Meyer Lansky. He has no problem with that. He understands that I am a lawyer, an advocate, and that is how I make my living—collecting fees for my services. You asked what Fidel and I discussed. It was actually a legal matter in Havana he wishes me to handle. It has to do with his family—his former wife, Mirta, and their son Fidelito. It is a complicated custody matter because Fidel did not get custody of Fidelito and subsequently kidnapped him, after which Fidelito was freed. Mirta remarried, moved to Spain, and then came back. It is all a mess and mostly involves Fidelito. I will have to work through other lawyers who do not know Fidel and be very careful. And I will receive no fees for this work as Fidel has no money for that—all available funds must go into the revolution."

"So why will you do it?"

"Because he is an old friend and because I believe he has a good chance of taking over Cuba." Roberto broke out in a wide grin. "It will certainly be wise to be on his good side if that happens. With me, it is all about the money and I must place bets on both horses in this race."

I stood as I thought about his answers. "Roberto, you never have told me where you stand politically."

"I just told you."

"You did?"

"Of course. Remember, I said with me it is all about the money. I am a capitalist. I fear Fidel is leaning toward becoming a communist. I know Raul already is one. If Fidel succeeds, I know I will receive much legal work and many fees. But to collect those fees, I will likely have to live under a communist regime. I would then have to decide if I love the money from the fees enough to stay in Cuba."

"You'd leave Cuba?"

We were alone with the ammunition boxes and no one was paying any attention to us. Roberto came closer and held me. "I do not know what is going to happen. I only know I treasure every moment

I am spending with you and that is all I wish to think about as long as you are in Cuba."

Our little hug concluded, I looked up at him. We had a fleeting "moment" of eye contact after which I said, "I hope I'm not *all* you think about while I'm here."

His look was still fervently amorous. "What else is there, my darling?" he asked.

I reached up, took his head in both my hands, and pulled our faces inches apart. "School buses, Roberto. School buses."

Chapter Thirty-Four

Hallie

She couldn't get it out of her mind. Yes, Rich had explained his answer about whether Albert Adams had invested or not, and yes he had offered to give all her money back right on the spot. But there was one thing that kept replaying in Hallie's mind. It was Albert Adams saying she should get a lawyer and an accountant to look at her investment and that she should liquidate it if possible.

She googled Albert Adams in the Tampa white pages. When she came up with nothing, she called Ian and asked him to look up Adams in his Palma Ceia Club directory.

"He's a non-resident member. Here's the number at his office in New York."

It was several hours before Adams called her back.

"Mr. Adams, I was just wondering if you could elaborate on what you told me at The Governor's Club."

There was a long pause. "Frankly, I deliberated on whether to return your call. I probably shouldn't have said what I did at the lunch table the other day."

"Why not?" Hallie asked.

"Because it's my understanding that you and Mr. Rodino are romantically involved and that's usually a losing battle."

She thought a moment. "Well, we're not married and I'm the one calling you. I just wonder why you think it's a bad investment?"

"Look, I don't think this conversation—"

"No, no, Mr. Adams, I'm not challenging you. It's just that I'm not financially astute and you have me wondering. I'd be truly grateful for any enlightenment you could provide. I'm serious."

A very long pause. In fact, Hallie wondered if they'd been cut off.

"Mr. Adams?"

"Yes, I'm here. I was just thinking how best to answer you. Let me ask you this: Why did you invest in the first place?"

"Because Rich said I should."

"Exactly as I thought. Here's a simple suggestion: Sit down with Mr. Rodino and ask him to explain his deals to you in detail and try your best to understand. If you want to call me back after that, I'll discuss it further."

"All right, that sounds like a good idea. When will you be in Tampa again? I tried to find a number for you here, but—"

"I have a condominium in Tampa I use when I visit my grandson or when I want to quail hunt at a nearby club I belong to, but there's no phone at the condo. Not sure when I'll be there next; call me here in New York when you've had your little talk."

That night, she stayed at Rodino's mansion and he cooked for her. As the main course he cooked risotto with bacon and kale. Risotto requires marathon stirring and he did it in his huge, restaurant-style kitchen to the steady beat of beach music played on his state-of-the-art sound system turned up very loud. He made Hallie laugh as he danced solo by the massive stainless steel Viking commercial stove while never allowing his wooden spoon to leave the risotto pan. The only moments he left his risotto-stirring was when Bruce Channel's "Hey Baby" came on and they both broke out in the shag in the middle of the kitchen floor. An excellent 2007 Amarone had plenty to do with their behavior.

As they dined, she found herself nervous about bringing up her topic.

"Rich, I want to talk to you about something serious."

He immediately leaned toward her. "I hope I know what it is."

She hated disappointing him. "No, not that. Not yet anyway. I was just wondering if you'd be willing to take the time to explain to me what you do. I want to understand it better. It might help me . . . you know, with that other question."

He leaned back. "Sure. I'm a lawyer. Rodino and Ross. Offices in Tampa and several other cities. Seventy lawyers, bunch of employees, great clients. What else?"

"You know what else. I want to understand those investments you sell. The ones I'm in."

"You do remember I told you I'd give you your money back."

"And I said I didn't want it. I invested that money with you because you said I should. But now I just want to understand it better, that's all."

In his office the next morning, he took her into his palatial conference room, fired up the enormous video screen at the end of the room and began giving her the presentation he gave potential investors.

"Large corporations and the people who run them sometimes do bad things," he began. "We started seeing two types of missteps: sexual harassment and whistle blowers."

"Whistle blowers?" she asked with a quizzical look.

"Say a company cheats on a big government contract. A whistle blower is an employee who calls his or her company on it. The moment whistle blowers do that, they become a potential plaintiff and the company becomes a potential defendant. Same with a victim of sexual harassment at the hands of an executive. We found that, instead of a messy lawsuit and the accompanying publicity, these parties are usually willing to enter into a settlement agreement where the potential plaintiff gets a wad of money paid by the potential defendant. And, given that we're dealing with large corporations or wealthy executives, it usually *is* a wad. Usually multiple millions."

"Wow. I already know more than I did," Hallie said.

"These settlement agreements are totally secret. The highest level of confidentiality possible, with strict attorney/client privilege. To protect this secrecy, these companies usually want to spread the payments out so they can make them more difficult to detect by shareholders and, in the cases where the executive must pay out of his own pocket, they sometimes *need* to spread it over time."

"So . . . how does that . . . ?"

"The potential plaintiffs—these victims, or whistle blowers—would rather get a lump sum *now* instead of waiting for the money or risking something like a death or bankruptcy and never getting it at all. So they accept a lesser, discounted amount of lump sum cash up front and it's over for them."

"Well, if the people who have to pay don't want to pay up front, where does the money come from to pay these people right away?"

Rodino broke out in a grin and held his index finger up. "Smart girl. See? You understand more of this than you thought you would. That's where our investors come in. They put up a negotiated amount equal to around sixty to seventy per cent of the money the potential plaintiff would get over time. That money goes immediately into that victim or whistle blower's pocket. Cash American." His grin broadened. "We, of course, get our rather substantial fees."

She nodded and smiled back. "Of course."

"Then, as the money comes in from the potential defendant— the company or the executive—since the potential plaintiff has already been paid, it goes back to the investors. And their return . . . well, you know what it is because you're an investor."

"It's never been less than twelve per cent," Hallie said.

"And you've always gotten a check, right?"

She nodded and smiled.

"Still want your money back?"

"You know I don't but I still don't understand why Mr. Adams is so down on your investment."

"I can tell you exactly why. He's a lawyer and is accustomed to grinding through every word of every document having to do with any deal. But he's never seen deals like ours."

"No? But he's some big lawyer—"

"Yes, but our deals are incredibly unique in one way. The secrecy that is almost always insisted upon by both parties to our settlement agreements. Under attorney/client privilege rules, we have no choice but to redact from these agreements anything that might identify the parties. The Florida Bar would take my license if I didn't."

"Redact is when you . . . ?"

"We take the biggest, boldest Sharpie pen and black out all the names or other identifiers on all the docs. Apparently that was something that Adams guy couldn't get past." He gave a big shrug. "C'est la vie."

Rodino had been standing at the video screen with a remote in his hand going through slides as he spoke. Now Hallie rose from her chair, went to him, and kissed him lightly on the lips. "Thank you, baby," she said, and headed for the door.

"How about that other little matter?" he asked.

She twirled and, throwing him a flirtatious smile over her shoulder, said, "Getting closer."

Chapter Thirty-Five

Albert Adams dressed at his Tampa condominium in his trademark Maus & Haufman blue blazer with grey slacks and Allen Edmonds cordovan loafers. Today he chose a yellow bow tie with small trout fishing flies all over it. His assistant in New York had made the lunch appointment for him two days ago after his telephoned instructions. Now it was time to go to the Palma Ceia Club.

His lunch guest was waiting for Adams in the lobby. He'd never met the man but knew instantly from his appearance he was Adams's expected guest. The man, who appeared to be in his mid-forties, was just under six feet, about twenty pounds overweight, square-jawed and short-haired. The lack of facial hair and the cheap grey suit completed the package.

"You're Higgins?" Adams said.

"Mr. Adams?" the man said.

Albert Adams extended his hand and the man took it while reaching in his suit pocket with the other. "Be happy to show you my ID if you'd like," he said.

"No, that's not . . . well, sure, I'd like to see what one looks like."

The man flopped his vinyl ID holder down so Adams could see. He squinted and read aloud, "Gerald R. Higgins, Special Agent in Charge, Tampa, Florida." He smiled at the man and said, "Shall we have some lunch?"

"Sure," Higgins said.

When they'd been seated, Adams said, "You do know this is a private club. Which means I'll have to buy. The FBI okay with that?"

Higgins grinned. "Long as there are no martinis involved."

"I gave up drinking at lunch forty years ago."

Menus came and, as the FBI agent studied his, Albert Adams tried to gather his thoughts. Agent Higgins didn't give him long as he made a quick ordering decision and closed his menu. "Mr. Adams, normally when we get a call like yours, we have you come to the office. But your assistant insisted you didn't want to do that; we checked you out, and so I'm making an exception. Thanks for buying lunch, by the way."

"My pleasure," Adams replied.

"Well, sir," Higgins said. "You have succeeded in arousing my curiosity. What exactly do you think could be a crime being committed that will make the national news when it breaks?"

Adams took a deep breath and began. "May I assume you live here in Tampa?"

"Sure do."

"Well, I suspect you have heard of a fellow named Rich Rodino. Rodino and Ross? The law firm?"

"Sure, who hasn't? Gave a pile of money to the university, they just named the Y after him, hangs with the governor, bunch of other stuff. Why?"

Their waiter interrupted. Higgins ordered a Reuben sandwich with french fries while Adams went with a Cobb salad.

"I strongly suspect he may be running a Ponzi scheme of mammoth proportions. Perhaps into the hundreds of millions of dollars."

Higgins almost choked on his iced water and just looked at Adams for several long moments. "Holy crap."

"I hope I'm wrong."

"Of course. But you have my attention. Only because, as I said, we checked you out."

"In addition to his charitable contributions, are you aware of his personal spending?"

Higgins shook his head. "Not really."

"His own jet, a yacht over a hundred feet, a collection of homes around the country, a mansion here in town, a garage full of Maseratis and Ferraris. Even one of those four million-dollar Bugattis. But he drives to his office in a scruffy old Bentley convertible. Art work, antiques, wine cellars, it goes on and on. He just about gave me the complete inventory recently when he invited me bonefishing in the Bahamas to try to sell me on his deals."

"So you're saying . . . ?"

"I'm saying do the math. Even silk stocking lawyers in New York—and I was one of them for years until I became an investor—can't generate *that* much cash."

"So where do you think the money's coming from?"

The waiter brought their beverages. Sweet iced tea for Higgins, a small bottle of San Pelligrino for Adams.

"It's coming from a range of private investors and, unfortunately, many of them are mom and pop folks who can't afford to lose their money. And I suspect they're about to."

"Investors? In what? I thought he was a lawyer."

Adams proceeded to lay out in detail the settlement agreement concept as it was pitched to him by Rodino. "The thing is, all the agreements he shows are totally redacted—not a single name or identifier. And there are some other documents from banks he presents which I suspect may be Photoshopped."

"Forged."

"Exactly. I strongly suspect that most, if not all, of these settlement agreements people are . . . 'investing' in . . . are non-existent. I mean, think about it. How could just one law firm end up with that many of these sexual harassment and whistle blower cases? Just doesn't compute."

Higgins took a long pull on his iced tea and looked reflectively at the ceiling for several moments before looking back at Adams and performing an extended exhale. "Mr. Adams, if what you say pans out, I need to be buying *you* lunch. Or a lot more. I don't mind telling you, this would *make* my career with the Bureau."

"Well, that's very nice, Agent Higgins, but my interest is in seeing this investigated and stopped before more victims lose money they can't afford to."

"Understand and agree. Now I just have to decide how to approach this."

Adams took a sip of San Pelligrino and dabbed his lips with his starched napkin. "I left my briefcase in my car because I don't think they allow them in here. I know they don't at the Yale Club in New York. But when we leave I'll give you a complete set of docs Rodino gave me for one of his deals. All redacted, as I said."

"That's excellent, sir."

"Should be a good start."

"Let me ask you this. You know of any investors?"

"Only one. And it will be tricky because it's his girlfriend. Wouldn't surprise me if they get married soon."

Higgins had a pen and pad out. "Got a name for me?"

"Hallie Duncan. We've met and we've talked. I've been expecting to hear from her again but she's gone radio silent." Adams then explained the fishing trip, the encounter with Hallie at lunch, and their phone call.

"Well, we need to get to her before she gets married and can avoid testifying. You willing to call her and see if she'll take a meeting with us? Much better than my guys and me showing up on her doorstep."

"I'll do my best. But you must remember that love is blind."

Chapter Thirty-Six

Dimple

I think Hallie looks and acts very energized today. Like there is something she's particularly excited about. She has that "look" that usually involves a man. I'm curious and ask her what's going on in her life right now and ask her about Rich. But she deflects the question while expressing her anticipation of hearing what happened after the meeting with Fidel Castro in the mountains, saying it will make one of the most interesting scenes in the book. So, I do what I've been doing amazingly well at lately: talk.

Well, Angel, after Roberto and I bid Castro adieu in those infernal mountains, we hiked back down through the rocks and mud with the man Roberto called Emilio who was really Faustino. By the time we reached the jeep, it was about dark. We actually waited a while to leave the camp to make sure of that. I'd forgotten how rough that damn jeep ride was but in short order I was sorely–and I mean just that–reminded.

We arrived at the same spot where Roberto had left his car and it felt so funny going in that shack and undergoing a metamorphosis. Me of all people had, over eighteen hours, become this battlefield person in fatigues, sleeping with scorpions, eating out of a tin bowl, and tee-teeing in the woods. And all of a sudden I was back in this dilapidated old *bohío* putting on a frilly dress, earrings, and high heels. And don't even ask me about my hair—ye gods.

When we got back to the Hotel Casa Grande in Santiago there was no thought of nightclubbing, hanky panky or even a mojito. We had room service send up some arroz con pollo, ate it quickly, and then just fell in the bed and slept like the dead until morning.

Well, it was hardly enough rest for me; I slept in the car a good bit of the way back to Havana. When we arrived at Roberto's apartment, he held me and kissed me very sweetly before he told me he would not be staying. I wasn't surprised. He'd had to drive that long way after what we'd already been through, and he looked so tired he seemed out on his feet. Despite that, he said he had to go by his office to catch up on a couple of things.

In a way I was relieved. I needed to decompress. And recharge too. But mainly I knew I had to call your daddy that night. I was going to be so nervous spouting a fresh bunch of lies to him and I surely didn't want Roberto anywhere near me then.

Well, I somehow got through the lying part of the call and I think I know why: Dallis wasn't really even listening to what I said because he couldn't wait to tell me his news. "Honey, you're not going to believe this." The excitement in his voice was electric.

"What?"

"I got the money!"

"But . . . but when did you go to Illinois?"

"I didn't."

"You—"

"The international sales manager got tired of rescheduling our meeting and finally told me to explain the situation over the phone. So I did. Apparently they've done this before in some underdeveloped countries so it wasn't that big a deal. The money's supposed to be wired in the morning. So I'll go to the bank, stuff my briefcase with the cash, and see you tomorrow night!"

It was a lot to process and I found myself remaining silent.

"Dorothy? Are you there? These damn Cuban phones, I—"

"Yes, Dallis, I'm here. Sorry."

"Well, what do you think of all that?"

Of course I thought it was wonderful because it sounded like we were close to the end of our financial worries. But, Angel, I confess I had the strangest emptiness overcome me as I realized that my trip to Santiago with Roberto had likely been my swan song with him. And, my goodness, the last two nights we hadn't even been together. It was a classic case of wanting my cake and eating it too. But why should I be surprised at myself? I mean, after all, I was now a lying, scheming adulteress and was conspiring with my husband to bribe government officials in a foreign country. On top of that, I had just lunched with an aspiring Communist revolutionary.

"Honey, that's just wonderful news!" I said. "I just can't believe it, and I can't *wait* to see you."

The next morning, I called Roberto at his office to tell him Dallis's news.

"Yes, I know," he said. "Dallis called me first thing this morning and told me. And I have already spoken with Sergio. The contracts are ready to be signed as soon as the marketing fees are established. So it looks as if this deal is going to happen. You and Dallis and I must celebrate tonight. I will pick you both up at eight."

My heart soared and sank at the same time. I was *thrilled* at success coming for Dallis and an end to our being broke. But when I thought about the three of us going out on the town together, I just wanted to go out on the street, find a manhole cover, lift it up and crawl in. How on *earth* was I going to sit there between the two of them knowing what I know, knowing Roberto knows it too, and knowing your poor daddy doesn't know anything?

"Roberto, I . . . I can't go out with you and Dallis and celebrate . . . I—"

"And why not, my darling?"

"First of all, you've got to stop calling me that."

"What? You mean 'my darling'?"

"Yes."

"But—"

"But nothing. Oh, Roberto, how did I let this happen to me?"

"What? Fall in love?" He laughed. "My darling, it just happens. It has happened to both of us and it has been wonderful, do you not agree?"

"I most certainly do not," I said, almost crossly. And then I pouted in silence.

"Dorothy?" he said when my silence continued. "What is the matter, my darling?"

I sighed, probably somewhat dramatically. "I guess men are different. Maybe you can tell me how I'm supposed to sit between two men I'm . . . *involved* with and carry on like nothing's happened. I just don't know how I'd be able to even *look* at either one of you. Especially wondering when you're going to slip up and call me 'darling'."

"Well, I am going to call you that right now, my darling, because that is what you are to me. I do love you and, because of that, I am going to give you the answer to your problem."

"Oh, really?" I said. I knew my voice was dripping with sarcasm.

"It is very simple. Tonight, and any other time the three of us are together, you should only be polite to me, nothing more. You should give all your attention to your husband. Your eyes should always be meeting his, not mine. Your hands should always be on him, not me. He is the one you are married to and he is a fine man. I envy him and I wish I were in his shoes, but that is the way it has to be and it is the way it should be."

I felt moisture come to my eyes.

"I will pick you both up at eight," Roberto said.

"Okay," I squeaked out in a tiny voice.

The next day found Dallis, Roberto and me at the lunch table at the Havana Country Club with E. Hawkins McHenry III. Through

Roberto, McHenry had invited Dallis and me for lunch and golf, and included Roberto for the lunch part.

Somehow I'd gotten through the previous night's celebration dinner. I guess the only way I did was by following Roberto's advice and showering Dallis with attention. I barely even looked at Roberto all night; I just couldn't. Dallis loved the attention and was very responsive. In fact, it was a wifely lesson to me because it made me realize what happens when you make your husband the focus of everything—it comes back to you in kind. I was only left alone with Roberto once when Dallis went to the men's room and Roberto was deliberately reserved and respectful. Didn't reach for my thigh under the table or anything. I loved him for it.

Hawkins McHenry—"Hawk"—and Dallis hit it off immediately. Even after it came out that Hawk was a great golfer, regularly shooting in the seventies. Dallis's score was usually around ninety. And me? Well, your daddy had a standing bet with me that if and when I broke a hundred he'd give me a hundred dollar bill. It hadn't happened yet and I was almost glad because I knew coming up with a hundred dollars would just *kill* Dallis. At least until we got this bus deal done.

"So," said Hawk, pausing to lift a glass of Hatuey beer with which he was washing down his lunch, "how is the school bus deal coming?" He didn't direct the question to anyone in particular.

Roberto answered with a broad grin. "I spoke with Sergio Baretto this morning and the contracts are ready to be signed."

"Hmmph," Hawk said. "That means there's a nice bag of money somewhere." He looked at Dallis. "You must have it. At the moment, at least."

Dallis's jaw dropped and he looked at Roberto with a pained expression. "I am not sure what you are referring to, Hawk," Roberto said with a very straight face.

Hawk laughed out loud, took another drink of his beer, and said, "Hogwash, old chap. We *all* know what I'm referring to." He sighed. "But . . . that's life in the tropics."

"Well, let me ask you a question then," Roberto said. "How are things at the Embassy? When is the new ambassador arriving?"

"Ha! He already has. Surprised the hell out of us. And he's hit the ground running. I was amazed, frankly."

"What is his name again?" Roberto asked.

"Smith," Hawk said. "Earl E. T. Smith. Business guy. Wall Street, actually. From Rhode Island, a Yalie."

"You say 'hit the ground running'?" Roberto asked.

"Well, the guy's never been a diplomat, doesn't speak a *syllable* of Spanish, so he decides to start by getting out and about. Decides to head to Santiago to take in the País funeral."

I was sitting there listening and wondering who País was but didn't have the gumption to ask. Dallis did.

"Frank País was nothing more than a kid," Hawk said. "Only twenty-two but a key leader of Castro's 26th of July Movement. Santiago police gunned him down in the street. Anyway, our new ambassador gets to see 200,000 people show up protesting País's shooting and shouting '*Libertad! Libertad!*' Even our esteemed new ambassador knows that means 'liberty' and that they want Batista out and Castro in. He also gets to watch the police go after the mob with truncheons and water cannons. Next thing you know he's giving his first press conference condemning excessive use of force by Batista's henchmen."

"Wow," said Roberto. It was the first time I'd heard him use such an American slang word.

"Wow is right," said Hawk. "I'm not sure if Washington knew about it or if Smith was acting on his own. If it's the former, we're talking about a pendulum swing. If it's the latter, our new man may get his nuts cut off by Ike."

"A pendulum swing toward Castro," Roberto said.

"Mmm, probably more like away from Batista." Then Hawk looked right at Roberto with a smirk on his face. "But you wouldn't know anything about Castro, would you?"

For the first time, I saw Roberto's face turn to fury. He stuck his finger very near Hawk's face. "Señor, this is the last time I am telling you. I have had no contact with the man in years and—"

"Oh, relax, old chap. I'm just joshing with you; I wouldn't say a word about that around anybody else."

Roberto was still hot. "You never know who is listening and it is a bad habit to develop. Perhaps you have not seen Batista's firing squads in action. I have."

Although he shouldn't have, Dallis spoke up. "You know Castro?"

"Not that well. He and I were in law school together but—"

"Castro's a lawyer?" Dallis asked with some incredulity.

Hawk chuckled. "Not only that, he went to boarding school."

"Anyway," Roberto continued. "I have had no contact with him in years and do not plan to have any unless, of course, he wins the revolution and takes power. Then, since he will need lawyers like everyone does, I will contact him and solicit his business and his fees. But in the meantime, for everyone's personal safety with El Presidente, we should not mention the name Fidel Castro."

Dallis began pointing to himself and to me. "You mean *our* safety, too?"

Roberto smiled gently at Dallis. "Yes, Dallis. You must remember that you are a big fan of President Fulgencio Batista. Never mind that he is a murderer."

"Right," Dallis said. "Got it."

Roberto turned to Hawk. "So have you talked to the new ambassador about his press conference remarks?"

"The bastard hasn't given me the time of day so far. Of course it's early, but I wouldn't let any grass grow under that bus deal if I were you."

Your daddy and Roberto *didn't* let any grass grow under their deal. Even Batista had a bureaucracy, but Roberto turned out to be very skilled at navigating through it all. The "marketing fees" were paid and the contract was signed. That was all wonderful, but Dallis wouldn't see a dime of his *very* sizable commission until the buses were shipped to Cuba and the money from the Cuban government was received in Illinois. I wondered how we were going to live until all that happened, both literally and figuratively.

And there was a lot more to it than I knew. I learned that international business was far more complicated than just selling something to somebody in Miami, sending them a bill, and getting a check back in the mail. Dallis had to learn about commercial invoices, certificates of origin, customs declarations, and irrevocable letters of credit. And he had to deal with Challenger's lawyers and a customs house in Miami. I understood none of all that. But I was soon to learn that there was one thing involved that was going to affect me.

Roberto was going to be coming to Miami.

Chapter Thirty-Seven

Hawk McHenry, after initially insulting me when we were introduced at the embassy, turned out to be charming and just plain fun. And oh, Angel, what a golfer. His swing was so effortless yet the ball just *flew* off his club. It made your daddy furious that somebody could be that much better than he but I just *loved* watching Hawk play, and playing with him. Dallis and I actually had two golf games with Hawk before it was time to go back to Miami.

I was with your daddy constantly in the days before leaving. There was only one time that we were apart and it was our last day in Havana when he had to meet with the fleet managers one last time. I'm not exactly sure about why he had to talk to them; I heard him mention parts inventories, operating manuals, and some other things. But I was preoccupied with something else: how to get at least a few minutes alone with Roberto to say goodbye.

Dallis had said he'd be gone most of that last day and asked me what I would do.

"Oh, maybe some shopping," I answered.

"Remember, honey, we don't have the commission money yet."

"I said shopping. I didn't say buying. I'll just look at everything and decide what I'll buy when we come back and we're rich." I said it gaily.

"Hmmph. You better get that idea out of your head right now or we'll be broke again and stay that way."

"Oh pooh on you," I said, playfully. "I promise I'll be frugal but there are things we've done without for *so* long."

At that moment your daddy took me by my shoulders and put his baby blues on me the way only he could do. "I know we have, honey, but I'm so damn tired of worrying where our next rent check is coming from. We've got to put aside some of this money we'll be getting. Anyway, we may need it for . . ."

"What?"

He really gave me his look then. "Do you still want to?"

"What?"

"You know."

"You mean start a family?" I felt my face brighten.

He nodded.

"Golly Pete, of course I do."

"Well, I do too. So that means we have to be—what did you say—frugal?"

We had the best hug in a long time. "Just call me Mrs. Skinflint." I said it with as much enthusiasm as I could muster which, frankly, wasn't much.

"That's my girl," he said. "Happy shopping. I've got to go."

The moment the door closed behind him, I picked up the phone to call Roberto. His English-speaking secretary said he was "in conference" and would call me back. A little over an hour later the phone rang. I figured it could only be Roberto or Dallis so I just said hello.

"Hello to you, my darling."

"Roberto, remember? You've *got* to stop calling me that."

I had a perfect picture in my mind of what he was doing at that moment—smiling that perfect, engaging smile of his. "That is only necessary when Dallis is around," he said.

I wasn't going to argue with him. "You . . . you do realize Dallis and I are leaving for Miami tomorrow."

"Of course I know that. And I also know that Dallis is meeting with the fleet managers today. I thought it best not to call but I was hoping you would call me. I will come right over and——"

"No!"

"No?"

"Roberto, you can't come here. Somehow Dallis would know it . . . *I* would know it."

"I have the answer," he said. "It is almost lunch time. Meet me at a place called Salon Miami. It's on the Malecon and—"

"I know. I went there for lunch by myself one day when I—"

"Well, perhaps you would rather go somewhere else."

"Oh no. I *loved* that place."

And I did love it and its elegant—what's that fancy word?—ambiance. Gentlemen that he was, Roberto was waiting for me when I arrived. Against my better judgment, we had daiquiris to start, then another, then a light lunch of lobster empanadas. We sat side by side on a banquette against the wall at a table that could have accommodated four, so we were very close to each other. That and the daiquiris caused a topic to come up that was on both our minds.

"The answer is clear," he said. "We will simply go to my apartment."

I knew Roberto lived in an apartment in Vedado but that's all I knew. I was ready. I figured it would be my last treasured interlude of intimacy with this delicious man who had somehow swept a happily married woman off her feet. On the taxi ride I was paying all my attention to Roberto. In fact, we were paying so much attention to each other, if you know what I mean, that the driver may have been embarrassed. We arrived at the building and I thought it looked vaguely familiar. But when we got out of the taxi, I realized it with a shock. Good grief, it was the building I had just left.

"Roberto, I told you I just *can't*—"

"Relax, my darling." He was holding my elbow and smiling. "My apartment is six floors higher than where you are staying."

He had never told me or Dallis. Not only was it six floors higher, it was virtually identical to the one Dallis and I were staying in. Obviously the same decorator. Later, when I lay in his arms for what I guess is called "pillow talk," I knew our time was very short because Dallis would be coming back before long. This is it, I told myself. It's over. And I became upset. He could tell.

"What is the matter?"

I told him.

"This is not 'it,'" he said.

"What do you mean?"

"When you get back to Miami, you should rent a post office box. When you get the number of the box write me a letter and tell me. Then we can secretly write each other."

I looked up at him and smiled gratefully. It was one of the more touching things he'd ever said to me. I was *thrilled.* Then he really surprised me.

"And my letters will be one of the ways you will know exactly when I will be coming to Miami."

I jerked myself straight up in bed. "What?"

He was smiling broadly. "What I am about to tell you is *very* confidential, so . . . ," He put his index finger to his lips.

"I promise," I said.

"Sergio has a problem with his school bus drivers. They are joy riding in the buses at high speeds and using them for personal travel, but he is having a difficult time proving it. He has ordered tachographs to install in many of these Challenger buses that will give him speed history, hours driven, info on fast acceleration, heavy braking and things like that. They are used now on some trucks in Norte America but these are new prototypes that provide more data and–here is what Sergio is interested in–they are concealed beneath the floorboard of the bus so the drivers will not know they are being recorded."

"Well, why does that mean you'll be coming to—"

"Sergio doesn't even want any of his *supervisors* to know these devices are being installed. So he wants me to oversee the installation and handle the payment to the supplier. It is a somewhat complicated transaction because the payments must be hidden within the government and because the supplier is a French company."

Angel, I don't recall ever experiencing a more polarized range of feelings as I did at that moment. On the one hand, I was ecstatic that I would see Roberto again. On the other, I felt trapped and oppressed by the knowledge that my skein of lying and cheating was not yet over. I had a little angel and a little devil inside me carrying on a fierce moral and emotional tug of war that I feared would some-how destroy or incapacitate me. I'm ashamed to tell you, my sweet daughter, that in a few moments, the devil got the upper hand as I pulled Roberto under the sheet with me again and treasured every sublime second of it.

Chapter Thirty-Eight

Hallie

"You taught me that writers aren't supposed to use clichés, but do you want mine for today?"

Hallie had phoned Ian Lightbourne. "Sure, let me have it," he said with a chuckle.

"Okay, here goes," she said. "Let's do lunch."

He laughed out loud. "Sounds superb. Somewhere near the university?"

"How about the Silver Ring Café at one? I'm overdue for my Cuban sandwich fix. After all, I *am* writing a book set in Cuba."

"Perfect. See you there."

Hallie's gaily-issued invitation to her professor and wannabe lover belied her real feelings about meeting him. The fact was she dreaded it. She knew she cared for him, she just didn't know exactly how, how much, or what it meant. And she became almost ill at the thought of hurting him in any way. But she had come to a decision and it was time to tell him.

They were at their table, each with half of a Cuban sandwich and a cup of black bean soup, when Hallie said, "I'm going to marry Rich."

She'd just blurted it out, otherwise fearing she'd lose her nerve. She unfortunately did so just as Ian had taken a huge bite of his

Cuban sandwich. She realized her poor timing, saw his eyes get a little buggy, and hoped she wouldn't have to use the Heimlich maneuver on him. He couldn't talk; he just put his sandwich down, dabbed his paper napkin to his mouth a couple of times, and chewed and chewed while staring at her. Finally, he could speak.

"I suppose I don't blame you," he said, his mouth still partially full of food.

Hallie didn't quite know how to take that. "What exactly do you mean?"

"Well, all that money."

She could tell he realized his mistake the very instant the words left his mouth, even before he saw the expression of fury on her face. He beat her to the punch. "Please," he said. "Strike that. It came out totally wrong."

"Then why did you say it and what did you mean?"

He was still finishing chewing and he took a sip of his hot tea. "You really want to know what I meant?"

"Of course I do."

"The answer is I don't know what I meant. I only know I've just learned he's the winner and I'm the loser so I lashed out in frustration, envy—all those unbecoming emotions. The remark certainly had nothing to do with you; I know you wouldn't marry somebody just for his money."

"What do you mean you're the loser?"

He put the sandwich down. "So you want me to spell it out for you? Okay, I will. I'm in love with you and if I thought I could win you, I'd leave my wife in a New York minute." He rolled his eyes and looked at the ceiling. "My God, the bloody clichés are raining on us today, aren't they?"

She smiled appreciatively.

"I assume you were already aware of what I just told you," he said.

She was dabbling at her cup of black bean soup. "Yes, I suppose I was."

"Well, I frankly don't want to hear any details like how much you love him, how wonderful he is, how you're flying around the world on his jet for your honeymoon. Oh, I'm aware that the chic, gentlemanly thing to do would be to confirm my love by insisting that you not be cut in half like Solomon's baby. That all I want is your happiness. But I *am* a human, you know. And reasonably competitive for a phlegmatic old college professor."

She was still toying with her black beans and in agony listening to him describe his hurt. He reached over and took her hands. "I've never met anyone like you, Hallie. And I have fallen deeply in love with you. I pray you will be happy with that man but I just ask you to be cautious. Not for me, but for you. Just make sure he's real."

She looked at him, quizzically, wondering. "What do you mean?"

He was still holding her hands. "I'm not sure. I only want you to know I'll be here for you, no matter what."

The remark was at the same time comforting and unsettling to her.

Then he said, "So what does this mean for the book? Do I lose that part of you, too?"

She smiled at him. "No. Nothing will stop me from finishing the book."

"I hate to be playing the part of Professor Negative, but what about your mother?"

Once again, he had said something that felt like a body blow. But it was valid. She had to think it over a moment or two before replying, "If she can't finish telling the story, my imagination will."

It struck Hallie that, in the same day, she was having lunch and dinner with two different men, both of whom were in love with her. At least she was accepting the marriage proposal of the one who was not married! She and Rich went to Mise en Place for dinner to celebrate their engagement. They ordered multiple culinary creations of Chef Marty and accompanied their dinner with a $1750 bottle of Chateau Petrus selected by Rodino.

Rodino didn't ask anything about her lunch with Ian Lightbourne because he didn't know it occurred and didn't know there was any reason for her to tell her professor about becoming engaged. But he did ask Hallie about her mother and about the book.

"She seems to be hanging on and the story keeps coming. I'm committing it to fiction as fast as it unfolds."

Then he caught her a little off guard. "So what does your professor think?"

She wondered if he caught the vulnerable expression she knew she showed him. A glance at him told her he might have.

"Oh my gosh, he *loves* it," she said, putting her palm to her chest. "His professional support for what I'm doing is what's keeping me going."

"I still want to meet this guy sometime." He broke into a grin. "You spend a lot of time with him. I'm trying to decide if I should be worried."

She held up her ring finger with the most enormous diamond she'd ever seen in her life. It caught the light and reflected it on Rodino's Roman nose. "I believe this should answer that question, sir."

He leaned forward, smiling broadly, and took her hands. "Let's talk about the wedding."

And they did. He wanted a "destination" wedding and mentioned Carmel, someplace in Napa, or maybe even Provence. She preferred staying in Tampa in the hope that her mother could somehow be taken to the ceremony and wheeled in. They decided to defer the decision until another night. Then, out of the blue, a thought came to Hallie.

"You know, baby," she said, "If I'm going to be your wife with no prenuptial agreement, when do I learn more about all this money I'm supposed to be getting half of?" She said it with a good-natured smile but still couldn't believe the question had come to her.

He threw back his head and laughed. "Whenever you want. But my suggestion is that you devote your time and effort to *spending* it, not worrying about how much there is."

She tucked her head inside her shoulder and peeked up at him with a flirtatious smile. "That doesn't sound too bad, Mr. Rodino."

He leaned over and kissed her lightly on the cheek. "Nothing will be too good for the future Mrs. Rodino."

She reached for the back of his neck with her hand and affectionately ruffled the three inches or so of hair that hung over his collar. "Well, could the future Mrs. Rodino ask how you and Thomas are coming on that fifty million-dollar investment you went to New York about?"

At that moment, Hallie saw something in her fiancé's face she didn't recall seeing before. It was a fixed, fake smile that she normally associated with people who were not completely telling the truth. "Still working on it," Rodino said, with the fake smile intact. "Shouldn't be a problem, though."

The next morning, the phone rang and Hallie couldn't believe the voice on the other end of the line. Realizing its identity gave her a start.

"This is Albert Adams calling. Is this Hallie?"

"Yes, this is Hallie. How are you, Mr. Adams?"

He chuckled. "Please. I'm Albert."

"Albert it is. What can I do for you?"

"Well, I thought I might hear back from you after our last phone conversation. Remember, you called me with some questions about Rich Rodino's investment packages and I suggested that you ask him for a detailed presentation? I was just wondering if you did and, if so, how it went."

When Rich had so effectively explained the investments to her in his conference room, she had totally forgotten about calling Adams back. She told him so and, while she was at it, briefly reviewed her newfound basic understanding of the Rodino settlement agreement investments. "And, by the way, Rich and I are officially engaged now," she added.

She was trying to decide if she heard Adams emit a barely discernible groan on the other end of the line but couldn't. What she was sure of is that the line had fallen silent.

"Mr. Adams? Er, I mean, Albert? You there?"

"Uh, yes . . . yes, I'm here. I was just trying to decide what to make of what you just told me. Certainly, congratulations on your engagement."

"Thank you, sir."

"Well," he said. "So." Both declarations were vocalized pauses as it was clear he was organizing his thoughts. There was more silence.

"Is there anything else I can help you with, Albert?" Hallie asked, trying to wrap up the conversation.

Another brief silence, then finally, "Yes, perhaps so. I have a friend who runs a substantial hedge fund in New York who could have an interest in Rich's deals. And I might even take a second look myself. Maybe you could have Rich give me a call and he and I could meet next time I'm in Tampa."

"Knowing Rich, he'll want to get on his plane and come to New York."

"No, no. Don't want to do that. I prefer to meet in Tampa. Helps justify some business expense of having my condominium there, you know."

"I understand. Sure, I'll ask him to call you; I still have your number in New York."

"Excellent. By the way, my hedge fund friend may want to speak with some other investors. Any problem with giving him your number?"

"No, of course not."

"Good. Do you know any other investors?"

Hallie thought a moment or two. Grace Lamont, her boss at the advertising agency came to mind, but she really didn't want to have a stranger calling her boss.

"I'm trying to think of somebody and can't seem to," she said. "I'm sorry."

"What about some of those folks who attended the presentation at Rich's house? Know any of them?"

"Not really. I stood next to a woman at the last one who raved about the investment. Said her CPA recommended it to her."

"You remember the CPA's name?"

"Sorry, no."

"Well, thanks. Nice to speak with you again, Hallie. And once again, congratulations."

When she hung up, Hallie reflected on the phone conversation and found her spirits lifted. Even if the fifty million-dollar man from New York passed, here was a new one that might be even bigger for Rich. Plus Albert Adams was interested again. Yes, with the exception of hurting Ian Lightbourne with her engagement news, things were looking up all around.

Chapter Thirty-Nine

Albert Adams entered the FBI's Tampa field office and asked for Gerry Higgins, who came out and fetched him from the waiting room after Adams went through the security procedures. Higgins ushered Adams to his corner office. There was another agent in Higgins's office waiting for them.

"Mr. Adams, meet Special Agent William Dixon."

An expressionless Dixon extended his hand and shook. "Mr. Adams," he said.

"How do you do?" Adams answered.

They sat at a round conference table in Higgins's office; after Adams declined an offer of coffee, they got to it.

"Well, I think I have some pretty good news," Adams said after adjusting his bow tie, which today had a Kelly green field with small flying mallards in the foreground. "I have the appointment with Rodino for next Monday. He agreed to have Thomas Herring there."

Higgins cut a glance over at Dixon and gave a little mini-fist pump. "That's really, really good, Mr. Adams. Any luck with that CPA?"

"As a matter of fact, yes. I followed your plan, calling Rodino's office and explaining that I attended his presentation at the mansion and met a lady by herself who has a son who is dying to go quail hunting at the Gilchrest Club where I belong. I told the person I spoke with that I lost the lady's contact information but I did remember that her accountant put her in the investment. They gave me her name and contact information."

Another mini-fist pump by Higgins, albeit less demonstrative. "And?"

"Would you like the accountant's name?"

"You bet."

After accepting the accountant's contact information, Higgins began discussing Adams's upcoming meeting with Rich Rodino and Thomas Herring.

"We're working real hard to develop enough probable cause to get a warrant for you to record your meeting with Rodino. If we can't get it in time, you may have to ask him to postpone the meeting. You understand that, right?"

"Certainly."

"I'm hoping we may get something from this accountant and that he may know of other accountants in the loop. If he was getting some kind of kickback from Rodino, we may get him to spill all his beans."

"That would be good," Adams said. Agent Dixon had not uttered a word since greeting Adams but he was about to.

"Okay, Agent Dixon here is going to show you how we're going to record Rodino. We rarely use what you may know as a 'wire' anymore. Now we just use an ordinary-looking ball point pen. It has a super-sensitive microphone and a transmitter. We'll hear everything in real time. It works just as well as a wire but, if somebody gets suspicious and rips your shirt off they find nothing. Make sense?"

"Indeed."

"You activate the mic and transmitter by simply pushing the button on top of the pen as you would to use any ball point pen. You must remember not to keep flicking it back and forth like a lot of us do or we'll only get a partial transmission. Now, here's the big thing: Take a note pad with you and be sure to use the pen—which actually works as a pen—to take notes. Then you have to leave the pen behind so we can hear what they say after you leave. Don't leave it on the table or they might try to give it back to you. Instead, leave it in your chair which, hopefully, will be an upholstered one that allows you to bury the pen in a crease. Don't worry about pushing it down too far, that mic is some kind of powerful."

Adams nodded with a wry smile. "Gentlemen, I'm duly impressed."

Agent Dixon went over the operation of the pen. Then he sent Adams across the street to the library with the pen in his pocket where he had a conversation with a librarian about a book he said he was looking for. When he returned to the FBI office, Adams listened to a perfectly clear recording of his conversation with the librarian.

"We have covert video devices as well, but we won't need that here," Higgins said. "Looks like we're all set. We'll be in touch as soon as we know something about the warrant. And I have to get the approval of my boss but that will be no problem."

Albert Adams's meeting with Rodino and Herring occurred late in the day the following Monday after all warrants and approvals came through. Higgins explained to Adams that the sworn statement of the CPA they called on was instrumental in obtaining the warrant.

"And, I hate to tell you this," Higgins had said. "This accountant has a half-dozen clients in the deal and they've all complained about their checks being late for the first time ever. Two months in a row with the second month later than the first. Looks like things are coming unbuttoned, which means it's major hurt time for some people who can't absorb it. And it also looks like Rodino's counting on your money to save him."

Adams groaned.

It was almost six p.m. Now, the meeting with Rodino having concluded earlier in the day, they were in Higgins's office, ready to go over the recording from the meeting. Higgins turned to the laptop computer, stroked a few keys, and two external speakers came alive.

"Albert, let me introduce you to my colleague, Thomas Herring."

"Pleasure to meet you, Thomas. Are you a lawyer as well?"

"Nope. CPA. The bean counter."

"Man, can this guy cast. I'm telling you, Thomas, when he came down and fished with me, we're talking eighty-foot casts right on that bonefish's nose."

They listened to additional pleasantries being exchanged before Rodino got down to business.

"I can't tell you how glad I am to hear you're willing to take another look at our settlement agreements. You got the package I overnighted to you with our latest package of deals, right?"

"I got them, but they look different from the agreements you showed me in the Bahamas."

"They are. Mainly, it's that they're for larger settlement amounts. This stack of agreements, in the aggregate, is worth a little over fifty mil in payouts."

"I don't understand how you get so many of these things."

"Well, for one thing, we're a decent-sized firm. Over seventy lawyers, offices in multiple cities—"

"Rich is being too modest, Mr. Adams. He's done a super job of cultivating referral relationships with some very large firms. Those connections are really paying off now."

"I see."

"Anyway, because these amounts are larger, it appears the returns will be, too. Thomas, what are the latest calculations?"

A pause occurred as the sound of rustling papers was heard.

"Looks like these will allow us pay out closer to sixteen percent instead of the usual twelve. Maybe more."

"Albert, does that sound like something your hedge fund friend would be interested in?"

"Frankly, it sounds like something I would be interested in. Which brings up a question: How might I be rewarded for bringing in this kind of money from my friend and from me?"

"Are you talking about the entire fifty million?"

"What if I did ten and my friend did forty?"

"Then we're ready for you. Thomas and I analyzed this opportunity and determined we can pay you a five percent finder's fee on top of everything else. And that's annual, not one time. So that means an extra two-and-a-half million for you every year if you can get this done. Add in the sixteen per cent on your ten million and that's over four million a year for you."

"That would certainly come in handy."

"And, don't forget, there'll be plenty more bonefishing trips taking the Citation *down to the Bahamas."*

"Well that certainly sounds good, too."

"So, what do you think?"

"It obviously sounds terrific, but I'm still hung up on the redaction of all the documents. How do I know you guys didn't just word process these things out of thin air and black out where the names are supposed to go?

"Albert, that question is just as valid now as it was when you raised it in the Bahamas. But I have a better answer for you now. Have a look at this."

A brief rustling of papers was heard.

"TD Bank, yep I know them."

"The letter you're looking at, duly signed by a senior vice president, guarantees the payment stream represented by these agreements. Since TD Bank is the paying agent, they have to look at the actual files for each deal. The Florida Bar says that, with the client's authorization, I can show the bank the actual files but not you, otherwise I'd get disbarred for violating attorney/client privilege."

"Well, how can the payment stream be guaranteed if the payments are to be made over time?"

"Because we pay the bank a fee for the guarantee. It's a calculated risk for them, an actuarial exercise like an interest rate swap option. A derivative. And we can easily afford the fee as lucrative as these deals are. And I think you'll admit these deals are pretty lucrative."

"Indeed they are."

A sound was heard similar to loud static from a radio. "You're pushing the pen down in the chair now, aren't you?" asked Higgins.

Adams grinned and nodded.

"Well, let me see what I can do and get back to you."

"Albert, there's something I need to tell you."

"Oh?"

"You and I became friends on our fishing trip so I feel comfortable telling you this: We have someone else strongly considering taking this entire package. You're not going to believe this but it's a New York-based hedge fund. Now, I know it's not your guy because I asked him if he knew you. The point is, they are very close to pulling the trigger. Now, here's what's important: Even if they beat you to the punch on these agreements, I will try to stall them a bit. Why? Because, while money is important to me—like you, I need a lot of it—relationships are too. And I've never waded a bonefish flat with those guys. You know what I'm saying?"

"I do, Rich, and I appreciate that. I'll work as fast as I can."

"Please do, Albert; I may not be able to stall these guys long. I'm sure we'll have more deals down the line for whichever one of you was late to the party, but these are really sweet ones and I'd like to see you get them."

"So how'd I do?" Adams asked Higgins.

Higgins had paused the recording and was grinning. "Outstanding. I only wish you'd asked for a copy of the bank letter."

"I thought about it, but worried it might make me come off as *too* suspicious. But I have the bank officer's name and, on the way over here, I called him."

"Really," Higgins said, then pursed his lips and widened his eyes, indicating he was impressed. "And?"

"Guy's name is Allen Bannister in Jacksonville. I told him I was considering Rodino's investment. When I asked him about the letter, he said he could confirm that Rodino and Ross is a customer, that he had corresponded with them, but beyond that he preferred not to interject himself in his customer's business. When I specifically asked if they were guaranteeing any payments, he repeated his prior answer."

"Excellent work, sir."

"Thank you."

"Okay, are you ready to get to the good stuff?" And he started the recording again.

"So what do you think, Rich?"

"I think he'd damn sure better come through for us. After that other New York guy crapped on us, Adams is all we've got. How late are we going to be with checks this month?"

A long period of rustling papers was heard.

"Ain't looking good, Kemo Sabe. If that guy in Jacksonville comes through with his two mil, we can actually pay about half the folks on time, but—"

"Just make sure Hallie's check is on time."

"Understand. When's the wedding, by the way?"

A long pause before Rodino's voice came on again.

"If we get this fifty mil, it'll be soon. If not, I may not even be able to afford a marriage license."

Another long pause, a shuffling of papers, and a very long pause.

"Is that it?" Adams asked.

"No," Higgins said. Presently, a voice was heard again.

"Rich."

"Yeah."

"Speaking of Hallie . . ."

"Yeah?"

"Well . . . what if the worst happens? What about her money she put in the deals?"

"I'll be broke and you and I will both be in jail. Who gives a rat's ass then?"

Chapter Forty

Dimple

It seems like I've been sleeping a lot lately. That's not good because the doctors keep telling me to try to stay active. The good news is everything upstairs seems to still be working at the level it has been since I began remembering my time in Cuba. And that's all I'm really living for now, to be able to help Hallie with her book.

It turns out I was right about how radiant she looked last time. I just knew *something* was up. Well, she came back later with Rich. What a charming boy—he actually asked me for Hallie's hand in marriage. I've never seen my sweet angel look so happy. I know I won't be able to go to the wedding but I can't wait to hear all the details. However, I know I can't allow myself to spend much time on that because I've got to press on with telling Hallie my story.

She's still radiant when she arrives today and pulls out her recorder and encourages me to start talking. So I take as deep a breath as I can these days and begin.

Well, let's see, where was I last time? Oh, yes, your daddy and I returned to Miami, which was one of the most deflating things that had ever happened to me. Except for my devotion to your daddy, my life there hadn't been much. See, back in those days women didn't work like they do now. I was a true housewife. And my time in Cuba was like a dream. I mean it was *living* the most amazing daydream you could ever conjure from watching romantic movies or reading books. On the flight home, I just stared out the window and replayed the entire thing. And I would do so many more times in the days that followed.

As soon as I returned to Miami, I went to the nearest post office and rented a box. Then I sat down and wrote Roberto a long letter. In it, I told him of feelings I had that, for some reason, I hadn't shared with him in Cuba. Even in all the time we were alone together, there really hadn't been time, if you know what I mean, because we were too busy having fun. In the letter, I told him I had fallen in love with him but that I was also still in love with my wonderful husband. And that, although I'd broken my vows by having an affair, there was no question but that I would stay married to Dallis. I did my best to explain the kaleidoscope of emotions it all subjected me to but I probably did a poor job of it. Anyway, I mailed the letter and then faithfully visited the post office every day. Finally, one day there was a letter! I ripped it open and *devoured* every word. It was very short and went something like this:

Hello, my darling Dimple.

I want you to know I miss you very much and that I still love you very much. I am happy to tell you that I will be in Miami very soon for the business reason I told you about. I suggest you ask Dallis about my schedule. I am sure the three of us can have dinner at least one night but, if we are lucky, you and I can find a moment to be together alone. I hope so.

Much love — Roberto

I re-read the letter–it was a note, really–a dozen or more times, trying to somehow divine something that was not apparent on each preceding reading. I did notice that he rather uncharacteristically used my "Dimple" nickname but the big thing was that he was coming to Miami, and it was only a week away. Of course I had to wait and let Dallis mention Roberto's visit. When he didn't, I finally had to ask if he'd heard from Roberto.

"Matter of fact, he's coming," he replied. "Be here two nights, but we'll only see him the first one. The second night he says he has to be with the French guy who's delivering and installing those recording thingamajigs on the buses. Says the guy came all the way from France and he can't just let him go to someplace like Wolfie's and eat by himself."

We met Roberto at Joe's Stone Crab restaurant on Miami Beach. He was actually staying on the beach at the posh Eden Roc. We were waiting for him in the terrazzo-floored lobby of Joe's—Roberto was on *Cubano* time—and, unlike the first time we had ever met, Roberto entered and didn't even look at me but went straight for Dallis and shook his hand vigorously. I watched it all while I tried not to faint.

Angel, I had forgotten how handsome he was. He was wearing a white sport coat and a navy tie and my peripheral vision caught two women at the bar whispering to each other behind cupped hands as they cut glances at him. Finally he looked at me, smiled broadly, and reached for my hand. I gave it to him and he bent and kissed it. Of course, that made a puddle out of me but I was glad it was not a hug; my constitution wouldn't have endured it.

We all went for the standard issue at Joe's: fresh cold stone crabs with their special mustard sauce, hash browns, and their special cole slaw. We washed it down with draught Heineken beer after starting with cocktails in the bar. The arrival of the husbands of the two women did not deter them from continuing to glance at Roberto. Overhearing his Cuban accent seemed to heighten their interest.

Not long after we were seated at our dining table, Dallis excused himself for the men's room and Roberto sprang into action. "Here. Put this in your purse quickly," he said, handing me a small piece of note paper.

"What is it?"

"It is my room number at the Eden Roc. Come at noon. I will have a bottle of champagne and a bit of lunch for us." He smiled at me while fixing his eyes on me in a way that made we want to meld myself into his arms that instant, regardless of whether your daddy or all the people with stone crab napkins tied around their necks were watching. Instead, I just looked at him. Looked at his eyes, reviewed again all the features of his face, reached out for his hands and looked them over. Just getting re-acquainted with the physical Roberto. Waves of emotion washed over me as I realized how much I had missed him.

"Well, my darling?" he said, still smiling. "Will you be there?"

"I'll be there."

Fortunately, I disengaged Roberto's hands just before Dallis returned to the table.

"So," Dallis said. "Tell me about tomorrow."

Our dinner had been served while Dallis was away and Roberto now had a Joe's logoed paper napkin tied around his neck and an expertly cracked stone crab in his hands. "You had twenty of the buses delivered to the warehouse I specified, correct?"

"They're sitting there waiting on you, but why just twenty?" Dallis asked.

"These are just the ones that will be immediately driven to Santiago de Cuba after they arrive in Havana, because that is where Sergio is having the problem he needs the tachographs for. As soon as the units are installed tomorrow, these buses will be sent to the port for shipment to Havana."

"How did those gizmos of his get here?"

"Ocean freight. They are supposed to be at the warehouse already. I am having breakfast with the Frenchman who has supplied these new prototype tachographs. After that, I will supervise his installation of the units on the buses. It will take all day. Then I will take him to dinner tomorrow night. After all, he came all the way from France."

"Well," Dallis said. "I trust installing those gadgets goes well and the buses get to the port and on the ship. It leaves day after tomorrow and, with our letter of credit in place, if that tub doesn't sink between here and Havana, we'll have our money shortly."

After dinner, we stood outside Joe's saying goodbyes and the same conversation was more or less repeated as Dallis and Roberto seemed to want to prolong savoring the deliciousness of their impending success.

Finally it was time to part.

"Don't be a stranger," Dallis said over his shoulder as we walked away. I just sort of waved over my shoulder, hoping I'd played my goodbye in a way that was plausible to Dallis.

"Do not worry, amigo," Roberto called after us, smiling and waving. "Goodbye, Dorothy."

Chapter Forty-One

Less than twenty-four hours later, I was in Roberto's arms in his room at The Eden Roc. Being with him again was heavenly but I started crying. When Roberto asked what was wrong, I said, "I just have the strangest feeling I'm not going to see you again."

I was cradled in his arms and he stroked my hair and cheek. "Shhh, do not talk in such a way. There is always some reason for me to come to Miami. And, anyway, you and Dallis will need to come back to Cuba to check on the fleet or you can just come on holiday."

"What if Fidel pulls off his little revolution thingy and doesn't let Americans come any more?" I let out a short sob.

Roberto laughed. "For one thing, it is not at all clear that the revolution will succeed. And for another, if Castro is in charge of Cuba, he would never refuse the American tourist dollar."

"What do you really think? Will he win?"

He looked at me earnestly. "If he can get the one thing he lacks."

"And that is?"

"Remember the boxes we sat on to eat lunch with Fidel?"

"Yes, but I've forgotten what—"

"They were empty ammunition boxes. Every time his rebels defeat Batista's soldiers—which is almost all the time now—they capture more excellent weapons. Even tanks. Many of these weapons were supplied by the United States but now they have stopped shipping them. But it is ammunition the rebels need and if Fidel can solve that problem, he will win quickly. It is what the outcome of the revolution hangs on."

"My goodness," I said. "So what's Fidel going to do?"

Roberto's room at the Eden Roc was a beautiful one with a spectacular view of the Atlantic Ocean. He gazed out at the sea for a moment before he answered. "I am not sure what he will do. But he is very resourceful. The most likely source is the United States but Hawk tells me there is much confusion in Washington. A lot of bickering over whether to support Batista or Castro. Even Eisenhower cannot make up his mind. It would not surprise me if Fidel turned to the Russians for help. I believe Raul and Che, who are both Marxist, are trying to move Fidel in that direction. But even if the Russians help him, it will be nearly impossible to get a large supply of ammunition into Cuba past Batista."

Well, Angel, it wasn't long after that when Dallis got his humongous commission check. Praise the Lord. Naturally, I wanted a new wardrobe and a bigger house. I actually didn't want a new car because I loved the one I had and didn't think it was replaceable. It was a Hillman Minx convertible—solid pink and perfectly adorable. But I did want to go to Cuba on holiday before the violence reached Havana. It was already bad in the provinces but Havana was still safe. It was thought that it would stay that way at least until Castro and his rebels arrived in the capital, and nobody knew when or if that would be.

Of course, your daddy had a totally different view of what to do with the money. He wanted to save it, maybe invest in some real estate, maybe start his own sales distributorship and represent other manufacturers in addition to Challenger. So, like most couples, I suppose, we had constant battles over money, even though we had way more of it than we used to. Which meant we finally had at least *some*.

Back in the fifties, the *Miami Herald* was a wonderful newspaper. Your daddy and I read it thoroughly. That was really the only way people got the news because network television news was still figuring itself out and there was no such thing as cable television. And the internet? It was still over forty years away.

Anyway, Dallis and I scoured every single page of the paper each day for *anything* having to do with Cuba. We were both keenly interested since he'd done business there, and I was interested for a reason Dallis knew nothing of; that was because of my time with Fidel Castro.

On New Year's Eve 1958, your daddy and I got invited to a party at the wonderful old Riviera Country Club in Coral Gables. Of course, we weren't members because, although we were breathing much easier, we still couldn't afford it. We'd been reading in the *Herald* about the remarkable progress Castro had been making in his revolutionary war. We learned that Batista had taken the desperate step of launching Operation Verano that was supposed to wipe out Castro and his rebel army which, amazingly, was still only about 300 men. Well, Batista sent thousands of troops for Operation Verano but, in the decisive Battle of La Plata, Castro and his rebels defeated a 500-man battalion, captured 240 Batista soldiers and only lost three rebels.

That seemed to be the turning point and Operation Verano ultimately failed. After that, Castro sent Che Guevara toward Havana on the offensive through the Escambray Mountains. He mowed down Batista's troops and took the city of Santa Clara. When Batista heard that, he panicked and, at his own New Year's Eve party, he announced to his friends that he was leaving Cuba. By three a.m., *former* President Fulgencio Batista of Cuba was on a plane with forty family members and supporters bound for the Dominican Republic. It's said that he took $300 million with him, mainly money from bribes and rake offs from the mafia-run casinos. And yes, some of that money came from Challenger Manufacturing to get our school bus deal done. Che Guevara entered Havana on New Year's Day and Castro simultaneously took control of Santiago. It was a week later before Fidel arrived in Havana to a crowd lining the streets that was estimated at a million devoted Cubans.

On New Year's Day 1959, the *Miami Herald* had a big story about Che Guevara's taking Santa Clara but I'll never forget their front-page headline on January 2. It was in the largest type I've ever seen in a newspaper and was just one word: **FIDEL!** The accompanying story told of Che's entering Havana and Batista fleeing in the middle of the night.

Three weeks later, I experienced the worst moment of my life. I only thank God Dallis wasn't there. It happened after the news that Castro had won and after he'd reached Havana and given interviews. At the grocery store, I picked up a copy of *Time*, the magazine. I bought it because it had a huge cover article on the Cuban revolution and when I got home I curled up with it to read every word.

I wish I hadn't.

When I got to the part about the war itself, I tried to wade through all the descriptions of the kinds of tanks and guns that were used and the military strategies. I didn't have much success at that, but there was one part that even I could understand: Castro had solved his biggest problem—a shortage of ammunition—by having huge quantities smuggled in from the Russians . . . on school buses Batista had ordered for his schools. It said twenty of the buses were supposed to be equipped with tachographs and sent to Santiago where it was believed the drivers were joyriding and using the buses for personal travel, but instead of installing the tachographs, large quantities of ammunition were concealed under the floorboards of the buses and smuggled in that way. The buses were driven to Santiago where, in the middle of the night, Fidel's rebels unloaded the ammunition, took it to the mountains, and that's what enabled them to win the revolution.

He . . . he used me, Angel. He just *used* me.

He used me in multiple ways. He used my body for his pleasure and he used Dallis and me to help his friend win his stupid revolution.

Angel, I *loved* him. And I thought he loved me. I mean he *told* me he did. I would have done *anything* for that man. Well, except leave your daddy. At least I don't think I would have. Anyway, I will never forget that day. I can still remember exactly where I was sitting when I read that magazine and how the pages felt in my hand. I tore the magazine into a million little pieces and threw them away. I decided I wouldn't mention it to Dallis in the hope that he'd be too busy to read anything about it either in the paper or a magazine. I was right; he didn't. As I thought about that, I wondered what his reaction would have been if he'd become aware of it. After all, were it not for that school bus deal, our financial problems would still exist. I just hoped nobody at Challenger would pick up on it.

But Dallis obviously knew something was wrong with me. It took the better part of two weeks before I wanted to speak to him or anybody, or even leave the house. Your daddy was concerned in the usual futile male way. I just told him I was having a particularly bad time of the month.

Angel, I know the Bible says we're not supposed to hate people. Of course, it also says we're not supposed to commit adultery! But the moment I read that magazine, I began to hate Roberto with every bone in my body. You just can't imagine what it feels like to have been duped and violated like that. Perhaps the worst thing was the knowledge that I would never get a chance for any kind of vengeance for this heinous act of his.

But it turned out that was not quite correct.

Chapter Forty-Two

Hallie

Hallie drove from The Meadows experiencing a range of emotions. When she thought of her sweet mother agonizing about her treatment at the hands of Roberto, she felt her heart break. At the same time, she loved the poignancy of it and couldn't wait to get in front of her laptop and write it into the book. So, absent her mother's hurt, and Ian Lightbourne's, the roll she was on seemed to be continuing—her engagement, setting Rich up with Albert Adams, the book. Only her finances continued to be a struggle, but that was about to change in a big way. Rich had told her that if either his original New York group or Albert Adams's friend with the hedge fund invested the fifty million, he would be thinking really big for the wedding and honeymoon. Perhaps Provence. But if one of those didn't come through, maybe something more modest in Tampa followed by taking the jet to someplace like Nevis or St. Barts. So at the moment, setting the date was being driven by Rich's business dynamics. But that was okay.

Yes, almost everything was okay—wonderful, in fact—as she drove from the nursing home to downtown Tampa and the advertising agency. She plugged her cell phone into the dash and went to music. She selected the Diana Krall tune "Peel Me A Grape," and sang along with it until she got downtown.

When she walked in Grace Lamont's office and sat down across from her desk, everything suddenly became anything *but* wonderful. The normally happy-go-lucky Grace wore a troubled expression. She stopped Hallie when Hallie tried to bring up a copywriting assignment she was working on.

"Let's talk about that later. Right now I want to ask you about something I've been very hesitant to bring up with you."

Hallie was caught off guard. "Please. Bring up anything. I thought you liked what I was doing on the—"

"It has nothing to do with your work."

"Well then—"

"The reason I've been so hesitant is that it involves the man who is now your fiancé."

Hallie's neurons and synapses instantly changed to alert status and she felt her pulse quicken. She didn't say anything; just spread her hands in a gesture that begged Grace to continue.

"Have your checks from Rich's settlement deals been late?"

"No, not at all. Right on time, as usual."

Grace's cell phone was sitting in front of her and it rang. She turned it off. "Well good for you. My check was a week late last month. I didn't think anything about it. Just administrative, I figured. But Hallie, I'm still waiting on this month's. It's ten days later than normal."

Hallie cupped her hand over her mouth and said, "Oh, my God." And began to softly weep.

Grace Lamont leaned forward in her desk chair. "What do you know that I don't?"

Hallie grabbed a tissue from the box on Grace's desk and dabbed her eyes. She was struck with a momentary flash of gratitude that her boss was a woman and therefore had the tissues available. "Nothing, Grace. I know nothing. I wish I didn't know what you just told me. Have you called Rich's office?"

"I thought about it but figured I'd see what you knew first."

"Do you know of anybody else whose checks have been late?"

"Yes, two others."

Hallie snuffled and daintily blew her nose. "Well, what did they say?"

"They know about my relationship with you. They're waiting to see what you say today."

Hallie began shaking her head back and forth in disbelief. Gaining some control, she said, "Look, why don't you do this: Pick up the phone and call a man named Thomas Herring. He's Rich's financial person. He's always been very nice and accommodating. Call him right now and ask him what's going on; I bet he'll know."

Grace reached for her phone and, to Hallie's surprise, got Herring on the phone. Grace put it on speaker.

"Thank you for calling, Ms. Lamont," Herring said over the phone. "We're sending out a letter explaining the *horrendous* computer problems we've been having that are causing some of our checks to be issued a little late."

"Mr. Herring, my check for this month isn't a little late, it's missing in action. When will I get it?"

"I am *so* sorry about that. We should have these problems resolved today and get your check out this afternoon. Once again, please accept our apologies."

Grace looked at Hallie and put her index finger to her lips for the "shhh" sign before saying, "Well, if you're having computer problems, why have some people received their checks and I haven't?"

"Uh . . . yes, I was aware of that. Our IT guys say it's some alphabetic anomaly that . . . well, I wish I understood it better. Once again, I'm so sorry, but I'm a financial guy, not a techie. I'll call you personally, say, day after tomorrow and follow up to make sure you received your check."

"Thank you, Mr. Herring. Good bye."

Grace and Hallie just looked at each other in silence for a long time. "Well, what do you make of that?" Hallie asked.

Grace rose and came around her desk to sit closer to Hallie in the adjacent desk chair. She was perched on the edge of the side chair and took Hallie's hands. "Listen, honey. You're more friend than employee. I have to tell you, I think that was the biggest bunch of crap I've ever heard in my life. Something is very wrong. I have a fair amount of money invested but thankfully I can afford to lose all of it. What worries me is that I don't think you can afford to lose *any* of it. And, of course, your stakes are much higher than just financial. You need to talk to Rich and sort this out."

A shaken Hallie left Grace's office and almost staggered to her tiny one. She called Rich's office and got his assistant, Karen.

"He's in the Orlando office all day today," she said. "In fact, I was just about to call you because he wanted me to tell you he may have to spend the night and have dinner with an investment prospect."

Hallie asked to be transferred to Thomas Herring. "Thomas, I was listening in when Grace Lamont called you." She fiercely fought to keep her composure but felt her voice rise anyway. "Thomas, what in the *hell* is going on? Why am I getting my checks and other people aren't?"

There was a long silence.

"Thomas?"

"Hallie, I don't know what to say."

"Thomas."

"Yes, Hallie."

"Thomas . . . there . . . there *are* no computer problems, are there?" She was on the brink of complete hysteria.

More silence before Herring said solemnly, "You'd better talk to Rich, Hallie."

Chapter Forty-Three

Dimple

Hallie looks totally different today, not radiant, more like ashen. When I ask her, she blames a pounding headache and gets out the recorder. I apologize for getting a little teary talking about that bastard Roberto yesterday and tell her I'm so glad she won't have a situation like that with Rich. The comment seems to make her look even more uncomfortable and she rather quickly turns on the recorder—my signal to start talking. So I do.

Well, after the revolution, my life in Miami with your daddy became sort of routine. I was still a housewife and your daddy kept selling buses and hearses in his Florida territory and doing better and better. And we had a little financial cushion from the big Cuba commission check. I was playing bridge, a little golf, and doing some volunteer work at Jackson Memorial Hospital. And we were trying to make a baby. Yes, Angel, during this time we tried to have you but couldn't seem to connect. That happened later, thank goodness.

But we continued to soak up any and all news from Cuba like a sponge. And, boy howdy, was there a lot of it; Castro didn't waste any time after he came into power. Pre-revolution, he bemoaned Batista's murder of thousands of Cuban citizens, mostly either anti-Batista activists or revolution sympathizers. But Castro turned around and did the same thing. His firing squads executed *throngs* of those who had clearly sided with Batista, and others got very long prison sentences. He even set up a militia—committees of informants to spy on fellow Cubans and report "suspicious" activity.

Fidel went to the U. S. and, in a speech, claimed he wasn't a communist. But everything he did said otherwise. He seized all kinds of private property—farms and industry—and nationalized all church property while declaring Cuba officially atheist. Free enterprise became a thing of the past and Cuba went from being the third-most prosperous nation in the hemisphere, behind the U. S. and Canada, to people not having enough food to eat, a dead economy, and crumbling buildings. Even with the restrictions on leaving the country, a half million Cubans defected to the United States between 1959 and 1980. A fourth of those were in 1980 when the Cuban government let pretty much anybody leave.

Cuba's relationship with the United States continued to deteriorate. The now-famous embargo happened in October 1960 and, in January 1961, the United States severed diplomatic relations with Cuba and the embassy closed. There were stories about the CIA planning to assassinate Castro and there was talk about some kind of invasion.

Well, Angel, that's when things got interesting for me.

One morning in January 1961, after I had just gotten home from volunteering at the hospital, the phone rang. A male voice said, "Well, Dimple, are you still hitting them long and straight?"

The voice sounded familiar but I couldn't quite place it, and I was really undone that someone whose voice I didn't immediately recognize knew my nickname. "Who is this, please?" I said.

The man on the other end laughed. "Forgotten your old golf partner already, eh? This is Hawk."

I let out a tiny squeal of delight before saying, "Hawk, you're a bird. Where are you calling from? Cuba?"

I was in social butterfly mode, ready to chat and catch up with our friend because Dallis and I had really enjoyed his company in Cuba. But his voice got suddenly flat and businesslike. "Dorothy, I'm in Miami and I need to see you. I need to talk to you about something and I don't want Dallis to know you're meeting me."

I didn't know what to make of that because Hawk had never seemed to be the masher type.

"Don't worry," he said. "I'm not trying to make a pass at you, I just need to talk. I need a favor and I can't go into it over the phone. Can you drive over to Miami Beach and meet me at Wolfie's for a spot of lunch? Say, in an hour?"

I couldn't imagine what he wanted. The first thing that came to mind was that he was in some kind of financial trouble. Maybe he figured we made a bundle on the bus deal and wanted to borrow some money. But why didn't he want Dallis to know? My curiosity consumed me on the drive over the Venetian Causeway to Miami Beach.

Wolfie's was a Miami Beach institution, a huge deli-style restaurant right on A1A, popular with tourists and locals alike. Hawk was wearing a business suit and waiting for me in a booth in the back of the place. He quickly rose and greeted me with a hug. I hadn't really gussied up for him or anything but he still gushed about how nice I looked. He was a truly charming and aristocratic gentleman New Englander.

We ordered lunch, then launched into some Cuba catch up. We chatted about golf. He asked about Dallis and whether he got his money from the bus deal. That made me decide this might indeed be about Hawk borrowing money.

I was dead wrong.

"Dimple, may I ask you a serious question?"

"Of course."

He seemed to study me carefully for a long moment before he continued. "Are you a patriot?"

I couldn't *imagine* what he was talking about and said so.

"I'm asking you if you love our country. America. The good old U. S. of A."

"Hawk, what kind of question is that? Of course I do. Don't you?"

"Yes I do, Dorothy. And that's why I've asked to see you today. To ask you to consider doing a little something for your country."

I was totally flummoxed with no clue what this was about. I said, "I think Dallis bought some U. S. savings bonds with some of the bus commission money. Is that the sort of thing you mean?"

Hawk's thin, aristocratic lips began to curl in amusement. "That's the Dimple we know and love," he said. "Innocent, vulnerable, and charming to the core."

I was getting a little irritated. "Hawk, what's this all about, anyway?"

"Let me tell you something you may not be aware of. Roberto has become Castro's chief legal advisor and is his co-chief of staff, along with Celia Sanchez."

I let out a small, ladylike gasp as I put my cupped hand to my mouth. "Why am I not surprised?" I said.

"Okay, the fact that you're not surprised tells me you're aware of what really happened with the buses."

I felt my face contort with disgust and a little fury thrown in. "The ammunition smuggling."

"Right. I think I see the answer already on your face but I must ask you: how do you feel about that?" About the way Roberto handled it?"

"Oh, I feel just *wonderful* about it. Why?" My tone was the most sarcastic one I could muster.

"I'm being a little too coy with you and I apologize. I need to tell you that I know all about your affair with Roberto. I know about your trip to Santiago with him, about your visit with Castro in the Sierra Maestra. All your other times with him. Everything."

I felt my eyes grow saucer-like as my hands went back to my mouth. "My God in heaven," I said. "How . . . What did . . . Who *are* you?"

"E. Hawkins McHenry III, at your service, ma'am."

"Come on, Hawk; how the hell did you know all that?" I was incensed.

His matzo ball soup had come and he paused to take a sip with his soup spoon. "Because knowing things like that is my business. My job."

He continued with his soup but I had zero interest in the pastrami sandwich in front of me. "But you're a diplomat; you work for—what—the State Department, right?"

Another spoonful of matzo ball. "I work *at* the embassy. But I don't work for State."

It was slowly sinking in. "You mean you're a . . . ?"

"Yes, Dimple, I am. But you must keep that fact strictly confidential. May I count on you for that?"

My head was spinning. "Why yes, of course."

He was really diving into his soup now, and began talking more rapidly. "Let me be a little more specific about why I came. Very simply it's this: We—your country—need for you to go undercover in Cuba and get certain information. This means re-establishing contact with Roberto."

I sat and looked at him with my jaw hanging down to my bosoms. My mouth was that wide open in astonishment. I didn't have the foggiest idea what to say and couldn't have gotten a word out if I had.

He leaned forward and lowered his voice to a whisper. "I have no choice but to tell you something that is one hundred percent classified. Repeating it to anyone would be a treasonous act on your part. Do you understand?"

I nodded, still in a catatonic state.

"The United States is planning to invade Cuba and depose Castro. It's technically and officially not the U.S. that will be doing it; it will be Cuba's counter-revolutionary movement. However, we're planning it, supplying most of the military assets, and controlling it. The Joint Chiefs are considering two possible landing locations: the Trinidad area or the Bay of Pigs. They're torn between the two as there are military and political advantages and disadvantages to both. The decision will rest upon intelligence we can gather about where Castro thinks we're coming. If we can acquire that intelligence, the

Joint Chiefs will choose their landing site accordingly and we should have a big advantage. Do you understand?"

I nodded, my hands on my cheeks in shock, wonderment, apoplexy, and several other feelings I can't remember right now.

"So, Dimple. Will you help us? Will you serve your country in this special way?"

My heart was pounding. This was the most upsetting thing that had happened to me since learning the truth about Roberto. The inside of Wolfie's seemed to be spinning. I felt light-headed. I couldn't talk.

"Dimple?" he said.

I think I was hyperventilating. I tried some deep breathing to calm myself where I could speak. "Hawk, this is ridiculous. I'm no *spy*, for goodness sake. What do you want me to do, call up Roberto in Cuba and ask him which of those places Castro thinks this invasion thing will happen? He'd hang up on me."

"Dorothy, perhaps I didn't make myself clear. We need for you to *go* to Cuba, revive your romance with Roberto, hang around him and Castro as much as you can, and listen, listen, listen."

"Oh my God," I said, my head back in my hands. "Hawk, why are you doing this to me? I can't do *any* of that."

"And why not, my dear Dimple?"

"I just . . . I just can't. If I saw Roberto again, I'd want to *kill* him—literally—not revive any . . . *romance*. Ugh!"

I saw Hawk's lips curl again, this time in more of a smirk. "Killing him would be fine; just make sure you get the intelligence first."

"Oh, Hawk!"

"I actually wasn't joking, but that's another matter. Now look. There are some technical details to work out. One is that you'll need a plausible story for Roberto, and I have one for you. Are you ready?"

I waved my hand at him in a half-hearted gesture to continue.

"You'll contact Roberto and tell him you and Dallis have separated. That Dallis is a traveling man, has always liked the skirts."

"That much is true but I'm not sure what he's ever done about it," I said.

"Tell Roberto you caught Dallis; you're furious about it, and the two of you have separated for a few months to try to figure the whole thing out. That you have conflicted feelings because you know you had your own affair. That you want to come down to Cuba for a month or so and try to find yourself again. Besides, you miss him."

"Yuck!" I said. "The only thing I miss is seeing him shot like the dog he is."

"The whole thing is contingent on him believing you're not aware that he smuggled the ammo in the buses. We think there's a better-than-even chance that will fly because, other than the *Granma*, the in-depth piece in *Time* is the only place we know of that ran the story."

"The *Granma?*"

"The Cuban state newspaper. Named after the broken-down yacht Castro and his rebels used to re-enter the country after his exile in Mexico."

I didn't say anything; I just sat there in agony, fully believing that I was getting the brunt of God's wrath for breaking His commandments forbidding adultery and bearing false witness. I knew I fully deserved all of it.

"Well, what do you think so far?" Hawk asked.

"I think I've always liked you but right now I wish I'd never heard of you."

He smiled. "I understand, but—"

"Hawk, it's not going to work anyway."

"Why?"

"Because I'm not fluent enough in Spanish. Roberto and that criminal Castro could talk about all this stuff in Spanish and I wouldn't have a clue."

"We've already thought of that and taken the liberty of enrolling you in the next Berlitz class. We know you're approaching the level of fluency you'll need to pick up the proper key words, and taking the class will assure it."

"Look, Hawk, I just can't—"

"Stop!" Hawk said, holding both hands up in the air. "Don't give me an answer now. All I ask is that you think about it a day or two."

I was still ignoring my pastrami sandwich but I put a potato chip in my mouth and ate it. When I'd swallowed it, I said, "Hawk, do you realize what you're asking? You're asking me to blow up my happy marriage. Because the only way I can go to Cuba for a month is to tell Dallis why I'm going and that means telling him about my affair with Roberto." I felt my eyes fill with tears.

He looked at me solemnly with what appeared to be bona fide empathy. "I know that. It's why I started by asking if you're a patriot. It would be a genuine sacrifice for your country. As I said, please just think about it. In the meantime, let me ask you about something else. I believe Dallis is in town, isn't he?"

"Yes," I said in a small voice as I looked down at my lap.

"I hope you both might be available for golf tomorrow. At Indian Creek."

I looked up. "Indian Creek?" I said. "Are you serious?"

I'd never been to Indian Creek and assumed I never would; it's perhaps the most exclusive private club in Miami.

"Yes. Our foursome will be you, me, Dallis, and your very own United States senator."

"Smathers? George Smathers?"

"We have a one p.m. tee time. I'll pick you and Dallis up."

Chapter Forty-Four

Dallis was *thrilled* when he found out Hawk was in town but when I told him we were going to play golf at Indian Creek with a sitting United States senator, I thought he was going to bust a gusset.

"What's Hawk doing in Miami?" he asked. "Castro run him off the island?"

"Some kind of government business, I think."

"I wish we were better golfers," Dallis said.

"Me too, but Indian Creek is Indian Creek."

And it was. The place is a true enclave, an island in Biscayne Bay surrounded by water and only accessible via a bridge guarded by a windowless, bunker-like structure that rivals anything on any military base. Hawk picked us up and, when we arrived at the gate's squawk box, a stern, flat-toned voice said simply, "Good afternoon."

"Mr. McHenry here to play golf with Senator Smathers," Hawk said.

No reply, the gate just opened and we drove through, crossed the bridge, and entered a world of which we were not familiar. Angel, every one of the thirty or so homes was a *mansion* and owned by a millionaire. At least that's what they were back then; now I think they're all *billionaires*. The houses are all on the bay ringing the island but a few of the golf holes are on the water, too. And the clubhouse? My stars, it was the most fabulous, majestic thing I've ever seen.

We pulled up to the porte cochère, where we were met by a small army of attendants who somehow knew who we were. "You're playing with Senator Smathers, right?" They were as nice as they could be and took care of our golf clubs and even parked Hawk's car.

I was as nervous as a prostitute in church and I could tell Dallis was, too. Both the place and our host were imposing and we really were not good golfers. But we were delighted to be there and told Hawk so.

"So how do you know Smathers?" Dallis asked.

"I don't," Hawk said.

"Then . . . how are we . . . ?"

"My boss owed me a favor and I happen to like you two."

We were walking through the Club from the entrance to the golf pro shop and, at Hawk's remark, Dallis stopped, mid-stride, and with a big grin extended his hand to Hawk. As they shook, Dallis said, "You're a gentleman and a scholar." And after a pause added, "Come to think of it, that's actually true." And laughed.

Hawk laughed too and, cryptically for Dallis but not so for me, said, "You don't know everything about me."

George Smathers was one of those bigger-than-life characters you occasionally meet. *Very* handsome, tall, and loaded with charm. He had an excellent physique; I later learned he played some kind of sport in college, maybe basketball.

"Senator Smathers, it's an honor just to meet you, and to play golf here with you is just *wonderful*."

"You're Dorothy, right?" he said.

"Yes, sir," I said.

"Well, if we're going to play golf together, I'm George. Okay?" He said it wearing a huge, engaging grin.

I was embarrassed but made myself say, "Okay, George it is."

"Well, shall we hit a few practice balls?" he said.

We did that, but it did little good because when we got to the first tee, I was so nervous I actually whiffed my first attempt at my drive. I was *so* embarrassed. It got a little better, but not much. Smathers was a pretty good golfer so the afternoon must have been agony for him. But we got through it and, at the end of the round, ended up in the bar for a drink. Female that I am, I picked up on some rather strange non-verbal communication that seemed to be going on between Smathers and Hawk, but as I nuzzled my second bourbon and soda, I dismissed it.

Then it happened.

Dallis excused himself to go to the men's room. I hadn't really freshened up after golf, so I said I'd like to visit the ladies' room. Hawk and Smathers both politely rose—gentlemen still did that back then—and Smathers said, "Just follow me, Dorothy; the ladies' locker room is a little tricky to find from here."

So, Angel, here I was, Dimple Duncan from Smithtown, Georgia, getting escorted to the potty to tinkle by a sitting United States senator. As I said, I was on my second drink and I almost burst out laughing at the near absurdity of it. When we got to the ladies' locker room, I was surprised to see three people just standing outside the door. Two were a couple of white-coated staff, perhaps attendants, and the third was a man who had on some kind of security uniform. "Good afternoon, Senator," they all said, almost in unison.

What was more surprising was that when I entered the ladies' locker room, there was not a solitary soul there, not even an attendant. I walked through the quiet of the large locker and card room area to the restrooms. After using the facilities and working on my hair, lipstick, and makeup, I emerged to the shock of my life. There, in the middle of the Indian Creek ladies' locker room, sitting at a card table smoking a cigarette, was United States Senator George A. Smathers. I'd just gone to the bathroom, but I swear I almost wet my pants.

"Senator," I said. "I mean, George."

He quickly rose and pulled out a chair for me at the card table. "Dorothy, please sit down," he said, and ground out his cigarette in an ash tray.

I rotated my head, looking all around. "But—"

"I assure you, no one will be coming in this locker room until you and I leave it."

"But how—"

"Not only am I a United States senator, but I'm also the current president of this club."

"Oh," I said in a small voice.

"Now, we don't have much time, because Dallis might get suspicious. So listen carefully, please."

It was clear this had nothing to do with anything naughty; his voice was serious and businesslike.

"I'd like to talk to you about the request Hawk made of you yesterday. President-elect Kennedy and I have worked closely in the Senate over the years and he is a very good personal friend of mine as well. He and I share an urgent concern about the spread of communism in our hemisphere, specifically in Cuba. Frankly, our country let this Castro thing get away from us with a lot of indecision and mismanagement. Now, as a result, we are exposed to the very grave danger of Soviet missiles being brought into Cuba and aimed at our shores just ninety miles away. The time has come for action and I believe Hawk has shared some classified information with you about the invasion."

"Yes sir."

He leaned forward, took my hands in his, and gave me one of the most earnest looks anyone has given me in my life. "Dorothy, your country needs you to take on this mission. President-elect Kennedy is aware that you and I are having this little meeting and he asked me to convey his personal request for your help. As you know, he'll be inaugurated tomorrow in Washington. I'm flying up as soon as I leave here. He told me to tell you that he'd appreciate it if you would watch his inauguration speech on television tomorrow and listen for a particular phrase. The phrase I'm talking about was in his speech anyway but he believes it particularly applies to the request he and I are making for your service. Will you be able to watch?"

I gulped and nodded.

"Dorothy, I'm not asking for an answer to our request right now, I'm just asking if you'll promise to give this prayerful consideration. Will you?"

I was struggling with my composure. I choked out, "Yes sir, I will."

The drive back to Miami from Surfside where Indian Creek is located is not a short one. I spent most of it staring out the window with my chin resting on my thumb and forefinger.

"Honey, you all right?" Dallis asked.

I fell back on the standard female answer. "Just a headache."

"Too bad," said Hawk, brightly. "I'd be up for treating for dinner. Figure out some way to charge it to the taxpayers."

Dallis laughed. I didn't answer; I just shook my head.

When we arrived at our house, Dallis profusely thanked Hawk again. I didn't say anything until Dallis was in the garage stowing our golf clubs and out of earshot.

"I've always heard there was no such thing as a free lunch," I said to Hawk, deadpan. "But I hadn't realized there was no such thing as a free golf game."

"I'm sorry I had to trick you," Hawk said. "But for secrecy and security, the senator felt it was the best way." He took my shoulders and kissed me lightly on the cheek. "May I call you tomorrow afternoon and get your answer?

I nodded and turned and went in the house.

Chapter Forty-Five

Of course I didn't sleep a wink. Realizing the futility, I finally went ahead and rose for the next day a couple of hours earlier than usual. Thankfully, Dallis was going up to West Palm Beach that day—Friday, January 20, 1961—on business. He had two excellent funeral home prospects he was calling on. The thought of hearses made me wish I could be *in* one instead of having to make my decision about what I was being asked to do. It was easily the worst day of my life.

I had a bridge game with some other girls but I canceled, pleading "tummy problems." I scoured the *Miami Herald* for any additional news on Cuba but there was nothing. But there was plenty about the inauguration of the new, young president. In those days, we didn't have cable news; that came years later, compliments of Ted Turner when he started CNN.

At noon, the networks came on with the ceremony and Kennedy's speech. It felt so strange sitting there in Miami, with the temperature around eighty, watching live pictures of Washington with snow everywhere and everybody bundled up so about all you could see were their noses. But I had to hand it to that Kennedy because he stood out there with no hat on and gave his speech. I devoured every word of it, waiting for the phrase I was supposed to recognize. It came almost at the end and, of course you know what it was: "Ask not what your country can do for you; ask what you can do for your country." The moment I heard it, I lost it. I wasn't sure if it was because of how much it touched me or if it was because I knew then the answer I must give Hawk.

When I called and told him I'd do it, after I uttered the words there was silence on the other end of the line. "Hawk?" I finally said.

"Yeah, I'm here," he said, in a tone I'd not heard before.

Angel, I actually think Mr. CIA officer got emotional for a moment. There was another brief pause during which I believe he gathered himself because his voice came again in its usual strong New England timbre. "Dorothy, you're a true patriot and I appreciate your service more than words can say."

"Thank you, Hawk. I'll try my best, but I can't guarantee any results."

"I know. And I know you *will* do your best. It's all I ask, my good lady." He cleared his throat. "Now we have to get down to business," he said, as he asked me to get a paper and pencil and take down information about the Berlitz class. He suggested I also spend a lot of time hanging around cafés in Little Havana and listening to Cuban-styled Spanish.

"Hawk, if I'm going to have to get lovey-dovey again with that bastard Roberto you need to send me to acting classes as well," I said, not entirely kidding.

"You'll do fine," he said. "When we get closer and your Spanish gets better, we'll go over more details including how to contact Roberto. You know, this operation is all based on him agreeing to let you come down. I personally believe he'll jump all over it, but we'll see."

"Yes we will," I said, repeating the obvious.

"One last thing. When are you going to tell Dallis?"

I didn't know what I dreaded more: telling Dallis about all this or getting involved with that dirty rat Roberto again. "Tonight, I guess," I said.

"Good luck. Remember, if he truly loves you he'll understand this and support you. And I believe he truly loves you."

I sighed. "I hope so."

"And let me tell you something else. I also believe Roberto loves you."

"What?" My tone was one of stark incredulity.

"Yep. I do. Dorothy, I know the guy pretty well. He's a patriot just like you except he's on the wrong side. The side of communism. He had to do what he had to do because his man Fidel had to have the ammo. But I truly believe his feelings for you were de-coupled from the mission he was executing. Plain and simple, he fell in love with you. I truly believe everything he told you about his feelings for you was true."

"Oh come on, Hawk; you're just saying that to try make it easier for me to get back in bed with him."

"Suit yourself. But I mean what I'm telling you, lady. I believe it. Good luck; I'll be in touch soon."

When Dallis got home, he gave me a little kiss on the forehead and then went directly to our little bar to fix a drink for us both. I asked him to postpone having a drink because I had something to talk to him about. He was holding the bourbon bottle in his hand in mid-air.

"What are you talking about? Friday night, been working all week; time for a pop."

"Dallis, please. I have something very serious to talk to you about. It's too important to have alcohol involved." Huntley and Brinkley were reporting the inauguration news on the television but I turned the set off.

He put the bottle down. "Okay. Let's have it." And he sat in his easy chair.

I decided to begin with the positive aspects and save the sordid ones for later.

"There was a reason Hawk came to Miami. It was to see us. And there's a reason we were invited to play golf at that fancy club with a senator."

Your daddy wore the most puzzled expression I've ever seen on his face. He spread his hands in a questioning gesture.

"Hawk never worked for the embassy or the State Department; he just worked *at* the embassy. Dallis, he's a spy."

"What?"

"Hawk works for the CIA."

"You're kidding. Wow, I can't believe I actually know a CIA agent."

"Most people call them agents but they're actually officers."

"Whatever, but what did he . . . ?"

"Roberto is in cahoots with Castro. Always was." I told him about the buses being used to smuggle the ammunition.

"That son of a bitch."

"Dallis, hold on. If he hadn't needed those buses to smuggle the bullets, we wouldn't have gotten that order and the commission that went with it."

"Hmmm, I guess you're right."

I then told him about Roberto's current position in Castro's government. I told him about the concern of the U.S. government over having a communist country and possibly Soviet missiles ninety miles from our shores. I told him about the planned invasion and the need to know where Cuba's defenses would be concentrated. I told him about Senator Smathers locking down the ladies' locker room so he could plead with me to go to Cuba on the mission. I finished with explaining how Jack Kennedy, now the leader of the free world, had personally sent a message through Smathers hoping I would go to Cuba and help them.

Dallis's next question was inevitable and he stated it with a look of profound puzzlement. "But how would you find out where Castro is expecting the invasion to come?"

"Through Roberto. By reconnecting with him down there." For a fleeting moment I wondered if it would somehow be possible to simply finesse the fact that I'd had the affair. The next question scotched that.

"But why would Roberto give you the time of day? I mean, the bus deal is over and . . ." He stopped mid-sentence and we just looked at each other. For a long time. I felt the tears start to come. "You . . . you mean you and Roberto?" he said. The tears were streaking my cheeks now. I couldn't talk; I just nodded as I experienced a feeling of doom that was crushingly oppressive to the point of inducing nausea.

I had to wait him out. He sat and stared at nothing for a few minutes, trying to process it. Then he went to the bar and poured about three fingers of bourbon in a glass without his customary ice and bolted it down in one swallow. Then he went into the kitchen. I heard a loud noise that startled and frightened me. (Later I saw the dent in the refrigerator door.) A few minutes later, he came out holding ice on his right hand.

"So. You going to tell me any details?"

"I really don't want to." I was softly crying again. "I'm so ashamed, and so sorry. It just happened; I was swept off my feet by him, by the place we were in. But Dallis, listen to me, please. I love you with all my heart and I always will."

"So you're not going down there to marry him and become a commie?"

"I've agreed to go down there and try to *fight* communism and try to trick Roberto like he tricked us."

"You don't love him?"

I couldn't lie to him anymore. "I fell a tiny bit in love with him, I suppose. Dallis, it's the only way I would have had an affair with him. I'm not the type of woman who falls in lust, just in love. If I hadn't fallen a little bit in love with him, nothing would have ever happened between us. I'm not sure men can understand that, but it's the way it is. Roberto told me I should keep loving you and stay devoted to you. He told me many times how much he likes and respects you."

"Hmmph. But not enough to keep from screwing my wife."

"Dallis, I would never have hurt you by telling you what happened with Roberto. He would have been out of our lives. But I'm risking the most precious thing I have—my marriage to you—to serve my country after being asked to do so by a senator and, indirectly, the president. I didn't feel like I could turn them down. I can just pray with all my heart that you'll understand and support me."

He stood again and went to the bar, repeating his shot of bourbon with no ice. Then he turned and stood at our little bar and looked at me. "Does this mean you'll have to go down there and start doing it with him again?" The pain on his face made me die inside.

"I'll do everything to avoid it, but I may not be able to and still get the information the CIA needs."

Then I explained my partial Spanish fluency he'd really not been aware of and the Berlitz course supplemented by time in Little Havana. He left the bar and sat in the chair again. He sat on the edge of it with his hands clasped, looking at the floor.

"Well, I'm in a bit of a spot here," he said. "For one thing, I can't very well tell you not to do what you can to keep our country safe from those commie missiles." He looked up at me. "The other thing is, I'm not in the best position to judge you for what you've done."

"You mean . . . ?"

He nodded as his face contorted, trying to hold back his own tears. "Those four walls of the hotel room get lonely at night, traveling all of Florida. None of it has meant anything. I didn't care about any of them. I couldn't tell you the name of even one of them. Just what you'd call . . . recreational sex, I guess. They'd ask if I was married and my answer was always the same: Yes, I'm married and I love my wife very much. But it seemed like that made them want to get in bed with me even more." The tears were on his cheeks now and he wiped them with the back of his hands. After he recovered somewhat, he looked up at me with a wan smile. "Guess it's true confessions night, huh?"

Angel, I was hardly surprised. Your daddy has stared at every wiggling bottom and every pair of bouncing bosoms he's ever seen, regardless of whether I was around or not. I went to him and climbed in the chair with him. He said, "Honey, I love you so much." He was crying hard now.

I held his face in my hands, looked at it through my tears, and replied, "I will always love you, Dallis Duncan."

"Hey," he said. "What do you say you go down there and beat the commies, save our country, and then let's be totally true to each other?"

I was sobbing now. All I could do was nod and then hug him.

Chapter Forty-Six

Hallie

Albert Adams was back in New York when Gerry Higgins called from the Tampa FBI office.

"We've gotten some good communication from CPAs who've been hustling the investment. A few of them took kickbacks, but that's another story. Apparently Rodino's starting to suck air because about half his payments are late. He's in Orlando now, begging some guy to fork over $2 million but the prospect is slow-walking him. We believe it's time to push Rodino over the brink and bring this thing to a head. We'd like you to call him—leave a message if you have to—and tell him your hedge fund guy whiffed. You should say that, despite the bank letter, your guy ultimately didn't like the redactions, and that has you spooked again, too. But thanks for showing us the deal again and you'd love to go fishing anytime, and so forth and so on. What do you say, Mr. Adams?"

"I say I'll make the call right now. I suspect that taking this step will shut down his fundraising, but we can only hope it will shut down his spending as well. Do you think he's a flight risk?"

"Absolutely we do, which is why we're watching his every move in Orlando. Our problem is stopping him if he tries to run because our file's not complete enough to get an arrest warrant at the moment.

When his payments totally stop, our hope is to confront him and get a confession."

When Hallie left The Meadows, she tried Rodino's cell phone again and it went directly to voice mail.

Next she called his assistant, Karen, who said, "Yes, I heard from him. He's still in Orlando and may have to spend another night there. He said that if you called, to tell you he'll call you tonight."

Next she called Grace Lamont. "Did you get your check?"

"Not yet, Hallie."

"How about your friends?"

"How did you know I checked with them? No, nothing."

"Well, did Thomas Herring call you?"

"Not a peep out of him."

Hallie felt like she'd fallen in a sinkhole and the earth was tumbling in on top of her. She didn't know what to say to Grace.

"Hallie, do you want to come in and talk about it?"

"Well, I have to come in anyway to finish up on that piece for the university, but Grace I . . . I don't know what I would talk about."

"Oh, honey, I'm so sorry—"

"I'm sorry for *you*," Hallie said.

"Yes, but remember, I can survive it. Have you talked to Rich?"

"No. He's in Orlando. Supposedly getting a check from a new investor. Maybe that will help him pay . . ." She stopped as the most horrible thought came to her. "Oh my God," she said.

"Hallie, is it possible the whole thing might be some kind of Ponzi scheme?"

Hallie's composure was teetering on the edge. "Grace, I've got to go. I'll call you later."

She was still upset when she got Thomas Herring on the phone. "Thomas, my boss, Grace Lamont, still doesn't have her check and she says you didn't call her like you said you would."

"Oh gosh, Hallie, I let that get away from me. I'm sorry, it's just that I've been so busy with these computer problems—"

"Thomas, that's crap! There are no computer problems, are there?"

"Hallie . . ."

She was near hysteria now. "Thomas, do you realize the money I have in this so-called investment is all the money I have in the world? Do you know that, Thomas?" She was yelling.

"Hallie, please calm down. I'm sure Rich would never let you lose that money, and anyway, when y'all get married, you'll have half of his wealth. So I wouldn't worry."

"What happened with the New York people Albert Adams brought in?"

There was a pause. "I'm not sure; why don't you ask Rich?"

"Because I can't *find* Rich, damn it."

"I wish I could be more helpful, Hallie."

"I do too. Goodbye, Thomas."

Chapter Forty-Seven

Dimple

I'm in my wheelchair in the solarium when Hallie comes. She looks terrible. She's obviously upset about something but is somehow still driven and focused. She seems almost abrupt as she wants to get right into recording, wanting to know if, back in Miami, I'm fluent in Spanish yet.

Angel, I don't know how those Berlitz people do it, but golly Pete does it work. Actually, I'm not sure hanging out in Little Havana for hours each day wasn't just as helpful. And, by the way, there was a lot of buzz in Little Havana about the possible invasion of Cuba. To answer your question, yes, I became pretty fluent in a very short time. Meanwhile, the invasion was getting closer and it was time to contact Roberto.

Angel, if I'd ever wavered about going through with things after I said I would—and I frankly suppose I *had* wavered—I was buoyed by something I received in the mail. It was a handwritten note on the most elegant executive stationery. Printed at the top was "The White House, Washington D.C." It very simply said: "Dear Mrs. Duncan, I want you know how much I appreciate your patriotism. Good luck and Godspeed, John F. Kennedy." I have a similar one from George Smathers. You'll find them in my things when I'm gone.

Hawk said Roberto had kept his law office open with just a part-time secretary. It took me two days of trying before I got somebody. I asked his secretary—speaking English, of course—to ask Roberto to call me. Hawk told me to instruct Dallis to never, ever answer the phone as we were supposed to be separated. The story would be that I caught Dallis cheating on me and sent him to a motel while we sort things out, and that my coming to Cuba would help my own sorting-out process. None of us were sure Roberto would call me back. A week after I placed the call to his law office, he did. The whole gambit hinged on whether Roberto still had a romantic interest in me and whether he believed I was unaware of the ammunition smuggling.

"Hello, my darling," he said when I answered.

Angel, I swear to goodness, I wanted to just throw up right on our cheap rug.

"I was very happy to get your message," he said. "I have been thinking about you constantly but I have been very busy."

"Well, I wondered about that," I said. "Because I had trouble getting anyone to answer at your office. What are you so busy doing these days? Did Fidel give you a lot of legal work after he took control?"

He laughed. "Haven't you heard?"

"Heard what?"

"I am now on Fidel's staff. His legal advisor and co-chief of staff with Celia. You remember her from the mountains."

"Yes, I do. She lit one cigarette with another."

He laughed again. "She still does. It worries me, but . . . So you did not know about this?"

"Roberto, the only thing I know is that Castro won the revolution and that he's apparently a communist."

The moment of truth had arrived; I knew he was too smart not to test me.

"Yes, thankfully, we did win the revolution. Fidel finally got the ammunition he needed. Remember, I told you that was his biggest problem?"

"Sure, I remember. We sat on the empty boxes. How did he finally get it?"

This was *really* the moment of truth. He paused a moment, obviously weighing his answer. "Fortunately, the Soviets smuggled it in."

"The Soviets," I repeated. On the one hand, I was monumentally relieved, but on the other I was disappointed. Because if he had discovered I knew he'd deceived me, I wouldn't have to go to Cuba. "Speaking of the Soviets," I said, "It seems like a lot of people in the U. S. are talking about a communist Cuba these days. And they don't seem very happy about it."

"How about you? How do you feel about it?"

This was going well because his question again confirmed he didn't know I knew about his despicable act of manipulating Dallis and me to get his ammunition to Castro.

"That's a good question," I said. "I don't know much about politics, I just don't want the Russians to nuke us. Do you think they will?"

He laughed. "I do not think so."

The conversation lulled into silence. My mind grappled for what to say next and I wondered if I should just wait for him.

"So tell me, my darling, to what do I owe the pleasure of this call?"

I remained silent for a long moment to add importance to my answer. "Roberto . . .," I feigned some emotion. "Dallis and I . . ." I paused.

"Yes?"

"Dallis and I have separated."

"I am sorry to hear that. I like Dallis. He is a fine man. A good businessman."

"But he's also a womanizer, Roberto. As you know, he travels all over the place selling buses and hearses and there are women in every city . . .," I feigned more emotion. "I just . . .," I let my voice trail off.

"So, did you tell him about us?"

"No. And I feel terribly guilty. After all, I'm no better than he is."

"Are you planning to get a divorce?"

"To tell you the truth, I don't know what I'm planning to do. I just need to sort all this out and maybe learn more about myself. You're not going to believe what I'm about to ask you. In fact, I don't believe it myself because it's a very tacky thing for a socially proper girl from South Georgia to do."

"Go ahead."

Well, I was just wondering . . . I was wondering if it might be possible for me to come back down to Cuba for a little while. Maybe just a few weeks. Just sort of hang out with you when you aren't real busy, just enjoy Cuba, and just talk to you and *think*. Do you think I'm terribly forward and brazen for even thinking such a thing?"

"Certainly not! It would be wonderful. You can stay at one of my apartments. I still have them. And if I am a lucky man, I may get to stay with you sometimes. You can even meet Fidel and Celia again and sit in a chair instead of on an ammunition box. My darling, this is excellent news. When can you come?"

My answer to Roberto was "The sooner, the better" and that's what happened. He told me to fly to Nassau and then book a flight to Havana; he would personally meet me at the airport and escort me. He said to use my passport to get to Nassau but that I wouldn't need it in Cuba and that it would not be stamped by Customs as he would just take me right around the Customs booth.

"How will you do that?" I asked.

He laughed. "I am Fidel's lawyer and co-chief of staff. I can do just about whatever I wish."

"Of course. I forgot."

I had a very teary goodbye with Dallis during which we repeat-edly re-affirmed our love and devotion for each other. A terrible part of the plan was that Dallis actually did have to move out of the house. Hawk insisted on it, explaining that Castro had spies all over Miami. So Dallis took up residence at the Flamingo Motel, a quintessential little 1950s-vintage place a mile up the Dixie Highway with a pleasant swimming pool.

When we had gotten Dallis's big commission check, I had finally bought some better dresses, shoes, and accessories. And I had the latest early-sixties do, kind of curled up at the bottom and with lots of hair spray. My commission check-funded wardrobe had been supplemented by some clothes I bought with government money Hawk had given me for that purpose. He also gave me the money for my plane tickets and a very generous additional amount for expenses. All cash, of course. And he bought me locks for my suitcases.

So off I went, "Dimple the Spy" on her secret mission. When I boarded the plane to Nassau and thought about it, I almost fell out. I spent most of the two flights thinking about how it was going to be with Roberto and how I was going to gird myself to even be nice to him, much less lovey-dovey. I tried to think about Hawk's comments about Roberto being a patriot, albeit a misguided one, and raising the possibility that he really *did* love me. But that didn't work for one minute. I found it impossible to swallow, and my torrid hate and revulsion for Roberto took over again. Despite the fact that my feelings kept bouncing from pillar to post like a weaving drunk person, I told myself that above all I had to remember one thing: that the president of the United States had personally asked me to do this and that I must not fail him.

When I arrived at the Havana airport, sure enough, Roberto was there waiting for me outside the Customs lines. Angel, I got the shock of my life. The handsomest man in the world looked like he was on his way to a costume party. And guess who he was going as? Fidel Castro! I mean, golly Ned, here was Roberto dressed in fatigues with his little conductor's hat and a full beard, albeit not quite of Fidel proportions. And he had some kind of pistol strapped to his belt. Were it not for his distinctive swagger and his captivating smile I would not have recognized him. I just stood there taking it all in, not being able to speak or react in any way. But he came to me immediately and just stopped in front of me. The trademark smile was still beaming its magic and, with the beard as a backdrop, his teeth gleamed like those of a model in a toothpaste ad. He just stood looking, studying, taking me all in, sort of reacquainting his eyes and his memory. I waited passively, letting it happen.

"Dorothy, my darling," he said.

At least it wasn't Dimple. Although it really wouldn't have made a difference.

"Hello, Roberto," I said. I didn't even want to risk an "hola" because my increased fluency in Spanish was the only secret weapon I possessed to use in "fighting" for my country.

"You look more beautiful than ever," he said.

I had not skimped on my arrival outfit. It was a haltered sun dress with a white field and large, splashy yellow sun flowers all over it. Really cute white shoes to match. After deplaning, I had stopped at the first ladies' room to fluff, put on fresh lipstick, and apply a hairspray touch up.

I decided to go clever and bold with my reply to his compliment. I mean why not? "I wish I could say the same for you," I said. I added a modest smile to make clear my facetiousness.

He threw his head back and laughed, one of his more endearing qualities, by the way. "I know what you are going to say," he said.

"I/you look like Fidel," we said in unison, and burst out laughing, also in unison. Then we hugged. More of a friendship-styled one, but it still nauseated me.

"Let's get your luggage," he said, a lilt of enthusiasm in his voice.

Not surprisingly, he had a driver fetch my luggage. Then we just totally bypassed Customs. All the uniformed guards did was sort of bow to Roberto; he was clearly a recognizable figure. When we reached the familiar apartment building in Vedado, we took the elevator but it was to the higher floor—his own apartment. The driver had toted—that's what we would have said in Smithtown, Georgia—my luggage, and Roberto directed him to place it in the master bedroom—Roberto's bedroom. Roberto gave him no tip and didn't even thank him. I guess his tip was that he didn't get shot.

I waited until the driver left to say, "The apartment Dallis and I stayed in was . . . ," and I pointed downward.

"Yes it was, but since you called, it has been rented. Actually, it is being used by an official of the new Cuban government." He smiled and said cheerfully, "But we have my apartment here."

"Roberto . . . I . . ."

"What is it, my darling?"

I strode to the window and looked out at the Malecon for a moment, then turned to face him. "Roberto, would you mind if I stayed in one of the guest bedrooms? This thing with Dallis has been very upsetting to me. As I said on the phone, I need to sort things out for a few days. I'm just not quite emotionally ready for . . . you know."

He frowned.

"Well, at least a *couple* of days," I said.

That concession turned his frown into a smile. I had decided that I was going to postpone as long as possible the disgust associated with performing my patriotic duty. May as well make him work for it this time, I figured. He responded by springing into action himself and moving my luggage to the largest of the two guest bedrooms.

"There," he said with cheer that could have been forced; I wasn't sure.

"Thank you, Roberto," I said. "I really appreciate your patience and understanding."

He came to me, took my shoulders in his hands, and gave me one of his looks. "Nothing is too good for you, my darling. You are the most special lady in the Western Hemisphere."

I felt the bile rising in my throat. All I could do was look down demurely because I didn't want him to see the revulsion in my eyes.

"But now, unfortunately, I will have to leave you for the evening. I have an important meeting to attend. In case you have not heard, your country is planning to invade Cuba, and Fidel is gathering our military to discuss strategy."

"An invasion?" I said, feigning what I hoped was the right measure of alarm. "Did I come at the wrong time? Will I be safe?"

He laughed. "Of course you will be safe. They will have to land somewhere on the coast and, even if they have success, it would take them a long time to reach Havana. Anyway, either way you will be safe because if the Americans gain control, you are an American, and if we retain control, your safety is guaranteed by me." He was smiling. "But we do not believe the Americans will succeed."

I tried to put on a semi-worried look. "Well, okay," I said. "If you say so."

He motioned me to follow him into the kitchen. "You may be tired after your trip and want to just stay in." He opened his refrigerator and showed me some leftover ropa vieja I could have for supper. "But tomorrow night we will dine with Fidel and Celia."

I let my countenance brighten fully at that news. I would be naturally excited to have dinner with a man who was now a world figure, but the real reason for my excitement was the possibility that the talkative Fidel might inadvertently reveal what I had come to find out.

"I do have some bad news," he said. "El Encanto was destroyed by fire just last night. Arson."

I put on a sad face and it took no effort because that truly was bad news.

"But you will have a nice day in the city tomorrow. I will have a car and driver waiting for you downstairs and at your disposal all day. He will be wearing a uniform and he will be armed. You will be perfectly safe."

Then he came to me and kissed me gently on the forehead the way he did the last time I was in Cuba. Then, it drove me crazy. Now, I found it revolting.

Chapter Forty-Eight

The next day was my "lady day" in Havana. Shopping, lunching, sightseeing. All by myself except for my driver and bodyguard. Havana was not yet in shambles as it is now, but there were distinct differences already, the most notable being the closing of all the casinos and the nationalization of the private clubs. But I had a nice day, all the while brimming with anticipation over the coming evening.

Angel, I'd brought some nice, tropical-styled dresses suitable for Havana in April but I was in a quandary. What do you wear to have dinner with a bunch of people wearing clothes that look like army uniforms? I finally decided the answer was the same thing as if they were wearing sport coats. So, at what I felt was a risk of overdressing, I chose a sort of casual pink suit of semi-shiny cotton with a removable jacket and a sleeveless white blouse. Spectator pumps completed my little ensemble.

Well, I *was* overdressed, particularly since we ended up having dinner at a table in the kitchen at the Habana Libre Hotel which was the new name for the Havana Hilton. I later learned that the hotel's penthouse was one of the places Castro lived and worked. The others were Celia Sanchez' apartment on Eleventh Street, a small office in the Plaza de la Revolución, and an office at INRA—the National Agrarian Reform Institute. When he wasn't working at one of those places, he was working out of a briefcase while in one of his motorcades comprised of either Soviet jeep-like vehicles or Mercedes-Benz limousines, depending upon his mood.

Angel, I was *so* nervous. This was way sooner than I had expected to have contact with anybody who might reveal the information my government had sent me for. I decided that, particularly since they'd had a meeting about the invasion the previous evening, tonight might be my best chance for success. Accordingly, I made up my mind that, if the information didn't come out tonight inadvertently, I would do my best to draw it out. Hopefully without compromising myself.

From personal experience, and by all other accounts I know of, Fidel Castro was one of the most brilliant men in the world. Never mind that he was a communist. He slept four hours a night and was a voracious reader of *everything*. In fact, to get a cigar out the pocket of his fatigues, he'd pulled out a copy of *The Remote Past* by somebody named Giovanni Papini and sort of absently set it on the dining table. I, of course, had never heard of either the book or the author.

Castro also had an elephantine memory. "You look very different than when we sat on ammunition boxes in the Sierra Maestra and talked of the revolution," he said in English, looking right at me when Roberto and I arrived at the table.

I surprised myself by smiling and replying, "I'll take that as a compliment, but I must say, you do not look different at all."

He threw his head back in laughter and pointed at me while looking at Roberto. "Very good, very good. You remember I told you to not let this woman out of your sight or I will move in. She is very beautiful." He gestured toward Celia Sanchez who, while not wearing fatigues, was not wearing a dress either. Instead, it was an earth-toned pants outfit that made her look like she was going fishing. "You remember Celia," Fidel said.

I smiled and greeted her in English. She smiled back and said, "Hello." It was obviously one of her few English words. The first two fingers of her right hand held the ever-present cigarette. I had remembered our other encounter and reached in my purse and pulled out a brand new pack of Luckies and handed it to her. "For you," I said, smiling.

She broke out in a refulgent grin, began nodding repeatedly, and said, "Muchas gracias, muchas gracias."

I didn't even say an English "you're welcome" because I didn't want to go so far as to reveal my understanding of her Spanish "thank you." So I just smiled and nodded.

"Please," said Fidel. "Sit down."

Castro was already working on a glass of Chivas Regal; I had seen the bottle nearby. I chose a rum and coke, or Cuba libre, while Roberto ordered a beer."

"So, you and your husband sold the buses to Batista," Castro said.

Suddenly, Roberto jumped in and said, "Recuerde que no sabe acerca de la municion."

With my new knowledge of Spanish, I knew he had said, "Remember, she does not know about the ammunition."

Castro took it in without nodding and said, "Sí."

"Yes, we did sell the buses and the commission came in very handy."

"That is very good, Señora; congratulations."

"Thank you . . . uh . . . excuse me, sir, but the last time I stupidly called you 'General.' What is correct now? President?"

Castro grinned widely in recollection. "I am prime minister of Cuba and commander-in-chief of the Cuban army. But I suggest you call me Fidel. Will you do that?"

I said yes even though I was intimidated by this complex, larger-than-life man. It occurred to me that, even if they shot me before I left, I would have achieved being on a first-name basis with a world leader.

"We are having steak tonight. Will that be good for you?" Fidel asked.

"Sounds wonderful," I said.

There was a lengthy pause in the conversation while Castro undertook the almost ritualistic process of lighting his enormous Cuban cigar. While this was going on, Roberto lit my Lucky for me and Celia lit a new cigarette with her old one. With the first blue plume of cigar smoke on its way to the ceiling, Fidel spoke again.

"I agreed to Roberto's suggestion of dinner tonight for two reasons. One is that I always like to be in the presence of beautiful women. But the other is the rare chance to get the perspective of an ordinary American citizen on our revolution." He paused and just looked at me, puffing on the cigar.

Hawk had coached me up on this possibility to a degree. I wish it had been more. "Well, Fidel," I said, as I smiled and blushed slightly at calling him that. "I'm no expert and actually know very little about American politics, but—"

"That is exactly what I want," he said. "The opinion of the average American housewife who plays canasta all day."

I knew there was an insult in there somewhere but I let it go. "I would say Americans are duly impressed by what you've done. I think I read somewhere that you defeated Batista's army with only a few hundred soldiers. That's amazing. But I also believe Americans are very concerned about the spread of communism."

Castro shifted in his chair. "What do you think they do not like about communism?"

"That's a good question. I can mainly only speak for myself. I don't understand everything I should about the loss of economic freedom that comes with communism but I think many Americans share my primary fear and that's nuclear proliferation. To be specific, there's a lot of talk about Soviet missiles ending up ninety miles from Key West and pointed right at America."

Castro then surprised me by launching into a mini version of one his speeches. One would not think that someone in his position would waste time preaching to an American housewife but I had read that he was famous for playing checkers and chess in public parks with ordinary Cuban citizens and engaging them in extemporaneous political discourse.

So, while more drinks were served and the first course of caldo gallego (turnip green soup with white beans) came and went, Fidel Castro ranted at length. He talked about the colonization of Cuba by America, the tyrant Batista, the domination of the choice agricultural lands by American companies, the poverty overlooked by America and Batista, the fact that, pre-revolution, Cuba was really run by the American ambassador, the rampant sickness of the average Cuban peoples, their lack of education, and the outrageous rents they had to pay. He went on to maintain that he was not a communist. But, of course, later in that year he announced that he was. I was mesmerized by the whole thing and, amazingly, Roberto listened intently as though he was hearing it all for the first time. Poor Celia, who understood no English, just ate her dinner.

He had eaten half his steak before he wound down a bit. "So, what is your reaction to what I've just said?" He directed the question at me.

"You said a lot," I answered. "But you didn't say anything about the Soviet Union, your relationship with them, and American concerns about Russia using Cuba as a way to attack the United States."

Castro had just put a huge wad of steak in his mouth and he talked as he chewed. It wasn't very attractive. "I keep hearing all this talk of missiles. There will never be missiles here. I keep hearing all this talk of attacking the United States." He pointed his fork at me. "But let me tell you who is attacking. It is the United States that is about to attack Cuba." He raised his voice. "Do you know about that?"

"I read one little thing in the *Miami Herald* about it, but it just made mention of it. Didn't say much at all."

He pointed his fork again. "Well, it is coming. And soon."

Angel, my heart was pounding. How could I keep this going? How could I extract what I needed? Surprisingly, Fidel fell silent, concentrating on the rest of his steak. I felt like I had to say something or the subject might die.

"I just really can't believe we'd invade your country. I mean, what are we going to do, sail right into Havana Harbor and have our soldiers climb over the seawall at the Malecon?"

Castro snorted with laughter, then jammed some more steak in his mouth. "The attack will come somewhere on the south coast. In fact, I held a meeting last night to study the possibilities."

"*Para espar perfectamente seguro yo no le diria nada,*" Roberto jumped in and said. (To be perfectly safe, I would not tell her anything.) He added, "*A menos que quieras decirle que es Trinidad.*" (Unless you want to tell her it's Trinidad.)

"Concluimos ayer por la noche que sera por la Bahia de Cochinos," Fidel said. (But we agreed last night it will be the Bay of Pigs.)

"Es para confundirla." (I mean as a decoy.)

Castro waved his hand dismissively. "Esta mujer es ama de casa. Podemos decirle cualquier cosa y no va a importar." (This woman is a housewife. We can tell her anything and it will not matter.)

Roberto shrugged, his body language saying: okay, suit yourself.

Castro was still chewing but, at this point, actually used his napkin. "We are not exactly sure where the Americans will invade. Somewhere on the south coast. We are still studying it. The reason you know so little about the invasion is that the CIA is managing it and they are trying to make it appear as if a small band of counter-revolutionaries are the attackers. In any event, it will not work. We will crush them."

I pretended to be pre-occupied with my steak but it was only to keep from breaking out in a broad grin. What I really wanted to do was scream at the top of my lungs because, Angel, I had it!

Hawk had coached me on what to listen for. The Trinidad alternative for the amphibious landing was near the city of the same name that lay only three miles from the Escambray Mountains. It had superb beaches located near hills running as high as four thousand feet and was protected from the north by a river that was impossible to ford. Plus there was a large concentration of anti-Castro guerrillas in the area.

The Bay of Pigs alternative was a hundred miles west of Trinidad. It was more remote, had an airfield that was closer, and fewer Castro forces nearby. However, the approach to the landing area was ribbed with dangerous coral reefs and thick swamps covered the area north of the projected landfall. So there were advantages and disadvantages associated with both options.

On the way back to the apartment, I was consumed by one overriding thought: I already had the information I was sent for and it only took me two days to get it. My objective became getting the intelligence to Hawk and then getting the hell out of Cuba and away from this slimeball I once thought I was in love with. And getting away *without* having to . . . well, you know.

First things first. When we arrived at the apartment, I told Roberto that Dallis had been very upset about our separation and had made me promise to call him tonight. Roberto gestured to the phone in his bedroom. "Sure, go ahead. I must take a shower."

Hawk had set up a coded communication system in case Roberto's phone was tapped. I called Miami for the Flamingo Motel and asked to be connected to Dallis's room. He answered.

I began a brief, but desultory conversation that we'd carefully planned because we assumed we would be recorded. I began by asking how he was doing. He replied, not so good, but he'd tell me more about that in a moment. Then, on cue, he asked how the weather was. I replied that it was lovely and that the bougainvillea were just beautiful. There. It was done. Bougainvillea meant the Bay of Pigs. Pretty frangipani would have meant Trinidad. Dallis would tell Hawk what I said and my mission was therefore complete. Now I had to figure out how to get out of there. As directed by Hawk, Dallis then began telling me more about "how he was doing." His answer would be the basis for my plan to escape from Cuba.

As I hung up with Dallis, I heard Roberto still in the shower. He was actually singing "Besame Mucho" at the top of his lungs and his voice was surprisingly good. I saw his fatigues piled on a chair. I also saw something else. Laying on top of his pile of clothes was his holster with the large pistol in it. I couldn't stop looking at it. I tried to look away, but my eyes kept returning to it as a feeling of calm came over me I had never before experienced. I knew absolutely nothing about guns. Had never even held one. But I kept staring at this one while the shower kept running and Roberto kept singing. Something made my hand slowly and deliberately reach for the holster. It had a snap that secured the pistol and it unsnapped easily. The gun slid out of the holster easily as well. The singing continued. A strange serenity overcame me as I felt my movements morph into a languid slow motion. I held the pistol in both hands and put my finger on the trigger. My hands were steady—no shaking whatsoever. I walked slowly into the bathroom, raised the gun, and pointed it at the shadow of Roberto behind the shower curtain.

I pulled the trigger.

Chapter Forty-Nine

Hallie

The needle on Hallie's "stress-o-meter" was red-lining. On top of her likely loss of *all* her money, and the likely loss of the man she thought she loved, her mother had just told her she had murdered a man in cold blood in Cuba. At least that's what it sounded like before her mother dozed off and couldn't be awakened. Hallie wondered how she would *live* until tomorrow morning when she could find out how her mother bumped off a prominent member of Fidel Castro's administration and got away with it.

But that was tomorrow. Today she had to try to find out what was going on with Rich. She called his assistant Karen again. When she came on the line, Hallie could tell she was upset. "Hallie, he's gone radio silent on me." Her voice cracked. "Frankly, I'm scared."

Hallie mustered all her bravado and said, "Don't worry, Karen; it'll be fine." But she didn't believe a word of it. "Is Thomas there?"

"I'll transfer you."

He came on the line. "Hello, Hallie." His tone was zombie-like.

"Thomas, where in the hell is my fiancé and what the hell is happening?"

"Can you meet me?"

"Where? When?"

"Wright's. The sandwich shop?"

"Yeah, when?"

"Soon as you can get there."

It was lunchtime, so they ordered. Hallie went with the chicken walnut salad, Herring with a Reuben. They sat in a booth in the back. Thomas Herring's demeanor matched his somber phone voice.

"It's over, Hallie."

Hallie's face bore a look that was beyond disbelief. "What are you saying, Thomas?"

"I'm saying it's over. All the money's gone, Rich is gone, and I'm going to jail."

"What?" She almost shrieked it, causing a couple at the nearest table to turn their heads. "What?" she repeated, more softly.

"Look, Hallie. I know you didn't know a thing. The whole settlement agreement business was a Ponzi scheme. We only actually did two or three of those agreements, the rest of them we just manufactured with word processing and Photoshopped the bank letters."

Hallie was holding her head in her hands, ignoring her salad, just looking at it but not seeing it. She looked up. "Thomas, please tell me you're—"

"I'm not kidding, Hallie. My lawyer and I are on the way to see the FBI this afternoon and try to cut a deal."

"Thomas, where is Rich?"

"You really want to know?"

"Of course I do. Remember? I'm supposed to be marrying him." She immediately regretted her sarcasm, but it was too late.

"Croatia."

"Croatia? My God, what the hell is he—"

"No extradition treaty with the U. S. and the fishing's good."

Hallie felt the room spinning as if she were as drunk as she'd ever been in her life. "Thomas, do you remember me telling you that all the money I have in the world is—"

"As a matter of fact, I do."

She was about to lose it altogether. "Well, what am I supposed to—"

"Stop," he said, holding his hand up. Then he reached in his pocket, pulling out an envelope. "This may extend my prison sentence if anybody finds out about it but I don't care. Here's a check for all the money you invested. The check is good at the moment but you should take it directly to your bank from here."

Hallie held the check and just stared at it. The amount was correct. Then she stared at Herring. "Thomas, why are you doing this for me?"

He just looked at her for several long moments, seeming to study her as if they'd just met. "Because you're you. Because you deserve it." He paused again and looked down at his plate. "Maybe because I'm stuck on you. Always have been."

"Oh, Thomas." She took his hand.

"Yep, 'fraid so. But I knew I could never compete with Rich. And now I'll be going to prison, so I'm really out of the picture." He smiled at her now. "Getting your money out is the best I could do."

Her phone call caught him in his office at the university.

"Hi," she said in a little voice.

"Well, hi yourself," Ian Lightbourne replied.

"Any chance I could come by?"

"I have about an hour. Come ahead."

After a stop at the bank to deposit the check Thomas Herring had given her, she arrived at Lightbourne's office. He stood and they briefly hugged as would old friends. He offered coffee and she took it. They sat on his office sofa.

"Something's wrong," he said.

She just studied her hands, turning Rich's engagement ring round and round her finger. She'd forgotten about the ring. It should bring a handsome sum and she couldn't think of a reason not to sell it and pocket the money.

"Well?" Lightbourne said.

"I bet on the wrong horse," she said.

"You're going to have to help me . . ."

"Oh, it's no big deal, really. Rich is a crook, was running a Ponzi scheme, and he's on the run. His right-hand man told me he's in Croatia where there's no extradition treaty with the U. S."

"Wow," Lightbourne said.

"Yep."

He stood and paced. "I know you don't want to hear this, but I'm not all that surprised. It just didn't all add up to me."

"You're right about it not adding up. A lot of people who can't afford to have lost a lot of money."

"Including you?"

She drank from her coffee cup. Ian had proper china, not just mugs. "Ian, you must promise me this is between us."

"Sure."

She told him about her lunch with Thomas Herring.

"Wow again," he said, as he sat down. "Well, I'm sorry you've lost your fiancé and sorry people lost their money. But, as I think you know, in one way I'm not all that sorry." He was smiling a hopeful kind of smile.

She smiled back and put her hand on his. "I know, Ian. I know. But I need time."

He was grinning broadly now. "And you shall have it, my dear."

Chapter Fifty

Dimple

I think Hallie looks different today. She seems stressed but hyper. In some kind of zone. I ask her about it but all she wants to talk about is my killing Roberto.

I can't help laughing as I begin to tell her.

Angel, I suppose I *would* have killed him except for one thing. When I pulled the trigger, nothing happened. I pulled it again and nothing happened. You know I don't know a *thing* about guns and I later found out that his pistol was some kind of automatic type that requires you to cock it somehow to put a bullet in the firing chamber.

Anyway, when I couldn't get the gun to fire, I came out of the trance of hate that had overcome me and concluded I'd just flunked Murder 101. And it's a good thing, because either Fidel would have had me executed or I'd still be in a dungeon somewhere under the streets of Havana and you wouldn't be here! Anyway, as far as I know, Roberto may still be alive. I lost interest in following up on him.

You probably want to know how I got out of Cuba. Well, when Roberto got out of the shower, I told him that when I spoke with your daddy on the phone, I learned he had appendicitis and had to have surgery the next afternoon. That I was the only one who could sign for him and take care of him. That we *were* still married and, despite our troubles, I felt obligated. I was finally putting the lying techniques I learned from having my affair with Roberto to good use. I further lied to him by telling him I wanted to come right back down to Cuba as soon as I could.

He didn't argue; in fact he was very sympathetic and said he'd get me on the morning flight. He made me promise to give his regards to Dallis, saying again how much he liked him. The only rough spot came when he, realizing it was my last night, reminded me with one of his smiles that he'd just taken a shower and was really, really clean.

"I can very easily move your things back in my room," he said, still smiling.

I took his hands and held them under my cheek. Then I gave him my sweetest, most earnest, female look and said, "Roberto, I'm so upset by this thing about Dallis, and just everything, really. I promise when I come back there won't be any delays, okay?"

One look at his face told me it was anything *but* okay and there was a protracted "moment" while our eyes locked and the wheels turned. When he finally said "okay," I wanted to leap in the air and click my heels, but I made myself act restrained.

I was indeed able to leave the next morning. A few weeks later, your daddy and I went to our church and renewed our wedding vows. Within a year, we had a wonderful little baby girl.

So, what about the invasion, you say? Why did we invade at the Bay of Pigs when I told the CIA that Castro was planning to put most of their defenses there?

Well, I asked Hawk about that afterwards and learned it was all politics. They were all set to go at Trinidad but at the last minute, Kennedy changed it to the Bay of Pigs. The reason was because it could be a night landing and, if things went badly, it would be easier to have U. S. personnel quickly fade away so it looked as if the entire operation was manned by Cuban counter-revolutionaries. Hawk explained to me the term "plausible deniability" and Kennedy felt like we'd have more of it at the Bay of Pigs. He didn't want to place himself in a position where Castro could go to the United Nations and tattle on us.

In fact, much later I learned we lost one of our pilots and it took us over twenty years to claim the body because we didn't want to admit any of our boys were there. The coral reef, the quicksand, and the swamps actually made it a poor choice, but politics are politics. However, the larger problem was the terrible planning and execution. Angel, it was not our country's finest hour.

Your daddy asked me if I felt the government casually used me for that mission, wasted my time, and put me in harm's way for nothing. I told him absolutely not. After all, the decision for the landing site was up in the air until the last minute. It could just as easily have been Trinidad, and if the invasion had been successful, resulting in Castro being deposed, maybe I'd be some kind of hero or something. A secret one. But, Angel, for me the best thing that came out of it was shoring up the foundation of my loving marriage to your wonderful father. Not to mention being able to have you, my sweet child. It was worth everything I went through just for that.

And knowing Hawk was a great experience. Not long after I got back from Cuba, he called. It was a brief conversation; he just thanked me for my service. Years later, after your daddy died, I got to thinking about Hawk and made a modest effort to see what became of him. But he was too much of a secret to be found.

Chapter Fifty-One

Hallie

Within a month, Ian Lightbourne had separated from his wife and started seeing Hallie regularly. One day he called Hallie, who was at the advertising agency working on a copywriting job.

"Hey there," she said.

"Hey, yourself," he said. "Thought you might want to know I just got a call from that literary agent I sent your final manuscript to."

Hallie almost jumped inside the telephone handset. "My God, Ian, what did she say?"

"If you'll meet me at The Silver Ring for a Cuban sandwich, I'll tell you."

The End

Acknowledgments

I'm upset with my parents for not living longer but far more upset with myself for not taking greater advantage of their presence here on earth. You see, my father actually was in the school bus business. Actually was a rep for a manufacturer—in Ohio, not Illinois. And he and my mother really did go to Cuba. A lot. Did he sell any buses to Batista? Well, because I was regrettably too wrapped up in my own life, I'm not really sure. But he was a marvelous salesman, so it's entirely possible. I think he and my mother mostly just went down there in search of mojitos, a good rhumba, and a little blackjack. And they were sure to tote a cache of their Lucky Strikes with them.

Beyond that, the plot of *A Lady in Havana* is purely the result of intravenous mainlining directly from my imagination.

My parents did have a Cuban friend named Roberto who came to visit when I was little. I even remember meeting him. Even vaguely remember what he looked like in his guayabera. To be clear, the character Dimple is definitely not my mother. Mainly because my mother would never, ever have climbed into bed with anybody other than my father. However, the refined, Southern lady aspects of Dimple, and her charming, vulnerable insouciance may be a composite of my mother and many of her dear Southern lady friends. They're all gone now, which is also upsetting as they were my last link to my parents.

For privacy, I only use given names in acknowledgments and I must start with my great friend Bill (sadly recently departed) who arranged for my spouse and me to go to Cuba with him and stay at a wonderful Havana boutique hotel called the Palacio de Pascua owned by his two adopted Cuban sons. New York City-based Bill was one of the top estate lawyers in the United States who spent a week every month in Havana and was a vast repository of data about Cuba, past and present. I am in his debt. And Bill's sons Yassel and Samuel contributed immensely to my knowledge and understanding of Cuba and Havana in particular. Moreover, Bill and his expert right-hand gal Pat introduced me to some other new friends who were helpful, most particularly Felipe who, in turn, introduced me to Lazaro.

I actually went to almost all the places in *A Lady in Havana*. Places like the Nacional, The Riviera, and El Floridita. Some of the places in the book are no longer there. The famous El Encanto department store is gone but I walked the streets of Galiano and San Rafael where it once was. I even spent a couple of nights at a "casa" (owned by Lazaro) on the shore of the Bay of Pigs. And, of course, I saw the show at Tropicana that still rivals Radio City in its execution, musicality, and visual impact.

While at Tropicana, even though I knew I wouldn't see it, I nevertheless looked for Liberace's piano table. Along with almost everything Cuban in *A Lady in Havana*, that table was a fact. And that includes Castro's ammunition shortage, though I found nothing to indicate that it was smuggled in on school buses.

Cuba is not the only place one can learn about Cuba. In my hometown, I have some wonderful Cuban friends, all expatriates. Like Mirtha and her husband and son (both named Sergio), Andy and Rosa, Lolly and Alex, and Emilio and Aida. All helped immeasurably. Mirtha, in particular, was a first reader and identified numerous ways to make the book more accurately "Cuban."

That's not to say I didn't do lots of digging on my own to try to get the facts right. I relied heavily on some superb historical books: *Fidel* by Ted Szulc, *Bay of Pigs* by Howard Jones, *Telex from Cuba* by Rachel Kushner, *Little Man* by Robert Lacey, and *Tropicana Nights* by Rosa Lowinger. And for accurate visual flavor, I obtained a copy of the 1950s film *Our Man in Havana* and watched it more than once.

There were numerous press archives available to me describing various flavors of Ponzi schemes. Rich Rodino and his con resulted from that research.

And I mustn't forget to mention my faithful "first readers." You all know who you are and I am in your debt. My most faithful and dedicated one, as always, was my wonderful spouse whom I love so dearly.

I never thought I'd say it, but visiting Cuba and doing the research was almost as stimulating as writing this book. I believe I've been accurate but I know I've taken a few liberties with certain time-lines to make the story work better. But hey, it *is* a story.

I can't end without a word about the Cuban people. To me, they are a paradox. They now have equality in that they are all equally impoverished. Except, that is, for the political class, some of whom live in comparative luxury. But they are a warm, charming, accommodating, loving people who seemed resigned to their circumstances. They're a joy to be with and being in their presence was a most pleasant and unexpected bonus that came from writing *A Lady in Havana*.